THE BLACK DOG

The

BLACK DOG

and other stories by

ALFRED EDGAR COPPARD

Short Story Index Reprint Series

BOOKS FOR LIBRARIES PRESS
FREEPORT, NEW YORK

First Published 1923
Reprinted 1970

STANDARD BOOK NUMBER:
8369-3312-5

LIBRARY OF CONGRESS CATALOG CARD NUMBER:
74-106275

PRINTED IN THE UNITED STATES OF AMERICA

to
GAY

Contents

THE BLACK DOG
Tales

The Black Dog

HAVING POCKETED HIS FARE THE freckled rustic took himself and his antediluvian cab back to the village limbo from which they had briefly emerged. Loughlin checked his luggage into the care of the porter, an angular man with one eye who was apparently the only other living being in this remote minute station, and sat down in the platform shade. July noon had a stark eye-tiring brightness, and a silence so very deep—when that porter ceased his intolerable clatter—that Loughlin could hear footsteps crunching in the road half a mile away. The train was late. There were no other passengers. Nothing to look at except his trunks, two shiny rails in the grim track, red hollyhocks against white palings on the opposite bank.

The holiday in this quiet neighbourhood had delighted him, but its crowning experience had been too brief. On the last day but one the loveliest woman he had ever known had emerged almost as briefly as that cabman. Some men are constantly meeting that woman. Not so the Honourable Gerald Loughlin, but no man turns his back tranquilly on destiny even if it is but two days old and already some half-dozen miles away. The visit had come to its end, Loughlin had come to his station, the cab had gone back to its lair, but on reflection he could find no other reasons for going away and denying himself the delight of this proffered experience. Time was his own, as much as he could buy of it, and he had an income that enabled him to buy a good deal.

Moody and hesitant he began to fill his pipe when the one-eyed porter again approached him.

"Take a pipe of that?" said Loughlin, offering him the pouch.

"Thanky, sir, but I can't smoke a pipe; a cigarette I take now and again, thanky, sir, not often, just to keep me from cussing and damming. My wife buys me a packet sometimes, she says I don't swear so much then, but I don't know, I has to knock 'em off soon's they make me feel bad, and then, dam it all, I be worsen ever. . . ."

"Look here," said the other, interrupting him, "I'm not going by this train after all. Something I have forgotten. Now look after my bags and I'll come along later, this afternoon." He turned and left the station as hurriedly as if his business was really of the high importance the porter immediately conceived it to be.

The Honourable Gerald, though handsome and honest, was not a fool. A fool is one who becomes distracted between the claims of instinct and common sense; the larger foolishness is the peculiar doom of imaginative people, artists and their kind, while the smaller foolishness is the mark of all those who have nothing but their foolishness to endorse them. Loughlin responded to this impulse unhesitatingly but without distraction, calmly and directly as became a well-bred bachelor in the early thirties. He might have written to the young beauty with the queer name, Orianda Crabbe, but that course teemed with absurdities and difficulties for he was modest, his romantic imagination weak, and he had only met her at old Lady Tillington's a couple of days before. Of this mere girl, just twenty-three or twenty-four, he knew nothing save that they had been immediately and vividly charming to each other. That was no excuse for presenting himself again to the old invalid of Tillington Park, it would be impossible for him to do so, but there had been one vague moment of their recalled intercourse, a glimmering intimation, which just now seemed to offer a remote possibility of achievement, and so he walked on in the direction of the park.

Tillington was some miles off and the heat was oppressive. At the end of an hour's stroll he stepped into " The Three Pigeons " at Denbury and drank a deep drink. It was quiet and deliciously cool in the taproom there, yes, as silent as that little station had been. Empty the world seemed to-day, quite empty; he had not passed a human creature. Happily bemused he took another draught. Eighteen small panes of glass in that long window and perhaps as many flies buzzing in the room. He could hear and see a breeze saluting the bright walled ivy outside and the bushes by a stream. This drowsiness was heaven, it made so clear his recollection of Orianda. It was impossible to particularize but she was in her way, her rather uncultured way, just perfection. He had engaged her upon several themes, music, fishing (Loughlin loved fishing), golf, tennis, and books; none of these had particularly stirred her but she had brains, quite an original turn of mind. There had been neither time nor opportunity to discover anything about her, but there she was, staying there, that was the one thing certain, apparently indefinitely, for she described the park in a witty detailed way even to a certain favourite glade which she always visited in the afternoons. When she had told him that, he could swear she was not finessing; no, no, it was a most engaging simplicity, a frankness that was positively marmoreal.

He would certainly write to her; yes, and he began to think of fine phrases to put in a letter, but could there be anything finer, now, just at this moment, than to be sitting with her in this empty inn. It was not a fair place, though it was clean, but how she would brighten it, yes! there were two long settles and two short ones, two tiny tables and eight spittoons (he *had* to count them), and somehow he felt her image flitting adorably into this setting, defeating with its native glory all the scrupulous beer-smelling impoverishment. And then, after a while, he would take her, and they would lie in the grass under a deep-bosomed tree and speak of love. How beautiful she would be. But she was not there, and so he left the inn and crossed the road to a church, pleasant and tiny and tidy, whitewalled and clean-ceilinged. A sparrow chirped in the porch, flies hummed in the nave, a puppy was barking in the vicarage garden. How trivial, how absurdly solemn, everything seemed. The thud of the great pendulum in the tower had the sound of a dead man beating on a bar of spiritless iron. He was tired of the vapid tidiness of these altars with their insignificant tapestries, candlesticks of gilded wood, the bunches of pale flowers oppressed by the rich glow from the windows. He longed for an altar that should be an inspiring symbol of belief, a place of green and solemn walls with a dark velvet shrine sweeping aloft to the peaked roof unhindered by tarnishing lustre and tedious linen. Holiness was always something richly dim. There was no more holiness here than in the tough hassocks and rush-bottomed chairs; not here, surely, the apple of Eden flourished. And yet, turning to the lectern, he noted the large prayer book open at the office of marriage. He idly read over the words of the ceremony, filling in at the gaps the names of Gerald Wilmot Loughlin and Orianda Crabbe.

What a fool! He closed the book with a slam and left the church. Absurd! You *couldn't* fall in love with a person as sharply as all that, could you ? But why not ? Unless fancy was charged with the lightning of gods it was nothing at all.

Tramping away still in the direction of Tillington Park he came in the afternoon to that glade under a screen of trees spoken of by the girl. It was green and shady, full of scattering birds. He flung himself down in the grass under a deep-bosomed tree. She had spoken delightfully of this delightful spot.

When she came, for come she did, the confrontation left him very unsteady as he sprang to his feet. (Confound that potation at " The Three Pigeons "! Enormously hungry, too!) But he was amazed, entranced, she was so happy to see him again. They sat down together, but he was still bewildered and his confusion left him all at sixes and sevens. Fortunately her own rivulet of casual chatter carried them on until he suddenly asked: " Are you related to the Crabbes of Cotterton—I fancy I know them ? "

" No, I think not, no, I am from the south country, near the sea, nobody at all, my father keeps an inn."

" An inn! How extraordinary! How very . . . very . . ."

" Extraordinary ?·" Nodding her head in the direction of the hidden mansion she added: " I am her companion."

" Lady Tillington's ? "

She assented coolly, was silent, while Loughlin ransacked his brains for some delicate reference that would clear him over this . . . this . . . cataract. But he felt stupid—that confounded potation at " The Three Pigeons "! Why, that was where he had thought of her so admirably, too. He asked if she cared for the position, was it pleasant, and so on. Heavens, what an astonishing creature for a domestic, quite positively lovely, a compendium of delightful qualities, this girl, so frank, so simple!

" Yes, I like it, but home is better. I should love to go back to my home, to father, but I can't, I'm still afraid—I ran away from home three years ago, to go with my mother. I'm like my mother, she ran away from home too."

Orianda picked up the open parasol which she had dropped, closed it in a thoughtful manner, and laid its crimson folds beside her. There was no other note of colour in her white attire; she was without a hat. Her fair hair had a quenching tinge upon it that made it less bright than gold, but more rare. Her cheeks had the colour of homely flowers, the lily and the pink. Her teeth were as even as the peas in a newly opened pod, as clear as milk.

" Tell me about all that. May I hear it ? "

" I have not seen him or heard from him since, but I love him very much now."

" Your father ? "

" Yes, but he is stern, a simple man, and he is so just. We live at a tiny old inn at the end of a village near the hills. ' The Black Dog.' It is thatched and has tiny rooms. It's painted all over with pink, pink whitewash."

" Ah, I know."

" There's a porch, under a sycamore tree, where people sit, and an old rusty chain hanging on a hook just outside the door."

" What's that for ? "

" I don't know what it is for, horses, perhaps, but it is always there, I always see that rusty chain. And on the opposite side of the road there are three lime trees and behind them is the yard where my father works. He makes hurdles and ladders. He is the best hurdle maker in three counties, he has won many prizes at the shows. It is splendid to see him working at the willow wood, soft and white. The yard is full of poles and palings, spars and fagots, and long shavings of the thin bark like seaweed. It smells so nice. In the spring the chaffinches and wrens are singing about him all day long ; the wren is lovely, but in the summer of course it's the whitethroats come chippering, and yellow-hammers."

" Ah, blackbirds, thrushes, nightingales ! "

" Yes, but it's the little birds seem to love my father's yard."

" Well then, but why did you, why did you run away ? "

" My mother was much younger, and different from father; she was handsome and proud too, and in all sorts of ways superior to him. They got to hate each other; they were so quiet about it, but I could see. Their only common interest was me, they both loved me very much. Three years ago she ran away from him. Quite suddenly, you know; there was nothing at all leading up to such a thing. But I could not understand my father, not then, he took it all so calmly. He did not mention even her name to me for a long time, and I feared to intrude; you see, I did not understand, I was only twenty. When I did ask about her he told me not to bother him, forbade me to write to her. I didn't know where she was, but he knew, and at last I found out too."

" And you defied him, I suppose ? "

" No, I deceived him. He gave me money for some purpose—to pay a debt—and I stole it. I left him a letter and ran away to my mother. I loved her."

" O well, that was only to be expected," said Loughlin. " It was all right, quite right."

" She was living with another man. I didn't know. I was a fool."

" Good lord! That was a shock for you," Loughlin said. " What did you do ? "

" No, I was not shocked, she was so happy. I lived with them for a year . . ."

" Extraordinary ! "

" And then she died."

" Your mother died ! "

" Yes, so you see I could not stop with my . . . I could not stay where I was, and I couldn't go back to my father."

" I see, no, but you want to go back to your father now."

" I'm afraid. I love him, but I'm afraid. I don't blame my mother, I feel she was right, quite right— it was such happiness. And yet I feel, too, that father was deeply wronged. I can't understand that, it sounds foolish. I should so love to go home again. This other kind of life doesn't seem to eclipse me— things have been extraordinary kind—I don't feel out of my setting, but still it doesn't satisfy, it is polite and soft, like silk, perhaps it isn't barbarous enough, and I want to live, somehow—well, I have not found what I wanted to find."

" What did you want to find ? "

" I shan't know until I have found it. I do want to go home now, but I am full of strange feelings about it. I feel as if I was bearing the mark of something that can't be hidden or disguised of what my mother did, as if I were all a burning recollection for him that he couldn't fail to see. He is good, a just man. He . . . he is the best hurdle maker in three counties."

While listening to this daughter of a man who made ladders the Honourable Gerald had been swiftly thinking of an intriguing phrase that leaped into his mind. Social plesiomorphism, that was it! Caste was humbug, no doubt, but even if it was conscious humbug it was there, really there, like the patterned frost upon a window pane, beautiful though a little incoherent, and conditioned only by the size and number of your windows. (Eighteen windows in that pub!) But what did it amount to, after all? It was stuck upon your clear polished outline for every eye to see, but within was something surprising as the sight of a badger in church—until you got used to the indubitable relation of such badgers to such churches. Fine turpitudes!

"My dear girl," he burst out, "your mother and you were right, absolutely. I am sure life is enhanced not by amassing conventions, but by destroying them. And your feeling for your father is right, too, rightest of all. Tell me . . . let me . . . may I take you back to him?"

The girl's eyes dwelt upon his with some intensity.

"Your courage is kind," she said, "but he doesn't know you, nor you him." And to that she added, "You don't even know me."

"I have known you for ten thousand years. Come home to him with me, we will go back together. Yes, you can explain. Tell him"—the Honourable Gerald had got the bit between his teeth now— "tell him I'm your sweetheart, will you—will you?"

"Ten thousand . . .! Yes, I know; but it's strange to think you have only seen me just once before!"

"Does that matter? Everything grows from that one small moment into a world of . . . well of . . . boundless admiration."

"I don't want," said Orianda, reopening her crimson parasol, "to grow into a world of any kind."

"No, of course you don't. But I mean the emotion is irresistible, 'the desire of the moth for the star,' that sort of thing, you know, and I immolate myself, the happy victim of your attractions."

"All that has been said before." Orianda adjusted her parasol as a screen for her raillery.

"I swear," said he, "I have not said it before, never to a living soul."

Fountains of amusement beamed in her brilliant eyes. She was exquisite; he was no longer in doubt about the colour of her eyes—though he could not describe them. And the precise shade of her hair was —well, it was extraordinarily beautiful.

"I mean—it's been said to me!"

"O damnation! Of course it's been said to you. Ah, and isn't that my complete justification? But you agree, do you not? Tell me if it's possible. Say you agree, and let me take you back to your father."

"I think I would like you to," the jolly girl said, slowly.

II

On an August morning a few weeks later they travelled down together to see her father. In the interim Orianda had resigned her appointment, and several times Gerald had met her secretly in the purlieus of Tillington Park. The girl's cool casual nature fascinated him not less than her appearance. Admiration certainly outdistanced his happiness, although that also increased; but the bliss had its shadow, for the outcome of their friendship seemed mysteriously to depend on the outcome of the proposed return to her father's home, devotion to that project forming the first principle, as it were, of their intercourse. Orianda had not dangled before him the prospect of any serener relationship; she took his caresses as naturally and undemonstratively as a pet bird takes a piece of sugar. But he had begun to be aware of a certain force behind all her charming naivete; the beauty that exhaled the freshness, the apparent fragility, of a drop of dew had none the less a savour of tyranny which he vowed should never, least of all by him, be pressed to vulgar exercise.

When the train reached its destination Orianda confided calmly that she had preferred not to write to her father. Really she did not know for certain whether he was alive or even living on at the old home she so loved. And there was a journey of three miles or more which Orianda proposed to walk. So they walked.

The road lay across an expanse of marshy country and approached the wooded uplands of her home only by numerous eccentric divagations made necessary by culverts that drained the marsh. The day was bright; the sky, so vast an arch over this flat land, was a very oven for heat; there were cracks in the earth, the grass was like stubble. At the mid journey they crossed a river by its wooden bridge, upon which a boy sat fishing with stick and string. Near the water was a long white hut with a flag; a few tethered boats floated upon the stream. Gerald gave a shilling to a travelling woman who carried a burden on her back and shuffled slowly upon the harsh road sighing, looking neither to right nor left; she did not look into the sky, her gaze was fastened upon her dolorous feet, one two, one two, one two; her shift, if she had such a garment, must have clung to her old body like a shrimping net.

In an hour they had reached the uplands and soon, at the top of a sylvan slope where there was shade and cooling air, Gerald saw a sign hung upon a sycamore tree, *The Black Dog by Nathaniel Crabbe*. The inn was small, pleasant with pink wash and brown paint, and faced across the road a large yard encircled by hedges, trees, and a gate. The travellers stood peeping into the enclosure which was stocked with new ladders, hurdles, and poles of various sizes. Amid them stood a tall burly man at a block, trimming with an axe the butt of a willow rod. He was about fifty, clad in rough country clothes, a white shirt, and a soft straw hat. He had mild simple features coloured, like his arms and neck, almost to the hue of a bay horse.

" Hullo! " called the girl. The man with the axe looked round at her unrecognizingly. Orianda hurried through the gateway. " Father! " she cried.

" I did not know. I was not rightly sure of ye," said the man, dropping the axe, " such a lady you've grown."

As he kissed his daughter his heavy discoloured hands rested on her shoulders, her gloved ones lay against his breast. Orianda took out her purse.

" Here is the money I stole, father."

25

She dropped some coins one by one into his palm. He counted them over, and saying simply " Thank you, my dear," put them into his pocket.

" I'm dashed ! "—thought Loughlin, who had followed the girl—" it's exactly how *she* would take it; no explanation, no apology. They do not know what reproach means. Have they no code at all ? "

She went on chatting with her father, and seemed to have forgotten her companion.

" You mean you want to come back ! " exclaimed her father eagerly, " come back here ? That would be grand, that would. But look, tell me what I am to do. I've—you see—this is how it is—"

He spat upon the ground, picked up his axe, rested one foot upon the axe-block and one arm upon his knee. Orianda sat down upon a pile of the logs.

" This is how it is . . . be you married ? "

" Come and sit here, Gerald," called the girl. As he came forward Orianda rose and said: " This is my very dear friend, father, Gerald Loughlin. He has been so kind. It is he who has given me the courage to come back. I wanted to for so long. O, a long time, father, a long time. And yet Gerald had to drag me here in the end."

" What was you afraid of, my girl ? " asked the big man.

" Myself."

The two visitors sat upon the logs. " Shall I tell you about mother ? " asked the girl.

Crabbe hesitated; looked at the ground.

" Ah, yes, you might," he said.

" She died, did you know ? "

26

The man looked up at the trees with their myriads of unmoving leaves; each leaf seemed to be listening.

"She died?" he said softly. "No, I did not know she died."

"Two years ago," continued the girl, warily, as if probing his mood.

"Two years!" He repeated it without emotion. "No, I did not know she died. 'Tis a bad job." He was quite still, his mind seemed to be turning over his own secret memories, but what he bent forward and suddenly said was: "Don't say anything about it in there." He nodded towards the inn.

"No?" Orianda opened her crimson parasol.

"You see," he went on, again resting one foot on the axe-block and addressing himself more particularly to Gerald: "I've . . . this is how it is. When I was left alone I could not get along here, not by myself. That's for certain. There's the house and the bar and the yard—I'd to get help, a young woman from Brighton. I met her at Brighton." He rubbed the blade of the axe reflectively across his palm— "And she manages house for me now, you see."

He let the axe fall again and stood upright. "Her name's Lizzie."

"O, quite so, you could do no other," Gerald exclaimed cheerfully, turning to the girl. But Orianda said softly: "What a family we are! He means he is living with her. And so you don't want your undutiful daughter after all, father?" Her gaiety was a little tremulous.

"No, no!" he retorted quickly, "you must come back, you must come back, if so be you can. There's

27

nothing I'd like better, nothing on this mortal earth. My God, if something don't soon happen I don't know what *will* happen." Once more he stooped for the axe. " That's right, Orianda, yes, yes, but you've no call to mention to her "—he glared uneasily at the inn doorway—" that . . . that about your mother."

Orianda stared up at him though he would not meet her gaze.

" You mean she doesn't know ? " she asked, " you mean she would want you to marry her if she did know ? "

" Yes, that's about how it is with us."

Loughlin was amazed at the girl's divination. It seemed miraculous, what a subtle mind she had, extraordinary! And how casually she took the old rascal's—well, what could you call it ?—effrontery, shame, misdemeanour, helplessness. But was not her mother like it too ? He had grasped nothing at all of the situation yet, save that Nathaniel Crabbe appeared to be netted in the toils of this housekeeper, this Lizzie from Brighton. Dear Orianda was " dished " now, poor girl. She could not conceivably return to such a menage.

Orianda was saying: " Then I may stay, father, mayn't I, for good with you ? "

Her father's eyes left no doubt of his pleasure.

" Can we give Gerald a bedroom for a few days ? Or do we ask Lizzie ? "

" Ah, better ask her," said the shameless man. " You want to make a stay here, sir ? "

" If it won't incommode you," replied Loughlin.

" O, make no doubt about that, to be sure no, I make no doubt about that."

" Have you still got my old bedroom ? " asked Orianda, for the amount of dubiety in his air was in prodigious antagonism to his expressed confidence.

" Why yes, it may happen," he replied slowly.

" Then Gerald can have the spare room. It's all wainscot and painted dark blue. It's a shrimp of a room, but there's a preserved albatross in a glass case as big as a van."

" I make no doubt about that," chimed in her father, straightening himself and scratching his chin uneasily, " you must talk to Lizzie."

" Splendid! " said Gerald to Orianda, " I've never seen an albatross."

" We'll ask Lizzie," said she, " at once."

Loughlin was experiencing not a little inward distress at this turn in the affair, but it was he who had brought Orianda to her home, and he would have to go through with the horrid business.

" Is she difficult, father ? "

" No, she's not difficult, not difficult, so to say, you must make allowance."

The girl was implacable. Her directness almost froze the blood of the Hon. Loughlin.

" Are you fond of her ? How long has she been here ? "

" O, a goodish while, yes, let me see—no, she's not difficult, if that's what you mean—three years, perhaps."

" Well, but that's long enough! "

(Long enough for what—wondered Loughlin ?)

" Yes, it is longish."

" If you really want to get rid of her you could tell her . . ."

" Tell her what ? "

" You know what to tell her! "

But her father looked bewildered and professed his ignorance.

" Take me in to her," said Orianda, and they all walked across to " The Black Dog." There was no one within; father and daughter went into the garden while Gerald stayed behind in a small parlour. Through the window that looked upon a grass plot he could see a woman sitting in a deck chair under a tree. Her face was turned away so that he saw only a curve of pink cheek and a thin mound of fair hair tossed and untidy. Lizzie's large red fingers were slipping a sprig of watercress into a mouth that was hidden round the corner of the curve. With her other hand she was caressing a large brown hen that sat on her lap. Her black skirt wrapped her limbs tightly, a round hip and a thigh being rigidly out-lined, while the blouse of figured cotton also seemed strained upon her buxom breast, for it was torn and split in places. She had strong white arms and holes in her stockings. When she turned to confront the others it was easy to see that she was a foolish, untidy, but still a rather pleasant woman of about thirty.

" How do you do, Lizzie ? " cried Orianda, offering a cordial hand. The hen fluttered away as, smiling a little wanly, the woman rose.

" Who is it, 'Thaniel ? " she asked.

Loughlin heard no more, for some men came noisily into the bar and Crabbe hurried back to serve them.

III

In the afternoon Orianda drove Gerald in the gig back to the station to fetch the baggage.

"Well, what success, Orianda?" he asked as they jogged along.

"It would be perfect but for Lizzie—that *was* rather a blow. But I should have foreseen her—Lizzies are inevitable. And she *is* difficult—she weeps. But, O I am glad to be home again. Gerald, I feel I shall not leave it, ever."

"Yes, Orianda," he protested, "leave it for me. I'll give your nostalgia a little time to fade. I think it was a man named Pater said: ' All life is a wandering to find home.' You don't want to omit the wandering?"

"Not if I have found my home again?"

"A home with Lizzie!"

"No, not with Lizzie." She flicked the horse with the whip. "I shall be too much for Lizzie; Lizzie will resume her wandering. She's as stupid as a wax widow in a show. Nathaniel is tired of Lizzie, and Lizzie of Nathaniel. The two wretches! But I wish she did not weep."

Gerald had not observed any signs of tearfulness in Lizzie at the midday dinner; on the contrary, she seemed rather a jolly creature, not that she had spoken much beyond " Yes, 'Thaniel, No, 'Thaniel," or Gerald, or Orianda, as the case had been. Her use of his Christian name, which had swept him at once

31

into the bosom of the family, shocked him rather pleasantly. But he did not know what had taken place between the two women; perhaps Lizzie had already perceived and tacitly accepted her displacement.

He was wakened next morning by unusual sounds, chatter of magpies in the front trees, and the ching of hammers on a bulk of iron at the smithy. Below his window a brown terrier stood on its barrel barking at a goose. Such common simple things had power to please him, and for a few days everything at " The Black Dog " seemed planned on this scale of novel enjoyment. The old inn itself, the log yard, harvesting, the chatter of the evening topers, even the village Sunday delighted him with its parade of Phyllis and Corydon, though it is true Phyllis wore a pink frock, stockings of faint blue, and walked like a man, while Corydon had a bowler hat and walked like a bear. He helped 'Thaniel with axe, hammer, and plane, but best of all was to serve mugs of beer nightly in the bar and to drop the coins into the drawer of money. The rest of the time he spent with Orianda whom he wooed happily enough, though without establishing any marked progress. They roamed in fields and in copses, lounged in lanes, looking at things and idling deliciously, at last returning home to be fed by Lizzie, whose case somehow hung in the air, faintly deflecting the perfect stream of felicity.

In their favourite glade a rivulet was joined by a number of springs bubbling from a pool of sand and rock. Below it the enlarged stream was dammed into a small lake once used for turning a mill, but now, since the mill was dismantled, covered with arrow heads and lily leaves, surrounded by inclining trees, bushes of rich green growth, terraces of willow herb, whose fairy-like pink steeples Orianda called " codlins and cream," and catmint with knobs of agreeable odour. A giant hornbeam tree had fallen and lay half buried in the lake. This, and the black poplars whose vacillating leaves underscored the solemn clamour of the outfall, gave to it the very serenity of desolation.

Here they caught sight of the two woodpeckers bathing in the springs, a cock and his hen, who had flown away yaffling, leaving a pretty mottled feather tinged with green floating there. It was endless pleasure to watch each spring bubble upwards from a pouch of sand that spread smoke-like in the water, turning each cone into a midget Vesuvius. A wasp crawled laboriously along a flat rock lying in the pool. It moved weakly, as if, marooned like a mariner upon some unknown isle, it could find no way of escape; only, this isle was no bigger than a dish in an ocean as small as a cartwheel. The wasp seemed to have forgotten that it had wings, it creepingly examined every inch of the rock until it came to a patch of dried dung. Proceeding still as wearily it paused upon a dead leaf until a breeze blew leaf and insect into the water. The wasp was overwhelmed by the rush from the bubbles, but at last it emerged, clutching the woodpecker's floating feather and dragged itself into safety as a swimmer heaves himself into a boat. In a moment it preened its wings, flew back to the rock, and played at Crusoe again. Orianda picked the feather from the pool.

C

" What a fool that wasp is," declared Gerald, " I wonder what it is doing ? "

Orianda, placing the feather in his hat, told him it was probably wandering to find home.

One day, brightest of all days, they went to picnic in the marshes, a strange place to choose, all rank with the musty smell of cattle, and populous with grasshoppers that burred below you and millions, quadrillions of flies that buzzed above. But Orianda loved it. The vast area of coarse pasture harboured not a single farmhouse, only a shed here and there marking a particular field, for a thousand shallow brooks flowed like veins from all directions to the arterial river moving through its silent leagues. Small frills of willow curving on the river brink, and elsewhere a temple of lofty elms, offered the only refuge from sun or storm. Store cattle roamed unchecked from field to field, and in the shade of gaunt rascally bushes sheep were nestling. Green reeds and willow herb followed the watercourses with endless efflorescence, beautiful indeed.

In the late afternoon they had come to a spot where they could see their village three or four miles away, but between them lay the inexorable barrier of the river without a bridge. There was a bridge miles away to the right, they had crossed it earlier in the day; and there was another bridge on the left, but that also was miles distant.

" Now what are we to do ? " asked Orianda. She wore a white muslin frock, a country frock, and a large straw hat with poppies, a country hat. They approached a column of trees. In the soft smooth

34

wind the foliage of the willows was tossed into delicate greys. Orianda said they looked like cockshy heads on spindly necks. She would like to shy at them, but she was tired. " I know what we *could* do." Orianda glanced around the landscape, trees, and bushes; the river was narrow, though deep, not more than forty feet across, and had high banks.

" You can swim, Gerald ? "

Yes, Gerald could swim rather well.

" Then let's swim it, Gerald, and carry our own clothes over."

" Can you swim, Orianda ? "

Yes, Orianda could swim rather well.

" All right then," he said. " I'll go down here a little way."

" O, don't go far, I don't want you to go far away, Gerald," and she added softly, " my dear."

" No, I won't go far," he said, and sat down behind a bush a hundred yards away. Here he undressed, flung his shoes one after the other across the river, and swimming on his back carried his clothes over in two journeys. As he sat drying in the sunlight he heard a shout from Orianda. He peeped out and saw her sporting in the stream quite close below him. She swam with a graceful overarm stroke that tossed a spray of drops behind her and launched her body as easily as a fish's. Her hair was bound in a handkerchief. She waved a hand to him. " You've done it! Bravo! What courage! Wait for me. Lovely." She turned away like an eel, and at every two or three strokes she spat into the air a gay little fountain of water. How extraordinary she was.

35

Gerald wished he had not hurried. By and by he slipped into the water again and swam upstream. He could not see her.

" Have you finished ? " he cried.

" I have finished, yes." Her voice was close above his head. She was lying in the grass, her face propped between her palms, smiling down at him. He could see bare arms and shoulders.

" Got your clothes across ? "

" Of course."

" All dry ? "

She nodded.

" How many journeys ? I made two."

" Two," said Orianda briefly.

" You're all right then." He wafted a kiss, swam back, and dressed slowly. Then as she did not appear he wandered along to her humming a discreet and very audible hum as he went. When he came upon her she still lay upon the grass most scantily clothed.

" I beg your pardon," he said hastily, and full of surprise and modesty walked away. The unembarrassed girl called after him: " Drying my hair."

" All right "—he did not turn round—" no hurry."

But what sensations assailed him. They aroused in his decent gentlemanly mind not exactly a tumult, but a flux of emotions, impressions, and qualms; doubtful emotions, incredible impressions, and torturing qualms. That alluring picture of Orianda, her errant father, the abandoned Lizzie! Had the water perhaps heated his mind though it had cooled his body ? He felt he would have to urge her, drag her if need be, from this " Black Dog." The setting was fair enough and she was fair, but lovely as she was not even she could escape the brush of its vulgarity, its plebeian pressure.

And if all this has, or seems to have, nothing, or little enough to do with the drying of Orianda's hair, it is because the Honourable Gerald was accustomed to walk from grossness with an averted mind.

" Orianda," said he, when she rejoined him, " when are you going to give it up. You cannot stay here . . . with Lizzie . . . can you ? "

" Why not ? " she asked, sharply tossing back her hair. " I stayed with my mother, you know."

" That was different from this. I don't know how, but it must have been."

She took his arm. " Yes, it was. Lizzie I hate, and poor stupid father loves her as much as he loves his axe or his handsaw. I hate her meekness, too. She has taken the heart out of everything. I must get her away."

" I see your need, Orianda, but what can you do ? "

" I shall lie to her, lie like a libertine. And I shall tell her that my mother is coming home at once. No Lizzie could face that."

He was silent. Poor Lizzie did not know that there was now no Mrs. Crabbe.

" You den't like my trick, do you ? " Orianda shook his arm caressingly.

" It hasn't any particular grandeur about it, you know."

" Pooh! You shouldn't waste grandeur on clearing up a mess. This is a very dirty Eden."

" No, all's fair, I suppose."

" But it isn't war, you dear, if that's what you mean. I'm only doing for them what they are naturally loth to do for themselves." She pronounced the word " loth " as if it rimed with moth.

" Lizzie," he said, " I'm sure about Lizzie. I'll swear there is still some fondness in her funny little heart."

" It isn't love, though; she's just sentimental in her puffy kind of way. My dear Honourable, you don't know what love is." He hated her to use his title, for there was then always a breath of scorn in her tone. Just at odd times she seemed to be—not vulgar, that was unthinkable—she seemed to display a contempt for good breeding. He asked with a stiff smile " What *is* love ? "

" For me," said Orianda, fumbling for a definition, " for me it is a compound of anticipation and gratitude. When either of these two ingredients is absent love is dead."

Gerald shook his head, laughing. " It sounds like a malignant bolus that I shouldn't like to take. I feel that love is just self-sacrifice. Apart from the taste of the thing or the price of the thing, why and for what this anticipation, this gratitude ? "

" For the moment of passion, of course. Honour thy moments of passion and keep them holy. But O, Gerald Loughlin," she added mockingly, " this you cannot understand, for you are not a lover; you are not, no, you are not even a good swimmer." Her mockery was adorable, but baffling.

" I do not understand you," he said. Now why in

the whole world of images should she refer to his swimming? He *was* a good swimmer. He was silent for a long time and then again he began to speak of marriage, urging her to give up her project and leave Lizzie in her simple peace.

Then, not for the first time, she burst into a strange perverse intensity that may have been love but might have been rage, that was toned like scorn and yet must have been a jest.

"Lovely Gerald, you must never marry, Gerald, you are too good for marriage. All the best women are already married, yes, they are—to all the worst men." There was an infinite slow caress in her tone but she went on rapidly. "So I shall never marry you, how should I marry a kind man, a good man? I am a barbarian, and want a barbarian lover, to crush and scarify me, but you are so tender and I am so crude. When your soft eyes look on me they look on a volcano."

"I have never known anything half as lovely," he broke in.

Her sudden emotion, though controlled, was unconcealed and she turned away from him.

"My love is a gentleman, but with him I should feel like a wild bee in a canary cage."

"What are you saying!" cried Gerald, putting his arms around her. "Orianda!"

"O yes, we do love in a mezzotinted kind of way. You could do anything with me short of making me marry you, anything, Gerald." She repeated it tenderly. "Anything. But short of marrying me I could make you do nothing." She turned from him again for a moment or two. Then she took his arm and as they walked on she shook it and said chaffingly, " And what a timid swimmer my Gerald is."

But he was dead silent. That flux of sensations in his mind had taken another twist, fiery and exquisite. Like rich clouds they shaped themselves in the sky of his mind, fancy's bright towers with shining pinnacles.

Lizzie welcomed them home. Had they enjoyed themselves—yes, the day had been fine—and so they had enjoyed themselves—well, well, that was right. But throughout the evening Orianda hid herself from him, so he wandered almost distracted about the village until in a garth he saw some men struggling with a cow. Ropes were twisted around its horns and legs. It was flung to the earth. No countryman ever speaks to an animal without blaspheming it, although if he be engaged in some solitary work and inspired to music, he invariably sings a hymn in a voice that seems to have some vague association with wood pulp. So they all blasphemed and shouted. One man, with sore eyes, dressed in a coat of blue fustian and brown cord trousers, hung to the end of a rope at an angle of forty-five degrees. His posture suggested that he was trying to pull the head off the cow. Two other men had taken turns of other rope around some stout posts, and one stood by with a handsaw.

" What are you going to do ? " asked Gerald.

" Its harns be bent, yeu see," said the man with the saw, " they be going into its head. 'Twill blind or madden the beast."

So they blasphemed the cow, and sawed off its crumpled horns.

When Gerald went back to the inn Orianda was
still absent. He sat down but he could not rest.
He could never rest now until he had won her
promise. That lovely image in the river spat fountains of scornful fire at him. " Do not leave me,
Gerald," she had said. He would never leave her,
he would never leave her. But the men talking in the
inn scattered his flying fiery thoughts. They dis-
coursed with a vacuity whose very endlessness was
transcendent. Good God! Was there ever a living
person more magnificently inane than old Tottel, the
registrar. He would have inspired a stork to protest.
Of course, a man of his age should not have worn a
cap, a small one especially; Tottel himself was small,
and it made him look rumpled. He was bandy: his
intellect was bandy too.

" Yes," Mr. Tottel was saying, " it's very interesting to see interesting things, no matter if it's man,
woman, or a object. The most interesting man as
I ever met in my life I met on my honeymoon.
Years ago. He made a lifelong study of railways,
that man, knew 'em from Alpha to . . . to . . . what
is it ? "

" Abednego," said someone.

" Yes, the trunk lines, the fares, the routs, the
junctions of anywheres in England or Scotland or
Ireland or Wales. London, too, the Underground.
I tested him, every station in correct order from
South Kensington to King's Cross. A strange thing!
Nothing to do with railways in 'imself, it was just his
'obby. Was a Baptist minister, really, but still a most
interesting man."

Loughlin could stand it no longer, he hurried away into the garden. He could not find her. Into the kitchen—she was not there. He sat down excited and impatient, but he must wait for her, he wanted to know, to know at once. How divinely she could swim! What was it he wanted to know? He tried to read a book there, a ragged dusty volume about the polar regions. He learned that when a baby whale is born it weighs at least a ton. How horrible!

He rushed out into the fields full of extravagant melancholy and stupid distraction. That! All that was to be her life here! This was your rustic beauty, idiots and railways, boors who could choke an ox and chop off its horns—maddening doubts, maddening doubts—foul-smelling rooms, darkness, indecency. She held him at arm's length still, but she was dove-like, and he was grappled to her soul with hoops of steel, yes, indeed.

But soon this extravagance was allayed. Dim loneliness came imperceivably into the fields and he turned back. The birds piped oddly; some wind was caressing the higher foliage, turning it all one way, the way home. Telegraph poles ahead looked like half-used pencils; the small cross on the steeple glittered with a sharp and shapely permanence.

When he came to the inn Orianda was gone to bed.

IV

The next morning an air of uneasy bustle crept into the house after breakfast, much going in and out and up and down in restrained perturbation.

42

Orianda asked him if he could drive the horse and trap to the station. Yes, he thought he could drive it.

"Lizzie is departing," she said, "there are her boxes and things. It is very good of you, Gerald, if you will be so kind. It is a quiet horse."

Lizzie, then, had been subdued. She was faintly affable during the meal, but thereafter she had been silent; Gerald could not look at her until the last dreadful moment had come and her things were in the trap.

"Good-bye, 'Thaniel," she said to the innkeeper, and kissed him.

"Good-bye, Orianda," and she kissed Orianda, and then climbed into the trap beside Gerald, who said "Click click," and away went the nag.

Lizzie did not speak during the drive—perhaps she was in tears. Gerald would have liked to comfort her, but the nag was unusually spirited and clacked so freshly along that he did not dare turn to the sorrowing woman. They trotted down from the uplands and into the windy road over the marshes. The church spire in the town ahead seemed to change its position with every turn of that twisting route. It would have a background now of high sour-hued down, now of dark woodland, anon of nothing but sky and cloud; in a few miles further there would be the sea. Hereabout there were no trees, few houses, the world was vast and bright, the sky vast and blue. What was prettiest of all was a windmill turning its fans steadily in the draught from the sea. When they crossed the river its slaty slow-going flow was broken into blue waves.

43

At the station Lizzie dismounted without a word and Gerald hitched the nag to a tree. A porter took the luggage and labelled it while Gerald and Lizzie walked about the platform. A calf with a sack over its loins, tied by the neck to a pillar, was bellowing deeply; Lizzie let it suck at her finger for a while, but at last she resumed her walk and talked with her companion.

"She's a fine young thing, clever, his daughter; I'd do anything for her, but for him I've nothing to say. What can I say? What could I do? I gave up a great deal for that man, Mr. Loughlin—I'd better not call you Gerald any more now—a great deal. I knew he'd had trouble with his wicked wife, and now to take her back after so many years, eh! It's beyond me, I know how he hates her. I gave up everything for him, I gave him what he can't give back to me, and he hates her; you know?"

"No, I did not know. I don't know anything of this affair."

"No, of course, you would not know anything of this affair," said Lizzie with a sigh. "I don't want to see him again. I'm a fool, but I got my pride, and that's something to the good, it's almost satisfactory, ain't it?"

As the train was signalled she left him and went into the booking office. He marched up and down, her sad case affecting him with sorrow. The poor wretch, she had given up so much and could yet smile at her trouble. He himself had never surrendered to anything in life—that was what life demanded of you —surrender. For reward it gave you love, this swarthy, skin-deep love that exacted remorseless penalties. What German philosopher was it who said Woman pays the debt of life not by what she does, but by what she suffers? The train rushed in. Gerald busied himself with the luggage, saw that it was loaded, but did not see its owner. He walked rapidly along the carriages, but he could not find her. Well, she was sick of them all, probably hiding from him. Poor woman. The train moved off, and he turned away.

But the station yard outside was startlingly empty, horse and trap were gone. The tree was still there, but with a man leaning against it, a dirty man with a dirty pipe and a dirty smell. Had he seen a horse and trap?

" A brown mare ? "

" Yes."

" Trap with yaller wheels ? "

" That's it."

" O ah, a young ooman druv away in that . . ."

" A young woman! "

" Ah, two minutes ago." And he described Lizzie. " Out yon," said the dirty man, pointing with his dirty pipe to the marshes.

Gerald ran until he saw a way off on the level winding road the trap bowling along at a great pace; Lizzie was lashing the cob.

" The damned cat! " He puffed large puffs of exasperation and felt almost sick with rage, but there was nothing now to be done except walk back to " The Black Dog," which he began to do. Rage gave place to anxiety, fear of some unthinkable disaster, some tragic horror at the inn.

45

" What a clumsy fool! All my fault, my own stupidity! " He groaned when he crossed the bridge at the half distance. He halted there: " It's dreadful, dreadful! " A tremor in his blood, the shame of his foolishness, the fear of catastrophe, all urged him to turn back to the station and hasten away from these miserable complications.

But he did not do so, for across the marshes at the foot of the uplands he saw the horse and trap coming back furiously towards him. Orianda was driving it.

" What has happened ? " she cried, jumping from the trap. " O, what fear I was in, what's happened ? " She put her arms around him tenderly.

" And I was in great fear," he said with a laugh of relief. " What has happened ? "

" The horse came home, just trotted up to the door and stood still. Covered with sweat and foam, you see. The trap was empty. We couldn't understand it, anything, unless you had been flung out and were bleeding on the road somewhere. I turned the thing back and came on at once." She was without a hat; she had been anxious and touched him fondly. " Tell me what's the scare ? "

He told her all.

" But Lizzie was not in the trap," Orianda declared excitedly. " She has not come back. What does it mean, what does she want to do ? Let us find her. Jump up, Gerald."

Away they drove again, but nobody had seen anything of Lizzie. She had gone, vanished, dissolved, and in that strong warm air her soul might indeed have been blown to Paradise. But they did not know

46

how or why. Nobody knew. A vague search was carried on in the afternoon, guarded though fruitless enquiries were made, and at laſt it seemed clear, tolerably clear, that Lizzie had conquered her mad impulse or intention or whatever it was, and walked quietly away across the fields to a ſtation in another direction.

v

For a day or two longer time resumed its sweet slow delightfulness, though its clarity was diminished and some of its enjoyment dimmed. A village woman came to assiſt in the mornings, but Orianda was now seldom able to leave the inn; she had come home to a burden, a happy, pleasing burden, that could not often be laid aside, and therefore a somewhat lonely Loughlin walked the high and the low of the country by day and only in the evenings sat in the parlour with Orianda. Hope too was slipping from his heart as even the joy was slipping from his days, for the spirit of vanished Lizzie, defrauded and indicting, hung in the air of the inn, an implacable obsession, a triumphant forboding that was proved a prophecy when some boys fishing in the mill dam hooked dead Lizzie from the pool under the hornbeam tree.

Then it was that Loughlin's soul discovered to him a mass of feelings—fine sympathy, futile sentiment, a passion for righteousness, morbid regrets—from which a tragic bias was born. After the dread ordeal of the inqueſt, which gave a passive verdict of Found Drowned, it was not possible for him to ſtem this disloyal tendency of his mind. It laid that drowned

47

figure accusatively at the feet of his beloved girl, and no argument or sophistry could disperse the venal savour that clung to the house of " The Black Dog." " To analyse or assess a person's failings or deficiencies," he declared to himself, " is useless, not because such blemishes are immovable, but because they affect the mass of beholders in divers ways. Different minds perceive utterly variant figures in the same being. To Brown Robinson is a hero, to Jones a snob, to Smith a fool. Who then is right ? You are lucky if you can put your miserable self in relation at an angle where your own deficiencies are submerged or minimized, and wise if you can maintain your vision of that interesting angle." But embedded in Loughlin's modest intellect there was a stratum of probity that was rock to these sprays of the casuist; and although Orianda grew more alluring than ever, he packed his bag, and on a morning she herself drove him in the gig to the station.

Upon that miserable departure it was fitting that rain should fall. The station platform was piled with bushel baskets and empty oil barrels. It rained with a quiet remorselessness. Neither spoke a word, no one spoke, no sound was uttered but the faint flicking of the raindrops. Her kiss to him was long and sweet, her good-bye almost voiceless.

" You will write ? " she whispered.

" Yes, I will write."

But he does not do so. In London he has not forgotten, but he cannot endure the thought of that countryside—to be far from the madding crowd is to be mad indeed. It is only after some trance of recollection, when his fond experience is all delicately and renewingly there, that he wavers; but time and time again he relinquishes or postpones his return. And sometimes he thinks he really will write a letter to his friend who lives in the country.

But he does not do so.

Alas, Poor Bollington!

"I WALKED OUT OF THE HOTEL, JUST as I was, and left her there. I never went back again. I don't think I intended anything quite so final, so dastardly; I had not intended it, I had not thought of doing so, but that is how it happened. I lost her, lost my wife purposely. It was heartless, it was shabby, for she was a nice woman, a charming woman, a good deal younger than I was, a splendid woman, in fact she was very beautiful, and yet I ran away from her. How can you explain that, Turner?"

Poor Bollington looked at Turner, who looked at his glass of whiskey, and that looked irresistible—he drank some. Bollington sipped a little from his glass of milk.

I often found myself regarding Bollington as a little old man. Most of the club members did so too, but he was not that at all, he was still on the sunny side of fifty, but *so* unassertive, no presence to speak of, no height, not enough hair to mention—if he had had it would surely have been yellow. So mild and modest he cut no figure at all, just a man in glasses that seemed rather big for him. Turner was different, though he was just as bald; he had stature and bulk, his very pince-nez seemed twice the size of Bollington's spectacles. They had not met each other for ten years.

"Well, yes," Turner said, "but that was a serious thing to do."

"Wasn't it!" said the other, "and I had no idea of the enormity of the offence—not at the time.

She might háve been dead, poor girl, and her executors advertising for me. She had money you know, her people had been licensed victuallers, quite wealthy. Scandalous!"

Bollington brooded upon his sin until Turner sighed: "Ah well, my dear chap."

"But you have no idea," protested Bollington, "how entirely she engrossed me. She was twenty-five and I was forty when we married. She was entrancing. She had always lived in a stinking hole in Balham, and it is amazing how strictly some of those people keep their children; licensed victuallers, did I tell you? Well I was forty, and she was twenty-five; we lived for a year dodging about from one hotel to another all over the British Isles, she was a perfect little nomad. Are you married, Turner?"

No, Turner was not married, he never had been.

"O, but you should be," cried little Bollington, "it's an extraordinary experience, the real business of the world is marriage, marriage. I was deliriously happy and she was learning French and Swedish—that's where we were going later. She was an enchanting little thing, fair, with blue eyes; Phoebe her name was."

Turner thoughtfully brushed his hand across his generous baldness, then folded his arms.

"You really should," repeated Bollington, "you ought to, really. But I remember we went from Killarney to Belfast, and there something dreadful happened. I don't know, it had been growing on her I suppose, but she took a dislike to me there, had

51

ftrange fancies, thought I was unfaithful to her. You see she was popular wherever we went, a lively little woman, in fact she wasn't merely a woman, she was a little magnet, men congregated and clung to her like so many tacks and nails and pins. I didn't object at all—on the contrary, 'Enjoy yourself, Phoebe,' I said, 'I don't expect you always to hang around an old fogey like me.' Fogey was the very word I used; I didn't mean it, of course, but that was the line I took, for she was so charming until she began to get so bad tempered. And believe me, that made her angry, furious. No, not the fogey, but the idea that I did not object to her philandering. It was fatal, it gave colour to her suspicions of me—Turner, I was as innocent as any lamb—tremendous colour. And she had such a sharp tongue! If you ventured to differ from her—and you couldn't help differing sometimes—she'd positively bludgeon you, and you couldn't help being bludgeoned. And she had a passion for putting me right, and I always seemed to be so very wrong, always. She would not be satisfied until she had proved it, and it was so monftrous to be made feel that because you were rather different from other people you were an impertinent fool. Yes, I seemed at laft to gain only the pangs and none of the prizes of marriage. Now there was a lady we met in Belfaft to whom I paid some attention . . ."

" O, good lord! " groaned Turner.

" No, but liften," pleaded Bollington, " it was a very innocent friendship—nothing was further from my mind—and she was very much like my wife, very much, it was noticeable, everybody spoke of it—

I mean the resemblance. A Mrs. Macarthy, a delightful woman, and Phoebe simply loathed her. I confess that my wife's innuendoes were so mean and persistent that at last I hadn't the strength to deny them, in fact at times I wished they were true. Love is idolatry if you like, but it cannot be complete immolation—there's no such bird as the phœnix, is there, Turner ? "

" What, what ? "

" No such bird as the phœnix."

" No, there is no such bird, I believe."

" And sometimes I had to ask myself quite seriously if I really hadn't been up to some infidelity! Nonsense, of course, but I assure you that was the effect it was having upon me. I had doubts of myself, frenzied doubts! And it came to a head between Phoebe and me in our room one day. We quarrelled, O dear, how we quarrelled! She said I was sly, two-faced, unfaithful, I was a scoundrel, and so on. Awfully untrue, all of it. She accused me of dreadful things with Mrs. Macarthy and she screamed out: ' I hope you will treat her better than you have treated me.' Now what did she mean by that, Turner ? "

Bollington eyed his friend as if he expected an oracular answer, but just as Turner was about to respond, Bollington continued: " Well, I never found out, I never knew, for what followed was too terrible. ' I shall go out,' I said, ' it will be better, I think.' Just that, nothing more. I put on my hat and I put my hand on the knob of the door when she said most violently: ' Go with your Macarthys, I

53

never want to see your filthy face again!' Extraordinary you know, Turner. Well, I went out, and I will not deny I was in a rage, terrific. It was raining but I didn't care, and I walked about in it. Then I took shelter in a bookseller's doorway opposite a shop that sold tennis rackets and tobacco, and another one that displayed carnations and peaches on wads of coloured wool. The rain came so fast that the streets seemed to empty, and the passers-by were horridly silent under their umbrellas, and their footsteps splashed so dully, and I tell you I was very sad, Turner, there. I debated whether to rush across the road and buy a lot of carnations and peaches and take them to Phoebe. But I did not do so, Turner, I never went back, never."

"Why, Bollington, you, you were a positive ruffian, Bollington."

"O, scandalous," rejoined the ruffian.

"Well, out with it, what about this Mrs. Macarthy?"

"Mrs. Macarthy? But, Turner, I never saw her again, never, I . . . I forgot her. Yes, I went prowling on until I found myself at the docks and there it suddenly became dark; I don't know, there was no evening, no twilight, the day stopped for a moment—and it did not recover. There were hundreds of bullocks slithering and panting and steaming in the road, thousands; lamps were hung up in the harbour, cabs and trollies rattled round the bullocks, the rain fell dismally and everybody hurried. I went into the dock and saw them loading the steamer, it was called s.s. *Frolic*, and really, Turner, the things they put into the belly of that steamer were rather funny: tons and tons of monstrous big chain, the links as big as soup plates, and two or three pantechnicon vans. Yes, but I was anything but frolicsome, I assure you, I was full of misery and trepidation and the deuce knows what. I did not know what I wanted to do, or what I was going to do, but I found myself buying a ticket to go to Liverpool on that steamer, and, in short, I embarked. How wretched I was, but how determined. Everything on board was depressing and dirty, and when at last we moved off the foam slewed away in filthy bubbles as if that dirty steamer had been sick and was running away from it. I got to Liverpool in the early morn, but I did not stay there, it is such a clamouring place, all trams and trollies and teashops. I sat in the station for an hour, the most miserable man alive, the most miserable ever born. I wanted some rest, some peace, some repose, but they never ceased shunting an endless train of goods trucks, banging and screeching until I almost screamed at the very porters. Criff was the name on some of the trucks, I remember, Criff, and everything seemed to be going criff, criff, criff. I haven't discovered to this day what Criff signifies, whether it's a station or a company, or a manufacture, but it was Criff, I remember. Well, I rushed to London and put my affairs in order. A day or two later I went to Southampton and boarded another steamer and put to sea, or rather we were ignominiously lugged out of the dock by a little rat of a tug that seemed all funnel and hooter. I was off to America, and there I stopped for over three years."

Turner sighed. A waiter brought him another glass of spirit.

"I can't help thinking, Bollington, that it was all very fiery and touchy. Of course, I don't know, but really it was a bit steep, very squeamish of you. What did your wife say?"

"I never communicated with her, I never heard from her, I just dropped out. My filthy face, you know, she did not want to see it again."

"Oh come, Bollington! And what did Mrs. Macarthy say?"

"Mrs. Macarthy! I never saw or heard of her again. I told you that."

"Ah, yes, you told me. So you slung off to America."

"I was intensely miserable there for a long while. Of course I loved Phoebe enormously, I felt the separation, I . . . O, it is impossible to describe. But what was worst of all was the meanness of my behaviour, there was nothing heroic about it, I soon saw clearly that it was a shabby trick, disgusting, I had bolted and left her to the mercy of . . . well, of whatever there was. It made such an awful barrier— you've no idea of my compunction—I couldn't make overtures—' Let us forgive and forget.' I was a mean rascal, I *was* filthy. That was the barrier—myself; I was too bad. I thought I should recover and enjoy life again, I began to think of Phoebe as a cat, a little cat. I went everywhere and did everything. But America is a big country, I couldn't get into contact, I was lonely, very lonely, and although two years went by I longed for Phoebe. Everything I did I wanted to do with Phoebe by my side. And then my cousin, my only relative in the world—he lived in England— he died. I scarcely ever saw him, but still he was my kin. And he died. You've no comprehension, Turner, of the truly awful sensation such a bereavement brings. Not a soul in the world now would have the remotest interest in my welfare. O, I tell you, Turner, it was tragic, tragic, when my cousin died. It made my isolation complete. I was alone, a man who had made a dreadful mess of life. What with sorrow and remorse I felt that I should soon die, not of disease, but disgust."

" You were a great ninny," ejaculated his friend. " Why the devil didn't you hurry back, claim your wife, bygones be bygones; why bless my conscience, what a ninny, what a great ninny! "

" Yes, Turner, it is as you say. But though conscience is a good servant it is a very bad master, it overruled me, it shamed me, and I hung on to America for still another year. I tell you my situation was unbearable, I was tied to my misery, I was a tethered dog, a duck without water—even dirty water. And I hadn't any faith in myself or in my case; I knew I was wrong, had always been wrong, Phoebe had taught me that. I hadn't any faith, I wish I had had. Faith can move mountains, so they say, though I've never heard of it actually being done."

" No, not in historical times," declared Turner.

" What do you mean by that ? "

" O well, time is nothing, it's nothing, it comes and off it goes. Has it ever occurred to you, Bollington, that in 5,000 years or so there will be nobody in the world speaking the English language, our very exist-ence even will be speculated upon, as if we were the Anthropophagi? O good lord, yes."

And another whiskey.

"You know, Bollington, you were a perfect fool. You behaved like one of those half-baked civil service hounds who lunch in a dairy on a cup of tea and a cream horn. You wanted some beef, some ginger. You came back, you must have come back because there you are now."

"Yes, Turner, I came back after nearly four years. Everything was different, ah, how strange! I could not find Phoebe, it is weird how people can disappear. I made enquiries, but it was like looking for a lost umbrella, fruitless after so long."

"Well, but what about Mrs. Macarthy?"

Mr. Bollington said, slowly and with the utmost precision: "I did not see Mrs. Macarthy again."

"O, of course, you did not see her again, not ever."

"Not ever. I feared Phoebe had gone abroad too, but at last I found her in London...."

"No," roared Turner, "why the devil couldn't you say so and done with it? I've been sweating with sympathy for you. O, I say, Bollington!"

"My dear Turner, listen. Do you know, she was delighted to see me, she even kissed me, straight off, and we went out to dine and had the very deuce of a spread and we were having the very deuce of a good time. She was lovelier than ever, and I could see all her old affection for me was returning, she was so . . . well, I can't tell you, Turner, but she had no

58

animosity whatever, no grievance, she would certainly have taken me back that very night. O dear, dear ... and then! I was anxious to throw myself at her feet, but you couldn't do that in a public café, I could only touch her hands, beautiful, as they lay on the white linen cloth. I kept asking: 'Do you forgive me?' and she would reply: 'I have nothing to forgive, dear, nothing.' How wonderful that sounded to my truly penitent soul—I wanted to die.

" ' But you don't ask me where I've been!' she cried gaily, ' or what I've been doing, you careless old Peter. I've been to France, and Sweden too!'

" I was delighted to hear that, it was so very plucky.

" ' When did you go?' I asked.

" ' When I left you,' she said.

" ' You mean when I went away?'

" ' Did you go away? O, of course, you must have. Poor Peter, what a sad time he has had.'

" I was a little bewildered, but I was delighted; in fact, Turner, I was hopelessly infatuated again, I wanted to wring out all the dregs of my detestable villainy and be absolved. All I could begin with was: ' Were you not very glad to be rid of me?'

" ' Well,' she said, ' my great fear at first was that you would find me again and make it up. I didn't want that then, at least, I thought I didn't.'

" ' That's exactly what I felt,' I exclaimed, ' but how could I find you?'

" ' Well,' Phoebe said, ' you might have found out and followed me. But I promise never to run away again, Peter dear, never.'

" Turner, my reeling intelligence swerved like a shot bird.

" ' Do you mean, Phoebe, that you ran away from *me* ? '

" ' Yes, didn't I ? ' she answered.

" ' But I ran away from *you*,' I said. ' I walked out of the hotel on that dreadful afternoon we quarrelled so, and I never went back. I went to America. I was in America nearly four years.'

" ' Do you mean you ran away from me ? ' she cried.

" ' Yes,' I said, ' didn't I ? '

" ' But that is exactly what I did—I mean, I ran away from you. *I* walked out of the hotel directly you had gone—*I* never went back, and I've been abroad thinking how tremendously I had served you out, and wondering what you thought of it all and where you were.'

" I could only say ' Good God, Phoebe, I've had the most awful four years of remorse and sorrow, all vain, mistaken, useless, thrown away.' And she said: ' And I've had four years—living in a fool's paradise after all. How dared you run away, it's disgusting! '

" And, Turner, in a moment she was at me again in her old dreadful way, and the last words I had from her were: ' Now I *never* want to see your face again, never, this *is* the end! '

" And that's how things are now, Turner. It's rather sad, isn't it ? "

" Sad! Why you chump, when was it you saw her ? "

"O, a long time ago, it must be nearly three years now."

"Three years! But you'll see her again!"

"Tfoo! No, no, no, Turner. God bless me, no, no, no!" said the little old man.

The Ballet Girl

ON THE LAST NIGHT OF HILARY term Simpkins left his father's shop a quarter before the closing hour in order to deliver personally a letter to John Evans-Antrobus, Esq., of St. Saviour's College. Simpkins was a clerk to his father, and the letter he carried was inscribed on its envelope as " Important," and a further direction, " Wait Answer," was doubly underlined. Acting as he was told to act by his father, than whom he was incapable of recognizing any bigger authority either in this world or, if such a slight, shrinking fellow could ever project his comprehension so far, in the next, he passed the porter's lodge under the archway of St. Saviour's, and crossing the first quadrangle, entered a small hall that bore the names J. Evans-Antrobus with half a dozen others neatly painted on the wall. He climbed two flights of wooden stairs, and knocking over a door whose lintel was marked " 5, Evans-Antrobus," was invited to " Come in." He entered a study, and confronted three hilarious young men, all clothed immaculately in evening dress, a costume he himself privily admired much as a derelict might envy the harp of an angel. The noisiest young gentleman, the tall one with a monocle, was his quarry; he handed the letter to him. Mr. Evans-Antrobus then read the letter, which invited him to pay instanter a four-year-old debt of some nine or ten pounds which he had inexplicably but consistently overlooked. And there was a half-hidden but unpleasant alternative suggested should

Mr. Evans-Antrobus fail to comply with this not unreasonable request. Mr. Evans-Antrobus said "Damn!" In point of fact he enlarged the scope of his vocabulary far beyond the limits of that modest expletive, while his two friends, being invited to read the missive, also exclaimed in terms that were not at all subsidiary.

"My compliments to Messrs. Bagshot and Buffle!" exclaimed the tall young man with the monocle angrily; "I shall certainly call round and see them in the morning. Good evening!"

Little Simpkins explained that Bagshot and Buffle were not in need of compliments, their business being to sell boots and to receive payment for them. Two of the jolly young gentlemen proposed to throw him down the stairs, and were only persuaded not to by the third jolly young gentleman, who much preferred to throw him out of the window. Whereupon Simpkins politely hinted that he would be compelled to interview the college dean and await developments in his chambers. Simpkins made it quite clear that, whatever happened, he was going to wait somewhere until he got the money. The three jolly young gentlemen then told little Simpkins exactly what they thought of him, exactly, omitting no shade of denunciation, fine or emphatic. They told him where he ought to be at the very moment, where he would quickly be unless he took himself off; in short, they told him a lot of prophetic things which, as is the way of prophecy, invited a climax of catastrophic horror.

"What is your name? Who the devil are you?"

"My name is Simpkins."

Then the three jolly young gentlemen took counsel together in whispers, and at last Mr. Evans-Antrobus said: " Well, if you insist upon waiting, Mr. Simpkins, I must get the money for you. I can borrow it, I suppose, boys, from Fazz, can't I ? "

Again they consulted in whispers, after which two of the young gents said they ought to be going, and so they went.

" Wait here for me," said Mr. Evans-Antrobus, " I shall not be five minutes."

But Mr. Simpkins was so firmly opposed to this course that the other relented. " Damn you! come along with me, then; I must go and see Fazz." So off they went to some rooms higher up the same flight of stairs, beyond a door that was marked " F. A. Zealander." When they entered Fazz sat moping in front of the fire; he was wrapped as deeply as an Esquimaux in some plaid travelling rugs girt with the pink rope of a dressing-gown that lay across his knees. The fire was good, but the hearth was full of ashes. The end of the fender was ornamented with the strange little iron face of a man whose eyes were shut but whose knobby cheeks fondly glowed. Fazz's eyes were not shut, they were covered by dim glasses, and his cheeks had no more glow than a sponge.

" Hullo, Fazz. You better to-day ? "

" No, dearie, I am not conscious of any improvement. This influenza's a thug; I am being deprived of my vitality as completely as a fried rasher."

" Oh, by the by," said his friend, " you don't know each other: Mr. Simpkins—Mr. Zealander."

The former bowed awkwardly and unexpectedly shook Mr. Zealander's hot limp hand. At that moment a man hurried in, exclaiming: " Mr. Evans-Antrobus, sir, the Dean wants to see you in his rooms at once, sir! "

" That is deuced awkward," said that gentleman blandly. " Just excuse me for a moment or two, Fazz."

He hurried out, leaving Simpkins confronting Mr. Zealander in some confusion. Fazz poked his flaming coal. " This fire! Did you ever see such a morbid conflagration ? "

" Rather nice, I thought," replied Simpkins affably; " quite cool to-night, outside, rather."

The host peered at him through those dim glasses. " There's a foggy humidity about everything, like the inside of a cream tart. But sit down," said Fazz, with the geniality of a man who was about to be hung and was rather glad that he was no longer to be exposed to the fraudulent excess of life, " and tell me a bawdy story."

Simpkins sank into an armchair and was silent.

" Perhaps you don't care for bawdy stories ? " continued Fazz. " I do, I do. I love vulgarity; there is certainly a niche in life for vulgarity. If ever I possess a house of my own I will arrange—-I will, upon my soul—one augustly vulgar room, divinely vulgar, upholstered in sallow pigskin. Do tell me something. You haven't got a spanner on you, I suppose ? There is something the matter with my bed. Once it was full of goose feathers, but now I sleep, as it were, on the bulge of a barrel; I must do

65   E

something to it with a spanner. I hate spanners—
such dreadful democratic tools; they terrify me, they
gape at you as if they wanted to bite you. Spanners
are made of iron, and this is a funny world, for it is
full of things like spanners."

Simpkins timidly rose up through the waves of this
discourse and asked if he could "do" anything.
He was mystified, amused, and impressed by this
person; he didn't often meet people like that, he
didn't often meet anybody; he rather liked him.
On each side of the invalid there were tables and
bottles of medicine.

"I am just going to take my temperature," said
Fazz. "Do have a cigarette, dearie, or a cigar. Can
you see the matches? Yes; now do you mind
surrounding me with my medicines? They give
such a hopeful air to the occasion. There's a phial
of sodium salicylate tabloids, I must take six of them
in a minute or two. Then there are the quinine
capsules; the formalin, yes; those lozenges I suck—
have one?—they are so comforting, and that depressing laxative; surround me with them. Oh,
glorious, benignant, isn't it? Now I shall take my
temperature; I shall be as stolid as the sphinx for
three minutes, so do tell me that story. Where is my
thermometer, oh!" He popped the thermometer
into his mouth, but pulled it out again. "Do you
know L. G.? He's a blithe little fellow, oh, very
blithe. He was in Jacobsen's rooms the other day—
Jacobsen's a bit of an art connoisseur, you know, and
draws and paints, and Jacobsen drew attention to the
portrait of a lady that was hanging on the wall. ' Oh,

dear,' said L. G., ' what a hag! Where did you get that thing ? ' just like that. Such a perfect fool, L. G. ' It's my mother,' says Jacobsen. ' Oh, of course,' explained L. G., ' I didn't mean *that*, of course, my dear fellow; I referred to the horrible treatment, entirely to the horrible treatment; it is a wretched daub.' ' I did it myself!' said Jacobsen. You don't know L. G.? Oh, he is very blithe. What were you going to tell me ? I am just going to take my temperature; yesterday it was ninety odd point something. I do hope it is different now. I can't bear those points, they seem so equivocal."

Fazz sat with the tube of the thermometer pro-jecting from his mouth. At the end of the test he regarded it very earnestly before returning it dis-consolately to the table. Then he addressed his visitor with considerable gloom.

" Pardon me, I did not catch your name."

" Simpkins."

" Simpkins!" repeated Fazz, with a dubious drawl. " Oh, I'm sorry, I don't like Simpkins, it sounds so minuscular. What are you taking ? "

" I won't take anything, sir, thank you," replied Simpkins.

" I mean, what schools are you taking ? "

" Oh, no school at all."

Fazz was mystified: " What college are you ? "

" I'm not at a college," confessed the other. " I came to see Mr. Evans-Antrobus with a note. I'm waiting for an answer."

" Where do you come from ? "

" From Bagshot and Buffle's." After a silence he added: " Bespoke boots."

" Hump, you are very young to make bespoke boots, aren't you, Simpkins, surely ? Are you an Agnostic ? Have a cigar ? You must, you've been very good, and I am so interested in your career; but tell me now what it exactly is that you are sitting in my room for ? "

Simpkins told him all he could.

" It's interesting, most fascinating," declared Fazz, " but it is a little beyond me all the same. I am afraid, Simpkins, that you have been deposited with me as if I were a bank and you were something not negotiable, as you really are, I fear. But you mustn't tell the Dean about Evans-Antrobus, no, you mustn't, it's never done. Tell me, why do you make bespoke boots ? It's an unusual taste to display. Wouldn't you rather come to college, for instance, and study . . . er . . . anthropology—nothing at all about boots in anthropology ? "

" No," said Simpkins. He shuffled in his chair and felt uneasy. " I'd be out of my depth." Fazz glared at him, and Simpkins repeated: " Out of my depth, that would be, sure."

" This is very shameful," commented the other, " but it's interesting, most fascinating. You brazenly maintain that you would rather study boots than . . . than books and brains ! "

" A cobbler must stick to his last," replied Simpkins, recalling a phrase of his father's.

" Bravo! " cried Fazz, " but not to an everlasting last! "

"And I don't know anything about all this; there's nothing about it I'd want to know, it wouldn't be any good to me. It's no use mixing things, and there's a lot to be learnt about boots—you'd be surprised. You got to keep yourself to yourself and not get out of your depth—take a steady line and stick to it, and not get out of your depth."

"But, dearie, you don't sleep with a lifebelt girt about your loins, do you now? I'm not out of my depth; I shouldn't be even if I started to make boots. . . ."

"Oh, wouldn't you?" shouted Simpkins.

"I should find it rather a shallow occupation; mere business is the very devil of a business; business would be a funny sort of life."

"Life's a funny business; you look after your business and that will look after you."

"But what in the world are we in the world at all for, Simpkins? Isn't it surely to do just the things we most intensely want to do? And you do boots and boots and boots. Don't you ever get out and about?—theatres—girls—sport—or do you insist on boot, the whole boot, and nothing but boot?"

"No, none of them," replied Simpkins. "Don't care for theatres, I've never been. Don't care for girls, I like a quiet life. I keep myself to myself—it's safer, don't get out of your depth then. I do go and have a look at the football match sometimes, but it's only because we make the boots for some of your crack players, and you want to know what you are making them for. Work doesn't trouble me, nothing troubles me, and I got money in the bank."

" Damme, Simpkins, you have a terrible conviction about you; if I listen to you much longer I shall bind myself apprentice to you. I feel sure that you make nice, soft, watertight, everlasting boots, and then we should rise in the profession together. Discourse, Simpkins; you enchant mine ears—both of them."

" What I say is," concluded Simpkins, " you can't understand everything. I shouldn't want to; I'm all right as it is."

" Of course you are, you're simply too true. This is a place flowing with afternoon tea, tutors, and clap-trap. It's a city in which everything is set upon a bill. You're simply too true, if we are not out of our depth we are in up to our ears—I am. It's most fascinating."

Soon afterwards Simpkins left him. Descending the stairs to the rooms of Evans-Antrobus he switched on the light. It was very quiet and snug in those rooms, with the soft elegant couch, the reading-lamp with the delicious violet shade, the decanter with whiskey, the box of chocolate biscuits, and the gramophone. He sat down by the fire, waiting and waiting. Simpkins waited so long that he got used to the room, he even stole a sip of whiskey and some of the chocolate biscuits. Then to show his independence, his contempt for Mr. Evans-Antrobus and his trickery, he took still more of the whiskey—a drink he had never tasted before—he really took quite a lot. He heaped coal upon the fire, and stalked about the room with his hands in his pockets or examined the books, most of which were

about something called Jurisprudence, and suchlike.
Simpkins liked books; he began reading:

That the Pleuronectidæ are admirably adapted by their
flattened and asymmetrical structure for their habits of life,
is manifest from several species, such as soles and flounders,
etc., being extremely common.

He did not care much for science; he opened
another:

It is difficult indeed to imagine that anything can
oscillate so rapidly as to strike the retina of the eye
831,479,000,000,000 in one second, as must be the case with
violet light according to this hypothesis.

Simpkins looked at the light and blinked his eyes.
That had a violet shade. He really did not care for
science, and he had an inclination to put the book
down as his head seemed to be swaying, but he
continued to turn the pages.

Snowdon is the highest mountain in England or Wales.
Snowdon is not so high as Ben Nevis.
Therefore the highest mountain in England or Wales is
not so high as Ben Nevis.

" Oh, my head! " mumbled Simpkins.

Water must be either warm or not warm, but it does not
follow that it must be warm or cold.

Simpkins felt giddy. He dropped the book, and
tottered to the couch. Immediately the room spun
round and something in his head began to hum, to
roar like an aeroplane a long way up in the sky. He
felt that he ought to get out of the room, quickly, and
get some water, either not or cold warm—he didn't

mind which! He clapped on his hat and, slipping into his overcoat, he reached a door. It opened into a bedroom, very bare indeed compared with this other room, but Simpkins rolled in; the door slammed behind him, and in the darkness he fell upon a bed, with queer sensations that seemed to be dividing and subtracting in him.

When he awoke later—oh, it seemed much later— he felt quite well again. He had forgotten where he was. It was a strange place he was in, utterly dark; but there was a great noise sounding quite close to him—a gramophone, people shouting choruses and dancing about in the adjoining room. He could hear a lady's voice too. Then he remembered that he ought not to be in that room at all; it was, why, yes, it was criminal; he might be taken for a burglar or something! He slid from the bed, groped in the darkness until he found his hat, unbuttoned his coat, for he was fearfully hot, and stood at the bedroom door trembling in the darkness, waiting and listening to that tremendous row. He *had* been a fool to come in there! How was he to get out—how the deuce was he to get out ? The gramophone stopped. He could hear the voices more plainly. He grew silently panic-stricken; it was awful, they'd be coming in to him perhaps, and find him sneaking there like a thief —he must get out, he must, he must get out; yes, but how ?

The singing began again. The men kept calling out " Lulu! Lulu! " and a lady's gay voice would reply to a Charley or a George, and so on, when all at once there came a peremptory knock at the outer door. The noise within stopped immediately. Deep silence. Simpkins could hear whispering. The people in there were startled; he could almost feel them staring at each other with uneasiness. The lady laughed out startlingly shrill. " Sh-s-s-sh! " the others cried. The loud knocking began again, emphatic, terrible. Simpkins' already quaking heart began to beat ecstatically. Why, oh why, didn't they open that door ?—open it! open it! There was shuffling in the room, and when the knocking was repeated for the third time the outer door was apparently unlocked.

" Fazz! Oh, Fazz, you brute! " cried the relieved voices in the room. " You fool, Fazz! Come in, damn you, and shut the door."

" Good gracious! " exclaimed the apparently deliberating Fazz, " what is that ? "

" Hullo, Rob Roy! " cried the lady, " it's me."

" Charmed to meet you, madame. How interesting, most fascinating; yes, I am quite charmed, but I wish somebody would kindly give me the loose end of it all. I'm suffering, as you see, dearies, and I don't understand all this, I'm quite out of my depth. The noise you've been making is just crushing me."

Several voices began to explain at once: " We captured her, Fazz, yes—Rape of the Sabines, what! —from the Vaudeville. Had a rag, glorious— corralled all the attendants and scene-shifters— rushed the stage—we did! we did!—everybody chased somebody, and we chased Lulu—we did! we did! "

" Oh, shut up, everybody! " cried out Fazz.

73

" Yes, listen," cried the voice of Evans-Antrobus.
" This is how it happened: they chased the eight
Sisters Victoria off the stage, and we spied dear little
Lulu—she was one of those eight Victorias—bolting
down a passage to the stage entrance. She fled into
the street just as she was—isn't she a duck ? There
was a taxi standing there, and Lulu, wise woman,
jumped in—and we jumped in too. (We did! We
did!) 'Where for ?' says taximan. 'Saviour's
College,' say we, and here you are—Lulu—what do
you think of her ? "

" Charming, utterly charming," replied Fazz.
" The details are most clarifying; but how did you
manage to usher her into the college ? "

" My overcoat on," explained one voice.

" And my hat," cried another.

" And we dazzled the porter," said a third. There
were lots of other jolly things to explain: Lulu had
not resisted at all, she had enjoyed it; it was a lark!

" Oh, beautiful! Most fascinating! " agreed
Fazz. " But how you propose to get her out of the
college I have no more notion than Satan has of
sanctity—it's rather late, isn't it ? "

Simpkins, in his dark room, could hear someone
rushing up the stairs with flying leaps that ceased at
the outer door. Then a breathless voice hissed out:
" You fellows, scat, scat! Police are in the lodge with
the proctors and that taximan! "

In a moment Evans-Antrobus began to groan.
" Oh, my God, what can we do with her ? We must
get her out at once—over the wall, eh, at once, quick!
Johnstone, quick, go and find a rope, quick, a rope."

74

And Fazz said: " It does begin to look a little foolish. Oh, I am feeling so damn bad—but you can't blame a fool for anything it does, can you ? But I am bad; I am going to bed instantly, I feel quite out of my depth here. Oh, that young friend of yours, that Simpkins, charming young person! Very blithe he was, dear Evans-Antrobus! "

Everybody now seemed to rush away from the room except the girl Lulu and Evans-Antrobus. He was evidently very agitated and in a bad humour. He clumped about the room exclaiming, " Oh, damnation, do hurry up, somebody. What am I to do with her, boozy little pig! Do hurry up! "

" Who's a pig ? I want to go out of here," shrilled Lulu, and apparently she made for the door.

" You can't go like that! " he cried; " you can't, you mustn't. Don't be a fool, Lulu! Lulu! Now, isn't this a fearful mess ? "

" I'm not going to stop here with you, ugly thing! I don't like it; I'm going now, let go."

" But you can't go, I tell you, in these things, not like that. Let me think, let me think, can't you! Why don't you let me think, you little fool! Put something on you, my overcoat; cover yourself up. I shall be ruined, damn you! Why the devil did you come here, you . . .! "

" And who brought me here, Mr. Antibus ? Oh yes, I know you; I shall have something to say to the vicar, or whoever it is you're afraid of, baby-face! Let me go; I don't want to be left here alone with you! " she yelled. Simpkins heard an awful scuffle. He could wait no longer; he flung open

75

the door, rushed into the room, and caught up a syphon, the first handy weapon. They saw him at once, and stood apart amazed.

"Fine game!" said the trembling Simpkins to the man, with all the sternness at his command. As nobody spoke he repeated, quite contemptuously: "Fine game!"

Lulu was breathing hard, with her hands resting upon her bosom. Her appearance was so startling to the boy that he nearly dropped the syphon. He continued to face her, hugging it with both hands against his body. She was clad in pink tights—they were of silk, they glistened in the sharper light from under the violet shade—a soft white tarlatan skirt that spread around her like a carnation, and a rose-coloured bodice. She was dainty, with a little round head and a little round face like a briar rose; but he guessed she was strong, though her beauty had apparently all the fragility of a flower. Her hair, of dull dark gold, hung in loose tidiness without pin or braid, the locks cut short to her neck, where they curved in to brush the white skin; a deep straight fringe of it was combed upon the childish brow. Grey were her surprised eyes, and wide the pouting lips. Her lovely naked arms—oh, he could scarcely bear to look at them. She stood now, with one hand upon her hip and the other lying against her cheek, staring at Simpkins. Then she danced delightfully up to him and took the syphon away.

"Look here," said Evans-Antrobus to Lulu—he had recovered his nerve, and did not express any astonishment at Simpkins' sudden appearance—"he is just your size, you dress up in his clothes, quick, then it's simple."

" No," said the girl.

" And no for me," said Simpkins fiercely—almost.

Just then the door was thrust partly open and a rope was flung into the room. The bringer of it darted away downstairs again.

" Hi! here! " called Evans-Antrobus, rushing to the door; but nobody stayed for him, nobody answered him. He came back and picked up the rope.

" Put on that coat," he commanded Lulu, " and that hat. Now, look here, not a word, not a giggle even, or we are done, and I might just as well screw your blessed neck! "

" Would you ? " snorted Simpkins, with not a little animosity.

" Yes, would you! " chimed Lulu, but nevertheless she obeyed and followed him down the stairs. When she turned and beckoned, Simpkins followed too. They crossed a dark quadrangle, passed down a passage that was utter darkness, through another quad, another passage, and halted in a gloomy yard behind the chapel, where Evans-Antrobus struck a match, and where empty boxes, bottles, and other rubbish had accumulated under a wall about ten feet high.

" You first, and quiet, quiet," growled Evans-Antrobus to Simpkins. No one spoke again. Night was thickly dark, the stars were dim, the air moist and chill. Simpkins, assisted by the other man, clambered over rickety boxes and straddled the high thick wall. The rope was hung over, too, and when the big man had jumped to earth again, dragging his weight against it, Simpkins slid down on the other side. He was now in a narrow street, with a dim lamp at one end that cast no gleam to the spot where he had descended. There were dark high-browed buildings looming high around him. He stood holding the end of the rope and looking up at the stars— very faint they were. The wall was much higher on this side, looked like a mountain, and he thought of Ben Nevis again. This was out of your depth, if you like, out of your depth entirely. It was all wrong somehow, or, at any rate, it was not all right; it couldn't be right. Never again would he mess about with a lot of lunatics. He hadn't done any good, he hadn't even got the money—he had forgotten it. He had not got anything at all except a headache.

The rope tightened. Lulu was astride the wall, quarrelling with the man on the other side.

" Keep your rotten coat! " She slipped it off and flung it down from the wall. " And your rotten hat, too, spider-face! " She flung that down from the wall, and spat into the darkness. Turning to the other side, she whispered: " I'm coming," and scrambled down, sliding into Simpkins' arms. And somehow he stood holding her so, embracing her quite tightly. She was all softness and perfume, he could not let her go; she had scarcely anything on— he would not let her go. It was marvellous and beautiful to him; the glimmer of her white face was mysterious and tender in the darkness. She put her arms around his neck:

" Oh . . . I rather love you," she said.

Simple Simon

THIS SIMPLE MAN LIVED LONELY IN A hut in the depths of a forest, just underneath three hovering trees, a pine tree and two beeches. The sun never was clear in the forest, but the fogs that rose in its unshaken shade were neither sweet nor sour. Lonely was Simon, for he had given up all the sweet of the world and had received none of the sweet of heaven. Old now, and his house falling to ruin, he said he would go seek the sweet of heaven, for what was there in the mortal world to detain him? Not peace, certainly, for time growled and scratched at him like a mangy dog, and there were no memories to cherish; he had had a heavy father, a mother who was light, and never a lay-by who had not deceived him. So he went in his tatters and his simplicity to the lord of the manor.

" I'm bound for heaven, sir," says Simon, " will you give me an old coat, or an odd rag or so? There's a hole in my shoe, sir, and good fortune slips out of it."

No—the lord of the manor said—he could not give him a decent suit, nor a shoe, nor the rags neither. Had he not let him dwell all life long in his forest? With not a finger of rent coming? Snaring the conies—(May your tongue never vex you, sir!)—and devouring the birds—(May God see me, sir!)—and cutting the fuel, snug as a bee in a big white hive. (Never a snooze of sleep, with the wind howling in the latch of it and the cracks gaping, sir!) What with the taxes and the ways of women—said the lord —he had but a scrimping time of it himself, so he

79

had. There was neither malt in the kiln nor meal in the hopper, and there were thieves in the parish. Indeed, he would as lief go with Simon, but it was such a diggins of a way off.

So Simon went walking on until he came to the godly man who lived in a blessed mansion, full of delights for the mind and eye as well as a deal of comfort for his belly.

No—the godly man said—he would not give him anything, for the Lord took no shame of a man's covering.

" Ah, but your holiness," said Simon, " I've a care to look decent when I go to the King of All."

" My poor man, how will you get there, my poor man ? " he said.

" Maybe," says Simon, " I'll get a lift on my way."

" You'll get no lift," the godly man said, " for it's a hard and lonely road to travel."

" My sorrow! And I heard it was a good place to go to! "

" It is a good place, my simple man, but the road to it is difficult and empty and hard. You will get no lift, you will lose your way, you will be taken with a sickness."

" Ah, and I heard it was a good kind road, and help in the end of it and warmth and a snap of victuals."

" No doubt, no doubt, but I tell you, don't be setting yourself up for to judge of it. Go back to your home and be at peace with the world."

" Mine's all walk-on," said Simon, and turning away he looked towards his home. Distant or near there was nothing he could see but trees, not a glint

80

of sea, and little of sky, and nothing of a hill or the roof of a friendly house—just a trap of trees as close as a large hand held before a large face, beeches and beeches, pines and pines. And buried in the middle of it was a tiny hut, sour and broken; in the time of storms the downpour would try to dash it into the ground, and the wind would try to tear it out. Well, he had had his enough of it, so he went to another man, a scholar for learning, and told him his intentions and his wishes.

" To heaven! " said the scholar. " Well, it's a fair day for that good-looking journey."

" It is indeed a fine day," said Simon. As clear as crystal it was, yet soft and mellow as snuff.

" Then content you, man Simon, and stay in it."

" Ah, sir," he says, " I've a mind and a will that makes me serve them."

" Cats will mouse and larks will sing," the scholar said, " but you are neither the one nor the other. What you seek is hidden, perhaps hidden for ever; God remove discontent and greed from the world: why should you look on the other side of a wall— what is a wall for ? "

The old man was silent.

" How long has this notion possessed you ? "

The old man quavered " Since . . . since . . ." but he could say no more. A green bird flew laughing above them.

" What bird is that—what is it making that noise for ? "

" It is a woodpecker, sir; he knows he can sing a song for sixpence."

The scholar stood looking up into the sky. His boots were old—well, that is the doom of all boots, just as it is of man. His clothes were out of fashion, so was his knowledge; stripped of his gentle dignity he was but dust and ashes.

"To travel from the world?" he was saying. "That is not wise."

"Ah, sir, wisdom was ever deluding me, for I'm not more than half done—like a poor potato. First, of course, there's the things you don't know; then there's the things you do know but can't understand; then there's the things you do understand but which don't matter. Saving your presence, sir, there's a heap of understanding to be done before you're anything but a fool."

"He is not a fool who is happy; mortal pleasures decline as the bubble of knowledge grows; that's the long of it, and it's the short of it too."

Simon was silent, adding up the buttons on the scholar's tidy coat. He counted five of them, they shone like gold and looked—oh, very well they looked.

"I was happy once," then he said. "Ah, and I remember I was happy twice, yes, and three times I was happy in this world. I was not happy since . . ."

"Yes, since what?" the scholar asked him: but the old man was dumb.

"Tell me, Simon, what made you happy."

"I was happy, sir, when I first dwelled in the wood and made with my own hands a house of boards. Why—you'd not believe—but it had a chimney then, and was no ways draughty then, and was not creaky then, nor damp then; a good fine house with a door and a half door, birds about it, magpies and tits and fine boy blackbirds! A lake with a score of mallards on it! And for conies and cushats you could take your oath of a meal any day in the week, and twice a day, any day. But 'tis falling with age and weather now, I see it go; the rain wears it, the moss rots it, the wind shatters it. The lake's as dry as a hen's foot, and the forest changes. What was bushes is timber now, and what was timber is ashes; the forest has spread around me and the birds have left me and gone to the border. As for conies, there's no contriving with those foxes and weasels so cunning at them; not the trace of a tail, sir, nothing but snakes and snails now. I was happy when I built that house; that's what I was; I was then."

"Ah, so, indeed. And the other times—the second time?"

"Why, that was the time I washed my feet in the lake and I saw...."

"What, man Simon, what did you see?"

Simon passed his hand across his brow. "I see ... ah, well, I saw it. I saw something ... but I forget."

"Ah, you have forgotten your happiness," said the scholar in a soft voice: "Yes, yes." He went on speaking to himself: "Death is a naked Ethiope with flaming hair. I don't want to live for ever, but I want to live."

He took off his coat and gave it to Simon, who thanked him and put it on. It seemed a very heavy coat.

" Maybe," the old man mumbled, " I'll get a lift on the way ? "

" May it be so. And good-bye to you," said the scholar, " 'Tis as fine a day as ever came out of Eden."

They parted so, and old Simon had not been gone an hour when the scholar gave a great shout and followed after him frantic, but he could not come up with him, for Simon had gone up in a lift to heaven— a lift with cushions in it, and a bright young girl guiding the lift, dressed like a lad, but with a sad ſtern voice.

Several people got into the lift, the moſt of them old ladies, but no children, so Simon got in too and sat on a cushion of yellow velvet. And he was near sleeping when the lift ſtopped of a sudden and a lady who was taken sick got out. " Drugs and lounge! " the girl called out, " Second to the right and keep ſtraight on. Going up ? "

But though there was a crowd of young people waiting nobody else got in. They slid on again, higher and much higher. Simon dropped into sleep until the girl ſtopped at the fourth floor: " Refreshments," she said, " and Ladies' Cloak Room! " All the passengers got out except Simon: he sat ſtill until they came to the floor of heaven. There he got out, and the girl waved her hand to him and said " Good-bye." A few people got in the lift. " Going down ? " she cried. Then she slammed the door and it sank into a hole and Simon never laid an eye on it or her from that day for ever.

Now it was very pleasant where he found himself, very pleasant indeed and in no ways different from the

fine parts of the earth. He went onwards and the
first place he did come to was a farmhouse with a
kitchen door. He knocked and it was opened. It
was a large kitchen; it had a cracked stone floor and
white rafters above it with hooks on them and shearing irons and a saddle. And there was a smoking
hearth and an open oven with bright charred wood
burning in it, a dairy shelf beyond with pans of
cream, a bed of bracken for a dog in the corner by the
pump, and a pet sheep wandering about. It had the
number 100 painted on its fleece and a loud bell was
tinkling round its neck. There was a fine young girl
stood smiling at him; the plait of her hair was thick
as a rope of onions and as shining with the glint in it.
Simon said to her: " I've been a-walking, and I seem
to have got a bit dampified like, just a touch o' damp
in the knees of my breeches, that's all."

The girl pointed to the fire and he went and dried
himself. Then he asked the girl if she would give
him a true direction, and so she gave him a true
direction and on he went. And he had not gone far
when he saw a place just like the old forest he had
come from, but all was delightful and sunny, and
there was the house he had once built, as beautiful
and new, with the shining varnish on the door, a
pool beyond, faggots and logs in the yard, and inside
the white shelves were loaded with good food, the
fire burning with a sweet smell, and a bed of rest in
the ingle. Soon he was slaking his hunger; then he
hung up his coat on a peg of iron, and creeping into
the bed he went into the long sleep in his old happy
way of sleeping.

But all this time the scholar was following after him, searching under the sun, and from here to there, calling out high and low, and questioning the travelling people: had they seen a simple man, an old man who had been but three times happy ?—but not a one had seen him. He was cut to the heart with anxiety, with remorse, and with sorrow, for in a secret pocket of the coat he had given to Simon he had left—unbeknown, but he remembered it now— a wallet of sowskin, full of his own black sins, and nothing to distinguish them in any way from any other man's. It was a dark load upon his soul that the poor man might be punished with an everlasting punishment for having such a tangle of wickedness on him and he unable to explain it. An old man like that, who had been happy but the three times! He enquired upon his right hand, and upon his left hand he enquired, but not a walking creature had seen him and the scholar was mad vexed with shame. Well, he went on, and on he went, but he did not get a lift on the way. He went howling and whistling like a man who would frighten all the wild creatures down into the earth, and at last he came by a back way to the borders of heaven. There he was, all of a day behind the man he was pursuing, in a great wilderness of trees. It began to rain, a soft meandering fall that you would hardly notice for rain, but the birds gave over their whistling and a strong silence grew everywhere, hushing things. His footfall as he stumbled through briars and the wild gardens of the wood seemed to thump the whole earth, and he could hear all the small noises like the tick of a beetle and the gasping of worms. In a grove of raspberry canes he stood like a stock with the wonder of that stillness. Clouds did not move, he could but feel the rain that he could not see. Each leaf hung stiff as if it was frozen, though it was summer. Not a living thing was to be seen, and the things that were not living were not more dead than those that lived but were so secret still. He picked a few berries from the canes, and from every bush as he pulled and shook it a butterfly or a moth dropped or fluttered away, quiet and most ghostly. " An old bit of a man "—he kept repeating in his mind—" with three bits of joy, an old bit of a man."

Suddenly a turtle dove with clatter enough for a goose came to a tree beside him and spoke to him! A young dove, and it crooed on the tree branch, croo, croo, croo, and after each cadence it heaved the air into its lungs again with a tiny sob. Well, it would be no good telling what the bird said to the scholar, for none would believe it, they could not; but speak it did. After that the scholar tramped on, and on again, until he heard voices close ahead from a group of frisky boys who were chasing a small bird that could hardly fly. As the scholar came up with them one of the boys dashed out with his cap and fell upon the fledgling and thrust it in his pocket.

Now, by God, that scholar was angry, for a thing he liked was the notes of birds tossed from bush to bush like aery bubbles, and he wrangled with the boy until the little lad took the crumpled bird out of his pocket and flung it saucily in the air as you would fling a stone. Down dropped the bird into a gulley as if it was shot, and the boys fled off. The scholar peered into the gulley, but he could not see the young finch, not a feather of it. Then he jumped into the gulley and stood quiet, listening to hear it cheep, for sure a wing would be broken, or a foot. But nothing could he see, nothing, though he could hear hundreds of grasshoppers leaping among the dead leaves with a noise like pattering rain. So he turned away, but as he shifted his foot he saw beneath it the shattered bird: he had jumped upon it himself and destroyed it. He could not pick it up, it was bloody; he leaned over it, sighing: " Poor bird, poor bird, and is this your road to heaven ? Or do you never share the heaven that you make ? " There was a little noise then added to the leaping of the grasshoppers—it was the patter of tears he was shedding from himself. Well, when the scholar heard that he gave a good shout of laughter, and he was soon contented, forgetting the bird. He was for sitting down awhile but the thought of the old man Simon, with that sinful wallet—a rare budget of his own mad joys— urged him on till he came by the end of the wood, the rain ceasing, and beyond him the harmony of a flock roaming and bleating. Every ewe of the flock had numbers painted on it, that ran all the way up to ninety and nine.

Soon he came to the farmhouse and the kitchen and the odd sheep and a kind girl with a knot of hair as thick as a twist of bread. He told her the thing that was upon his conscience.

" Help me to come up with him, for I'm a day to the bad, and what shall I do ? I gave him a coat, an old coat, and all my sins were hidden in it, but I'd forgotten them. He was an old quavering man with but three spells of happiness in the earthly world." He begged her to direct him to the man Simon. The smiling girl gave him a good direction, the joyful scholar hurried out and on, and in a score of minutes he was peeping in the fine hut, with his hand on the latch of the half door, and Simon snoring in bed, a quiet decent snore.

"Simon!" he calls, but he didn't wake. He shook him, but he didn't budge. There was the coat hanging down from the iron peg, so he went to it and searched it and took out the wallet. But when he opened it—a black sowskin wallet it was, very strong with good straps—his sins were all escaped from it, not one little sin left in the least chink of the wallet, it was empty as a drum. The scholar knew something was wrong, for it was full once, and quite full.

"Well, now," thought he, scratching his head and searching his mind, " did I make a mistake of it ? Would they be by chance in the very coat that is on me now, for I've not another coat to my name ? " He gave it a good strong search, in the patch pockets and the inside pockets and in the purse on his belt, but there was not the scrap of a tail of a sin of any sort, good or bad, in that coat, and all he found was a few cachous against the roughening of his voice.

" Did I make another mistake of it," he says again, " and put those solemn sins in the fob of my fancy waistcoat ? Where are they ? " he shouts out.

Simon lifted his head out of sleeping for a moment.

" It was that girl with the hair," Simon said. " She took them from the wallet—they are not allowed in this place—and threw them in the pigwash."

With that he was asleep again, snoring his decent snore.

" Glory be to God," said the scholar, " am I not a great fool to have come to heaven looking for my sins! "

He took the empty wallet and tiptoed back to the world, and if he is not with the saints yet, it is with the saints he will be one day—barring he gets another budget of sins in his eager joy. And *that* I wouldn't deny him.

The Tiger

THE TIGER WAS COMING AT LAST; the almost fabulous beast, the subject of so much conjecture for so many months, was at the docks twenty miles away. Yak Pedersen had gone to fetch it, and Barnabe Woolf's Menagerie was about to complete its unrivalled collection by the addition of a full-grown Indian tiger of indescribable ferocity, newly trapped in the forest and now for the first time exhibited, and so on, and so on. All of which, as it happened, was true. On the previous day Pedersen the Dane and some helpers had taken a brand new four-horse exhibition waggon, painted and carved with extremely legendary tigers lapped in blood—even the bars were gilded—to convey this unmatchable beast to its new masters. The show had had to wait a long time for a tiger, but it had got a beauty at last, a terror indeed by all accounts, though it is not to be imagined that everything recorded of it by Barnabe Woolf was truth and nothing but truth. Showmen do not work in that way.

Yak Pedersen was the tamer and menagerie manager, a tall, blonde, angular man about thirty-five, of dissolute and savage blood himself, with the very ample kind of moustache that bald men often develop; yes, bald, intemperate, lewd, and an interminable smoker of Cuban cigarettes, which seemed constantly to threaten a conflagration in that moustache. Marie the Cossack hated him, but Yak loved her with a fierce deep passion. Nobody knew why she was called Marie the Cossack. She came from Canning Town—everybody knew that, and her proper name was Fascota, Mrs. Fascota, wife of Jimmy Fascota, who was the architect and carpenter and builder of the show. Jimmy was not much to look at, so little in fact that you couldn't help wondering what it was Marie had seen in him when she could have had the King of Poland, as you might say, almost for the asking. But still Jimmy was the boss ganger of the show, and even that young gentleman in frock coat and silk hat who paraded the platform entrance to the arena and rhodomontadoed you into it, often against your will, by the seductive recital of the seven ghastly wonders of the world, all certainly to be seen, to be seen inside, waiting to be seen, must be seen, roll up—even he was subject to the commands of Jimmy Fascota when the time came to dismantle and pack up the show, although the transfer of his activities involved him temporarily in a change, a horrid change, of attire and language. Marie was not a lady, but she was not for Pedersen anyway. She swore like a factory foreman, or a young soldier, and when she got tipsy she was full of freedoms. By the power of God she was beautiful, and by the same gracious power she was virtuous. Her husband knew it; he knew all about master Pedersen's passion, too, and it did not even interest him. Marie did feats in the lion cages, whipping poor decrepit beasts, desiccated by captivity, through a hoop or over a stick of wood and other kindergarten disportings; but there are, people must live, and Marie lived that way. Pedersen was always wooing her. Sometimes he was gracious and kind, but at other times when his failure wearied him he would be cruel and sardonic, with a suggestive tongue whose vice would have scourged her were it not that Marie was impervious, or too deeply inured to mind it. She always grinned at him and fobbed him off with pleasantries, whether he was amorous or acrid.

"God Almighty!" he would groan, "she is not good for me, this Marie. What can I do for her? She is burning me alive and the Skaggerack could not quench me, not all of it. The devil! What can I do with this? Some day I shall smash her across the eyes, yes, across the eyes."

So you see the man really loved her.

When Pedersen returned from the docks the car with its captive was dragged to a vacant place in the arena, and the wooden front panel was let down from the bars. The marvellous tiger was revealed. It sprung into a crouching attitude as the light surprised the appalling beauty of its smooth fox-coloured coat, its ebony stripes, and snowy pads and belly. The Dane, who was slightly drunk, uttered a yell and struck the bars of the cage with his whip. The tiger did not blench, but all the malice and ferocity in the world seemed to congregate in its eyes and impress with a pride and ruthless grandeur the colossal brutality of its face. It did not move its body, but its tail gradually stiffened out behind it as stealthily as fire moves in the forest undergrowth, and the hair along the ridge of its back rose in fearful spikes. There was the slightest possible distension of the lips, and it fixed its marvellous baleful gaze upon

93

Pedersen. The show people were hushed into silence, and even Pedersen was startled. He showered a few howls and curses at the tiger, who never ceased to fix him with eyes that had something of contempt in them and something of a horrible presage. Pedersen was thrusting a sharp spike through the bars when a figure stepped from the crowd. It was an old negro, a hunchback with a white beard, dressed in a red fez cap, long tunic of buff cotton, and blue trousers. He laid both his hands on the spike and shook his head deprecatingly, smiling all the while. He said nothing, but there was nothing he could say —he was dumb.

"Let him alone, Yak; let the tiger alone, Yak!" cried Barnabe Woolf. "What is this feller?"

Pedersen with some reluctance turned from the cage and said: "He is come with the animal."

"So?" said Barnabe. "Vell, he can go. Ve do not vant any black feller."

"He cannot speak—no tongue—it is gone," Yak replied.

"No tongue! Vot, have they cut him out?"

"I should think it," said the tamer. "There was two of them, a white keeper, but that man fell off the ship one night and they do not see him any more. This chap he feed it and look after it. No information of him, dumb you see, and a foreigner; don't understand. He have no letters, no money, no name, nowheres to go. Dumb, you see, he has nothing, nothing but a flote. The captain said to take him away with us. Give a job to him, he is a proposition."

"Vot is he got you say?"

"Flote." Pedersen imitated with his fingers and lips the actions of a flute-player.

"O ya, a vloot! Vell, ve don't want no vloots now; ve feeds our own tigers, don't ve, Yak?" And Mr. Woolf, oily but hearty—and well he might be so for he was beautifully rotund, hair like satin, extravagantly clothed, and rich with jewellery— surveyed first with a contemplative grin, and then compassionately, the figure of the old negro, who stood unsmiling with his hands crossed humbly before him. Mr. Woolf was usually perspiring, and usually being addressed by perspiring workmen, upon whom he bellowed orders and such anathemas as reduced each recipient to the importance of a potato, and gave him the aspect of a consumptive sheep. But to-day Mr. Woolf was affable and calm. He took his cigar from his mouth and poured a flood of rich grey air from his lips. "O ya, look after him a day, or a couple of days." At that one of the boys began to lead the hunchback away as if he were a horse. "Come on, Pompoon," he cried, and thenceforward the unknown negro was called by that name.

Throughout the day the tiger was the sensation of the show, and the record of its ferocity attached to the cage received thrilling confirmation whenever Pedersen appeared before the bars. The sublime concentration of hatred was so intense that children screamed, women shuddered, and even men held their breath in awe. At the end of the day the beasts were fed. Great hacks of bloody flesh were forked into the bottoms of the cages, the hungry victims pouncing and snarling in ecstasy. But no sooner

were they served than the front panel of each cage
was swung up, and the inmate in the seclusion of his
den slaked his appetite and slept. When the public
had departed the lights were put out and the doors
of the arena closed. Outside in the darkness only
its great rounded oblong shape could be discerned,
built high of painted wood, roofed with striped
canvas, and adorned with flags. Beyond this match-
box coliseum was a row of caravans, tents, naphtha
flares, and buckets of fire on which suppers were
cooking. Groups of the show people sat or lounged
about, talking, cackling with laughter, and even
singing. No one observed the figure of Pompoon
as he passed silently on the grass. The outcast,
doubly chained to his solitariness by the misfortune of
dumbness and strange nationality, was hungry. He
had not tasted food that day. He could not understand it any more than he could understand the
speech of these people. In the end caravan, nearest
the arena, he heard a woman quietly singing. He
drew a shining metal flute from his breast, but stood
silently until the singer ceased. Then he repeated
the tune very accurately and sweetly on his flute.
Marie the Cossack came to the door in her green
silk tights and high black boots with gilded fringes;
her black velvet doublet had plenty of gilded buttons
upon it. She was a big, finely moulded woman, her
dark and splendid features were burned healthily by
the sun. In each of her ears two gold discs tinkled and
gleamed as she moved. Pompoon opened his mouth
very widely and supplicatingly; he put his hand
upon his stomach and rolled his eyes so dreadfully

that Mrs. Fascota sent her little daughter Sophy down to him with a basin of soup and potatoes. Sophy was partly undressed, in bare feet and red petticoat. She stood gnawing the bone of a chicken, and grinning at the black man as he swallowed and dribbled as best he could without a spoon. She cried out: " Here, he's going to eat the bloody basin and all, mum! " Her mother cheerfully ordered her to " give him those fraggiments, then! " The child did so, pausing now and again to laugh at the satisfied roll of the old man's eyes. Later on Jimmy Fascota found him a couple of sacks, and Pompoon slept upon them beneath their caravan. The last thing the old man saw was Pedersen, carrying a naphtha flare, unlocking a small door leading into the arena, and closing it with a slam after he had entered. Soon the light went out.

II

After a week the show shifted and Pompoon accompanied it. Mrs. Kavanagh, who looked after the birds, was, a little fortunately for him, kicked in the stomach by a mule and had to be left at an infirmary. Pompoon, who seemed to understand birds, took charge of the parakeets, love birds, and other highly coloured fowl, including the quetzal with green mossy head, pink breast, and flowing tails, and the primrose-breasted toucans with bills like a butcher's cleaver.

The show was always moving on and moving on. Putting it up and taking it down was a more entertaining affair than the exhibition itself. With

G

Jimmy Fascota in charge, and the young man of the frock coat in an ecstasy of labour, half-clothed husky men swarmed up the rigged frameworks, dismantling poles, planks, floors, ropes, roofs, staging, tearing at bolts and bars, walking at dizzying altitudes on narrow boards, swearing at their mates, staggering under vast burdens, sweating till they looked like seals, packing and disposing incredibly of it all, furling the flags, rolling up the filthy awnings, then Right O! for a market town twenty miles away.

In the autumn the show would be due at a great gala town in the north, the supreme opportunity of the year, and by that time Mr. Woolf expected to have a startling headline about a new tiger act and the intrepid tamer. But somehow Pedersen could make no progress at all with this. Week after week went by, and the longer he left that initial entry into the cage of the tiger, notwithstanding the comforting support of firearms and hot irons, the more remote appeared the possibility of its capitulation. The tiger's hatred did not manifest itself in roars and gnashing of teeth, but by its rigid implacable pose and a slight flexion of its protruded claws. It seemed as if endowed with an imagination of blood-lust, Pedersen being the deepest conceivable excitation of this. Week after week went by and the show people became aware that Pedersen, their Pedersen, the unrivalled, the dauntless tamer, had met his match. They were proud of the beast. Some said it was Yak's bald crown that the tiger disliked, but Marie swore it was his moustache, a really remarkable piece of hirsute furniture, that he would not have parted with for a pound of gold—so he said. But whatever it was—crown, mouſtache, or the whole conglomerate Pedersen—the tiger remarkably loathed it and displayed his loathing, while the unfortunate tamer had no more success with it than he had ever had with Marie the Cossack, though there was at leaſt a good humour in her treatment of him which was horribly absent from the attitude of the beaſt. For a long time Pedersen blamed the hunchback for it all. He tried to elicit from him by geſticulations in front of the cage the secret of the creature's enmity, but the barriers to their intercourse were too great to be overcome, and to all Pedersen's illuſtrative frenzies Pompoon would only shake his sad head and roll his great eyes until the Dane would cuff him away with a curse of disguſt and turn to find the eyes of the tiger, the dusky, smooth-skinned tiger with bitter bars of ebony, fixed upon him with tenfold malignity. How he longed in his raging impotence to transfix the thing with a sharp spear through the cage's gilded bars, or to bore a hole into its vitals with a red-hot iron! All the traditional treatment in such cases, combined firſt with ſtarvation and then with rich feeding, proved unavailing. Pedersen always had the front flap of the cage left down at night so that he might, as he thought, eſtablish some kind of working arrangement between them by the force of propinquity. He tried to sleep on a bench juſt outside the cage, but the horror of the beaſt so penetrated him that he had to turn his back upon it. Even then the intense enmity pierced the back of his

99

brain and forced him to seek a bench elsewhere out of range of the tiger's vision.

☞ Meanwhile, the derision of Marie was not concealed—it was even blatant—and to the old contest of love between herself and the Dane was now added a new contest of personal courage, for it had come to be assumed, in some undeclarable fashion, that if Yak Pedersen could not tame that tiger, then Marie the Cossack would. As this situation crystallized daily the passion of Pedersen changed to jealousy and hatred. He began to regard the smiling Marie in much the same way as the tiger regarded him.

" The hell-devil! May some lightning scorch her like a toasted fish! "

But in a short while this mood was displaced by one of anxiety; he became even abject. Then, strangely enough, Marie's feelings underwent some modification. She was proud of the chance to subdue and defeat him, but it might be at a great price—too great a price for her. Addressing herself in turn to the dim understanding of Pompoon she had come to perceive that he believed the tiger to be not merely quite untamable, but full of mysterious dangers. She could not triumph over the Dane unless she ran the risk he feared to run. The risk was colossal then, and with her realization of this some pity for Yak began to exercise itself in her; after all, were they not in the same boat ? But the more she sympathized the more she jeered. The thing had to be done somehow.

Meanwhile Barnabe Woolf wants that headline for the big autumn show, and a failure will mean a nasty interview with that gentleman. It may end by Barnabe kicking Yak Pedersen out of his wild beast show. Not that Mr. Woolf is so gross as to suggest that. He senses the difficulty, although his manager in his pride will not confess to any. Mr. Woolf declares that his tiger is a new tiger; Yak must watch out for him, be careful. He talks as if it were just a question of giving the cage a coat of whitewash. He never hints at contingencies; but still, there is his new untamed tiger, and there is Mr. Yak Pedersen, his wild beast tamer—at present.

III

One day the menagerie did not open. It had finished an engagement, and Jimmy Fascota had gone off to another town to arrange the new pitch. The show folk made holiday about the camp, or flocked into the town for marketing or carousals. Mrs. Fascota was alone in her caravan, clothed in her jauntiest attire. She was preparing to go into the town when Pedersen suddenly came silently in and sat down.

"Marie," he said, after a few moments, "I give up that tiger. To me he has given a spell. It is like a mesmerize." He dropped his hands upon his knees in complete humiliation. Marie did not speak, so he asked: "What you think?"

She shrugged her shoulders, and put her brown arms akimbo. She was a grand figure so, in a cloak of black satin and a huge hat trimmed with crimson feathers.

"If *you* can't trust him," she said, "who can?"

" It is myself I am not to trust. Shameful! But that tiger will do me, yes, so I will not conquer him. It's bad, very, very bad, is it not so ? Shameful, but I will not do it! " he declared excitedly.

" What's Barnabe say ? "

" I do not care, Mr. Woolf can think what he can think! Damn Woolf! But for what I do think of my own self . . . Ah! " He paused for a moment, dejected beyond speech. " Yes, miserable it is, in my own heart very shameful, Marie. And what you think of me, yes, that too! "

There was a note in his voice that almost confounded her—why, the man was going to cry! In a moment she was all melting compassion and bravado.

" You leave the devil to me, Yak. What's come over you, man ? God love us, I'll tiger him! "

But the Dane had gone as far as he could go. He could admit his defeat, but he could not welcome her all too ready amplification of it.

" Na, na, you are good for him, Marie, but you beware. He is not a tiger; he is beyond everything, foul—he has got a foul heart and a thousand demons in it. I would not bear to see you touch him; no, no, I would not bear it! "

" Wait till I come back this afternoon—you wait! " cried Marie, lifting her clenched fist. " So help me, I'll tiger him, you'll see! "

Pedersen suddenly awoke to her amazing attraction. He seized her in his arms. " Na, na, Marie! God above! I will not have it."

" Aw, shut up! " she commanded, impatiently, and

pushing him from her she sprang down the steps and proceeded to the town alone.

She did not return in the afternoon; she did not return in the evening; she was not there when the camp closed up for the night. Sophy, alone, was quite unconcerned. Pompoon sat outside the caravan, while the flame of the last lamp was perishing weakly above his head. He now wore a coat of shag-coloured velvet. He was old and looked very wise, often shaking his head, not wearily, but as if in doubt. The flute lay glittering upon his knees and he was wiping his lips with a green silk handkerchief when barefoot Sophy in her red petticoat crept behind him, unhooked the lamp, and left him in darkness. Then he departed to an old tent the Fascotas had found for him.

When the mother returned the camp was asleep in its darkness and she was very drunk. Yak Pedersen had got her. He carried her into the arena, and bolted and barred the door.

IV

Marie Fascota awoke next morning in broad daylight; through chinks and rents in the canvas roof of the arena the brightness was beautiful to behold. She could hear a few early risers bawling outside, while all around her the caged beasts and birds were squeaking, whistling, growling, and snarling. She was lying beside the Dane on a great bundle of straw. He was already awake when she became aware of him, watching her with amused eyes.

" Yak Pedersen! Was I drunk ? " Marie asked

dazedly in low husky tones, sitting up. "What's this, Yak Pedersen? Was I drunk? Have I been here all night?"

He lay with his hands behind his head, smiling in the dissolute ugliness of his abrupt yellow skull so incongruously bald, his moustache so profuse, his nostrils and ears teeming with hairs.

"Can't you speak?" cried the wretched woman. "What game do you call this? Where's my Sophy, and my Jimmy—is he back?"

Again he did not answer; he stretched out a hand to caress her. Unguarded as he was, Marie smashed down both her fists full upon his face. He lunged back blindly at her and they both struggled to their feet, his fingers clawing in her thick strands of hair as she struck at him in frenzy. Down rolled the mass and he seized it; it was her weakness, and she screamed. Marie was a rare woman—a match for most men—but the capture of her hair gave her utterly into his powerful hands. Uttering a torrent of filthy oaths, Pedersen pulled the yelling woman backwards to him and grasping her neck with both hands gave a murderous wrench and flung her to the ground. As she fell Marie's hand clutched a small cage of fortune-telling birds. She hurled this at the man, but it missed him; the cage burst against a pillar and the birds scattered in the air.

"Marie! Marie!" shouted Yak, "listen! listen!"

Remorsefully he flung himself before the raging woman who swept at him with an axe, her hair streaming, her eyes blazing with the fire of a thousand angers.

" Drunk, was I!," she screamed at him. " That's how ye got me, Yak Pedersen ? Drunk, was I ! "

He warded the blow with his arm, but the shock and pain of it was so great that his own rage burst out again, and leaping at the woman he struck her a horrible blow across the eyes. She sunk to her knees and huddled there without a sound, holding her hands to her bleeding face, her loose hair covering it like a net. At the pitiful sight the Dane's grief conquered him again, and bending over her imploringly he said: " Marie, my love, Marie! Listen! It is not true! Swear me to God, good woman, it is not true, it is not possible! Swear me to God! " he raged distractedly. " Swear me to God ! " Suddenly he stopped and gasped. They were in front of the tiger's cage, and Pedersen was as if transfixed by that fearful gaze. The beast stood with hatred concentrated in every bristling hair upon its hide, and in its eyes a malignity that was almost incandescent. Still as a stone, Marie observed this, and began to creep away from the Dane, stealthily, stealthily. On a sudden, with incredible agility, she sprang up the steps of the tiger's cage, tore the pin from the catch, flung open the door, and, yelling in madness, leapt in. As she did so, the cage emptied. In one moment she saw Pedersen grovelling on his knees, stupid, and the next. . . .

All the hidden beasts, stirred by instinctive knowledge of the tragedy, roared and raged. Marie's eyes and mind were opened to its horror. She plugged her fingers into her ears; screamed; but her voice was a mere wafer of sound in that pandemonium. She heard vast crashes of someone smashing in the small door of the arena, and then swooned upon the floor of the cage.

The bolts were torn from their sockets at last, the slip door swung back, and in the opening appeared Pompoon, alone, old Pompoon, with a flaming lamp and an iron spear. As he stepped forward into the gloom he saw the tiger, dragging something in its mouth, leap back into its cage.

Mordecai and Cocking

TWO MEN SAT ONE AFTERNOON beside a spinney of beeches near the top of a wild bare down. Old shepherd Mordecai was admonishing a younger countryman, Eustace Cocking, now out of work, who held beside him in leash a brindled whippet dog, sharp featured and lean, its neck clipped in a broad leather collar. The day was radiant, the very air had bloom; bright day is never so bright as upon these lonely downs, and the grim face of storm never so tragic elsewhere. From the beeches other downs ranged in every direction, nothing but downs in beautiful abandoned masses. In a valley below the men a thousand sheep were grazing; they looked no more than a handful of white beach randomly scattered.

" The thing's forbidden, Eustace; it always has and always will be, I say, and thereby 'tis wrong."

" Well, if ever I doos anything wrong I allus feel glad of it next morning."

" 'Tis against law, Eustace, and to be against law is the downfall of mankind. What I mean to say—I'm a national man."

" The law! Foo! That's made by them as don't care for my needs, and don't understand my rights. Is it fair to let them control your mind as haven't got a grip of their own ? I worked for yon farmer a matter of fourteen years, hard, I tell you, I let my back sweat . . ."

The dog at his side was restless; he cuffed it impatiently: " and twice a week my wife she had to

107

go to farmhouse; twice a week; doing up their washing and their muck—' Lie down! ' " he interjected sternly to the querulous dog—" two days in every seven. Then the missus says to my wife, ' I shall want you to come four days a week in future, Mrs. Cocking; the house is too much of a burden for me.' My wife says: ' I can't come no oftener, ma'am; I'd not have time to look after my own place, my husband, and the six children, ma'am.' Then missus flew into a passion. ' Oh, so you won't come, eh! '

" ' I'd come if I could, ma'am,' my wife says, ' and gladly, but it ain't possible, you see.'

" ' Oh, very well! ' says the missus. And that was the end of that, but come Saturday, when the boss pays me: ' Cocking,' he says, ' I shan't want you no more arter next week.' No explanation, mind you, and I never asked for none. I know'd what 'twas for, but I don't give a dam. What meanness, Mordecai! Of course I don't give a dam whether I goes or whether I stops; you know my meaning—I'd much rather stop; my home's where I be known; but I don't give a dam. 'Tain't the job I minds so much as to let him have that power to spite me so at a moment after fourteen years because of his wife's temper. 'Tis not decent. 'Tis under-grading a man.' "

There was no comment from the shepherd. Eustace continued: " If that's your law, Mordecai, I don't want it. I ignores it."

" And that you can't do," retorted the old man. " God A'mighty can look after the law."

" If He be willing to take the disgrace of it, Mordecai Stavely, let Him."

The men were silent for a long time, until the younger cheerfully asked: " How be poor old Harry Mixen ? "

" Just alive."

Eustace leaned back, munching a strig of grass reflectively and looking at the sky: " Don't seem no sign of rain, however ? "

" No."

The old man who said " No " hung his melancholy head, and pondered; he surveyed his boots, which were of harsh hard leather with deep soles. He then said: " We ought to thank God we had such mild weather at the back end of the year. If you remember, it came a beautiful autumn and a softish winter. Things are growing now; I've seen oats as high as my knee; the clover's lodged in places. It will be all good if we escape the east winds—hot days and frosty nights."

The downs, huge and bare, stretched in every direction, green and grey, gentle and steep, their vast confusion enlightened by a small hanger of beech or pine, a pond, or more often a derelict barn; for among the downs there are barns and garners ever empty, gone into disuse and abandoned. They are built of flint and red brick, with a roof of tiles. The rafters often bear an eighteenth-century date. Elsewhere in this emptiness even a bush will have a name, and an old stone becomes a track mark. Upon the soft tufts and among the triumphant furze live a few despised birds, chats and finches and that blithe screamer the lark, but above all, like veins upon the down's broad breast, you may perceive the run-way of the hare.

"Why can't a man live like a hare?" broke out the younger man. "I'd not mind being shot at a time and again. It lives a free life, anyway, not like a working man with a devil on two legs always cracking him on."

"Because," said Mordecai, "a hare is a vegetarian creature, what's called a rubinant, chewing the cud and dividing not the hoof. And," he added significantly, "there be dogs."

"It takes a mazin' good dog to catch ever a hare on its own ground. Most hares could chase any dog ever born, believe you me, if they liked to try at that."

"There be traps and wires!"

"Well, we've no call to rejoice, with the traps set for a man, and the wires a choking him."

At that moment two mating hares were roaming together on the upland just below the men. The doe, a small fawn creature, crouched coyly before the other, a large nut-brown hare with dark ears. Soon she darted away, sweeping before him in a great circle, or twisting and turning as easily as a snake. She seemed to fly the faster, but when his muscular pride was aroused he swooped up to her shoulder, and, as if in loving derision, leaped over her from side to side as she ran. She stopped as sharply as a shot upon its target and faced him, quizzing him gently with her nose. As they sat thus the dark-eared one perceived not far off a squatting figure; it was another hare, a tawny buck, eyeing their dalliance.

The doe commenced to munch the herbage; the nut-brown one hobbled off to confront this wretched, rash, intruding fool. When they met both rose upon their haunches, clawing and scraping and patting at each other with as little vigour as mild children put into their quarrels—a rigmarole of slapping hands. But, notwithstanding the delicacy of the treatment, the interloper, a meek enough fellow, succumbed, and the conqueror loped back to his nibbling mistress.

Yet, whenever they rested from their wooing flights, the tawny interloper was still to be seen near by. Hapless mourning seemed to involve his hunched figure; he had the aspect of a deferential, grovelling man; but the lover saw only his provocative, envious eye—he swept down upon him. Standing up again, he slammed and basted him with puny velvet blows until he had salved his indignation, satisfied his connubial pride, or perhaps merely some strange fading instinct—for it seemed but a mock combat, a ritual to which they conformed.

Away the happy hare would prance to his mate, but as often as he came round near that shameless spy he would pounce upon him and beat him to the full, like a Turk or like a Russian. But though he could beat him and disgrace him, he could neither daunt nor injure him. The vanquished miscreant would remain watching their wooing with the eye of envy—or perhaps of scorn—and hoping for a miracle to happen.

And a miracle did happen. Cocking, unseen, near the beeches released his dog. The doe shot away over the curve of the hill and was gone. She did not merely gallop, she seemed to pass into ideal flight, the shadow of wind itself. Her fawn body, with half-cocked ears and unperceivable convulsion of the leaping haunches, soared across the land with the steady swiftness of a gull. The interloping hare, in a blast of speed, followed hard upon her traces. But Cocking's hound had found at last the hare of its dreams, a nut-brown, dark-eared, devil-guided, eluding creature, that fled over the turf of the hill as lightly as a cloud. The long leaping dog swept in its track with a stare of passion, following in great curves the flying thing that grew into one great throb of fear all in the grand sunlight on the grand bit of a hill. The lark stayed its little flood of joy and screamed with notes of pity at the protracted flight; and bloodless indeed were they who could view it unmoved, nor feel how sweet a thing is death if you be hound, how fell a thing it is if you be hare. Too long, O delaying death, for this little heart of wax; and too long, O delaying victory, for that pursuer with the mouth of flame. Suddenly the hound faltered, staggered a pace or two, then sunk to the grass, its lips dribbling blood. When Cocking reached him the dog was dead. He picked the body up.

" It's against me, like everything else," he muttered.

But a voice was calling " Oi! Oi! " He turned to confront a figure rapidly and menacingly approaching.

" I shall want you, Eustace Cocking," cried the gamekeeper, " to come and give an account o' yourself."

The Man from Kilsheelan

IF YOU KNEW THE MAN FROM KIL-
sheelan it was no use saying you did not believe in
fairies and secret powers; believe it or no, but
believe it you should; there he was. It is true he was
in an asylum for the insane, but he was a man with age
upon him so he didn't mind; and besides, better men
than himself have been in such places, or they ought
to be, and if there is justice in the world they will be.

" A cousin of mine," he said to old Tom Tool one
night, " is come from Ameriky. A rich person."

He lay in the bed next him, but Tom Tool didn't
answer so he went on again: " In a ship," he said.

" I hear you," answered Tom Tool.

" I see his mother with her bosom open once, and
it stuffed with diamonds, bags full."

Tom Tool kept quiet.

" If," said the Man from Kilsheelan, " if I'd the
trusty comrade I'd make a break from this and go
seek him."

" Was he asking you to do that ? "

" How could he an' all and he in a ship ? "

" Was he writing fine letters to you then ? "

" How could he, under the Lord ? Would he give
them to a savage bird or a herring to bring to me so ? "

" How did he let on to you ? "

" He did not let on," said the Man from Kilsheelan.

Tom Tool lay long silent in the darkness; he had
a mistrust of the Man, knowing him to have a for-
getful mind; everything slipped through it like rain

through the nest of a pigeon. But at last he asked him: " Where is he now ? "

" He'll be at Ballygoveen."

" You to know that and you with no word from him ? "

" O, I know it, I know; and if I'd a trusty comrade I'd walk out of this and to him I would go. Bags of diamonds! "

Then he went to sleep, sudden; but the next night he was at Tom Tool again: " If I'd a trusty comrade," said he; and all that and a lot more.

" 'Tis not convenient to me now," said Tom Tool, " but to-morrow night I might go wid you."

The next night was a wild night, and a dark night, and he would not go to make a break from the asylum, he said: " Fifty miles of journey, and I with no heart for great walking feats! It is not convenient, but to-morrow night I might go wid you."

The night after that he said: " Ah, whisht wid your diamonds and all! Why would you go from the place that is snug and warm into a world that is like a wall for cold dark, and but the thread of a coat to divide you from its mighty clasp, and only one thing blacker under the heaven of God and that's the road you walk on, and only one thing more shy than your heart and that's your two feet worn to a tissue tramping in dung and ditches . . ."

" If I'd a trusty comrade," said the Man from Kilsheelan, " I'd go seek my rich cousin."

" . . . Stars gaping at you a few spans away, and the things that have life in them, but cannot see or speak, begin to breathe and bend. If ever your hair stood up it is then it would be, though you've no more than would thatch a thimble, God help you."

" Bags of gold he has," continued the Man, " and his pockets stuffed with the tobacca."

" Tobacca! "

" They were large pockets and well stuffed."

" Do you say, now! "

" And the gold! large bags and rich bags."

" Well, I might do it to-morrow."

And the next day Tom Tool and the Man from Kilsheelan broke from the asylum and crossed the mountains and went on.

Four little nights and four long days they were walking; slow it was for they were oldish men and lost they were, but the journey was kind and the weather was good weather. On the fourth day Tom Tool said to him: " The Dear knows what way you'd be taking me! Blind it seems, and dazed I am. I could do with a skillet of good soup to steady me and to soothe me."

" Hard it is, and hungry it is," sighed the Man; " starved daft I am for a taste of nourishment, a blind man's dog would pity me. If I see a cat I'll eat it; I could bite the nose off a duck."

They did not converse any more for a time, not until Tom Tool asked him what was the name of his grand cousin, and then the Man from Kilsheelan was in a bedazement, and he was confused.

" I declare, on my soul, I've forgot his little name. Wait now while I think of it."

" Was it McInerney then ? "

" No· not it at all."

" Kavanagh ? the Grogans ? or the Duffys ? "

" Wait, wait while I think of it now."

Tom Tool waited; he waited and all until he thought he would burst.

" Ah, what's astray wid you ? Was it Phelan— or O'Hara—or Clancy—or Peter Mew ? "

" No, not it at all."

" The Murphys. The Sweeneys. The Moores."

" Divil a one. Wait while I think of it now."

And the Man from Kilsheelan sat holding his face as if it hurt him, and his comrade kept saying at him: " Duhy, then ? Coman ? McGrath ? " and driving him distracted with his O this and O that, his Mc he—s and Mc she—s.

Well, he could not think of it; but when they walked on they had not far to go, for they came over a twist of the hills and there was the ocean, and the neat little town of Ballygoveen in a bay of it below, with the wreck of a ship lying sunk near the strand. There was a sharp cliff at either horn of the bay, and between them some bullocks stravaiging on the beach.

" Truth is a fortune," cried the Man from Kil- sheelan, " this it is."

They went down the hill to the strand near the wreck, and just on the wing of the town they saw a paddock full of hemp stretched drying, and a house near it, and a man weaving a rope. He had a great cast of hemp around his loins, and a green apron. He walked backwards to the sea, and a young girl stood turning a little wheel as he went away from her.

" God save you," said Tom Tool to her, " for who are you weaving this rope ? "

" For none but God himself and the hangman," said she.

Turning the wheel she was, and the man going away from it backwards, and the dead wreck in the rocky bay; a fine sweet girl of good dispose and no ways drifty.

" Long life to you then, young woman," says he. " But that's a strong word, and a sour word, the Lord spare us all."

At that the rope walker let a shout to her to stop the wheel; then he cut the rope at the end and tied it to a black post. After that he came throwing off his green apron and said he was hungry.

" Denis, avick! " cried the girl. " Come, and I'll get your food." And the two of them went away into the house.

" Brother and sister they are," said the Man from Kilsheelan, " a good appetite to them."

" Very neat she is, and clean she is, and good and sweet and tidy she is," said Tom Tool. They stood in the yard watching some white fowls parading and feeding and conversing in the grass; scratch, peck, peck, ruffle, quarrel, scratch, peck, peck, cock a doodle doo.

" What will we do now, Tom Tool ? My belly has a scroop and a screech in it. I could eat the full of Isknagahiny Lake and gape for more, or the Hill of Bawn and not get my enough."

Beyond them was the paddock with the hemp drying across it, long heavy strands, and two big stacks of it beside, dark and sodden, like seaweed. The girl came to the door and called: " Will ye take a bite ? " They said they would, and that she should eat with spoons of gold in the heaven of God and Mary. " You're welcome," she said, but no more she said, for while they ate she was sad and silent.

The young man Denis let on that their father, one Horan, was away on his journeys peddling a load of ropes, a long journey, days he had been gone, and he might be back to-day, or to-morrow, or the day after.

" A great strew of hemp you have," said the Man from Kilsheelan. The young man cast down his eyes; and the young girl cried out: " 'Tis foul hemp, God preserve us all! "

" Do you tell me of that now," he asked; but she would not, and her brother said: " I will tell you. It's a great misfortune, mister man. 'Tis from the wreck in the bay beyant, a good stout ship, but burst on the rocks one dark terror of a night and all the poor sailors tipped in the sea. But the tide was low and they got ashore, ten strong sailor men, with a bird in a cage that was dead drowned."

" The Dear rest its soul," said Tom Tool.

" There was no rest in the ocean for a week, the bay was full of storms, and the vessel burst, and the big bales split, and the hemp was scattered and torn and tangled on the rocks, or it did drift. But at last it soothed, and we gathered it and brought it to the field here. We brought it, and my father did buy it of the salvage man for a price; a Mexican valuer he was, but the deal was bad, and it lies there; going rotten it is, the rain wears it, and the sun's astray, and the wind is gone."

" That's a great misfortune. What is on it ? "
said the Man from Kilsheelan.

" It is a great misfortune, mister man. Laid out
it is, turned it is, hackled it is, but faith it will not dry
or sweeten, never a hank of it worth a pig's eye."

" 'Tis the devil and all his injury," said Kilsheelan.

The young girl, her name it was Christine, sat
grieving. One of her beautiful long hands rested on
her knee, and she kept beating it with the other.
Then she began to speak.

" The captain of that ship lodged in this house with
us while the hemp was recovered and sold; a fine
handsome sport he was, but fond of the drink, and
very friendly with the Mexican man, very hearty they
were, a great greasy man with his hands covered with
rings that you'd not believe. Covered! My father
had been gone travelling a week or a few days when
a dark raging gale came off the bay one night till the
hemp was lifted all over the field."

" It would have lifted a bullock," said Denis,
" great lumps of it, like trees."

" And we sat waiting the captain, but he didn't
come home and we went sleeping. But in the
morning the Mexican man was found dead murdered
on the strand below, struck in the skull, and the two
hands of him gone. 'Twas not long when they came
to the house and said he was last seen with the captain, drunk quarrelling; and where was he ? I said
to them that he didn't come home at all and was away
from it. ' We'll take a peep at his bed,' they said,
and I brought them there, and my heart gave a strong
twist in me when I see'd the captain stretched on it,

119

snoring to the world and his face and hands smeared with the blood. So he was brought away and searched, and in his pocket they found one of the poor Mexican's hands, juſt the one, but none of the riches. Everything to be so black againſt him and the assizes juſt coming on in Cork! So they took him there before the judge, and he judged him and said it's to hang he was. And if they asked the captain how he did it, he said he did not do it at all."

" But there was a bit of iron pipe beside the body," said Denis.

" And if they asked him where was the other hand, the one with the rings and the mighty jewels on them, and his budget of riches, he said he knew nothing of that nor how the one hand got into his pocket. Placed there it was by some schemer. It was all he could say, for the drink was on him and nothing he knew.

" ' You to be so drunk,' they said, ' how did you get home to your bed and nothing heard ? '

" ' I don't know,' says he. Good sakes, the poor lamb, a gallant ſtrong sailor he was! His mind was a blank, he said. ' 'Tis blank,' said the judge, ' if it's as blank as the head of himself with a gap like that in it, God reſt him! ' "

" You could have put a pound of cheese in it," said Denis.

" And Peter Corcoran cried like a loony man, for his courage was gone, like a ſtream of water. To hang him, the judge said, and to hang him well, was their intention. It was a pity, the judge said, to rob a man because he was foreign, and deſtroy him for riches and the drink on him. And Peter Corcoran swore he was innocent of this crime. ' Put a clean shirt to me back,' says he, ' for it's to heaven I'm going.' "

" And," added Denis, " the peeler at the door said ' Amen.' "

" That was a week ago," said Chriſtine, " and in another he'll be ſtretched. A handsome sporting sailor boy."

" What . . . what did you say was the name of him ? " gasped the Man from Kilsheelan.

" Peter Corcoran, the poor lamb," said Chriſtine.

" Begod," he cried out as if he was choking, " 'tis me grand cousin from Ameriky! "

True it was, and the grief on him so great that Denis was after giving the two of them a lodge till the execution was over. " Reſt here, my dad's away," said he, " and he knowing nothing of the murder, or the robbery, or the hanging that's coming, nothing. Ah, what will we tell him an all ? 'Tis a black ſtory on this house."

" The blessing of God and Mary on you," said Tom Tool. " Maybe we could do a hand's turn for you; me comrade's a great wonder with the miracles, maybe he could do a ſtroke would free an innocent man."

" Is it joking you are ? " asked Chriſtine ſternly.

" God deliver him, how would I joke on a man going to his doom and deſtruction ? "

The next day the young girl gave them jobs to do, but the Man from Kilsheelan was deſtroyed with trouble and he shook like water when a pan of it is struck.

"What is on you?" said Tom Tool.

"Vexed and waxy I am," says he, "in regard of the great journey we's took, and sorra a help in the end of it. Why couldn't he do his bloody murder after we had done with him?"

"Maybe he didn't do it at all."

"Ah, what are you saying now, Tom Tool? Wouldn't anyone do it, a nice, easy, innocent crime. The cranky gossoon to get himself stretched on the head of it, 'tis the drink destroyed him! Sure's there's no more justice in the world than you'd find in the craw of a sick pullet. Vexed and waxy I am for me careless cousin. Do it! Who wouldn't do it?"

He went up to the rope that Denis and Christine were weaving together and he put his finger on it.

"Is that the rope," says he, "that will hang my grand cousin?"

"No," said Denis, "it is not. His rope came through the post office yesterday. For the prison master it was, a long new rope—saints preserve us—and Jimmy Fallon the postman getting roaring drunk showing it to the scores of creatures would give him a drink for the sight of it. Just coiled it was, and no way hidden, with a label on it, 'O.H.M.S.'"

"The wind's rising, you," said Christine. "Take a couple of forks now, and turn the hemp in the field. Maybe 'twill scour the Satan out of it."

"Stormy it does be, and the bay has darkened in broad noon," said Tom Tool.

" Why wouldn't the whole world be dark and a man to be hung ? " said she.

They went to the hemp so knotted and ſtinking, and begun raking it and raking it. The wind was roaring from the bay, the hulk twitching and tottering; the gulls came off the wave, and Chriſtine's clothes ſtretched out from her like the wings of a bird. The hemp heaved upon the paddock like a great beaſt burſting a snare that was on it, and a ſtrong blaſt drove a heap of it upon the Man from Kilsheelan, twiſting and binding him in its clasp till he thought he would not escape from it and he went falling and yelping. Tom Tool unwound him, and sat him in the lew of the ſtack till he got his ſtrength again, and then he began to moan of his misfortune.

" Stint your shouting," said Tom Tool, " isn't it as hard to cure as a wart on the back of a hedgehog ? "

But he wouldn't ſtint it. " 'Tis large and splendid talk I get from you, Tom Tool, but divil a deed of ſtrength. Vexed and waxy I am. Why couldn't he do his murder after we'd done with him. What a cranky cousin. What a foolish creature. What a silly man, the devil take him! "

" Let you be aisy," the other said, " to heaven he is going."

" And what's the gain of it, he to go with his neck ſtretched ? "

" Indeed, I did know a man went to heaven once," began Tom Tool, " but he did not care for it."

" That's queer," said the Man, " for it couldn't be anything you'd not want, indeed to glory."

" Well, he came back to Ireland on the head of it. I forget what was his name."

" Was it Corcoran, or Tool, or Horan ? "

" No, none of those names. He let on it was a lonely place, not fit for living people or dead people, he said; nothing but trees and streams and beasts and birds."

" What beasts and birds ? "

" Rabbits and badgers, the elephant, the dromedary, and all those ancient races; eagles and hawks and cuckoos and magpies. He wandered in a thick forest for nights and days like a flea in a great beard, and the beasts and the birds setting traps and hooks and dangers for a poor feller; the worst villains of all was the sheep."

" The sheep ! What could a sheep do then ? " asked Kilsheelan.

" I don't know the right of it, but you'd not believe me if I told you at all. If you went for the little swim you was not seen again."

" I never heard the like of that in Roscommon."

" Not another holy soul was in it but himself, and if he was taken with the thirst he would dip his hand in a stream that flowed with rich wine and put it to his lips, but if he did it turned into air at once and twisted up in a blue cloud. But grand wine to look at, he said. If he took oranges from a tree he could not bite them, they were chiny oranges, hard as a plate. But beautiful oranges to look at they were. To pick a flower it burst on you like a gun. What was cold was too cold to touch, and what was warm was too warm to swallow, you must throw it up, or die."

" Faith, it's no region for a Christian soul, Tom Tool. Where is it at all ? "

" High it may be, low it may be, it may be here, it may be there."

" What could the like of a sheep do ? A sheep! "

" A devouring savage creature it is there, the most hard to come at, the most difficult to conquer, with the teeth of a lion and a tiger, the strength of a bear and a half, the deceit of two foxes, the run of a deer, the . . ."

" Is it heaven you call it! I'd not look twice at a place the like of that."

" No, you would not, no."

" Ah, but wait now," said Kilsheelan, " wait till the day of Judgment."

" Well, I will not wait then," said Tom Tool sternly. " When the sinners of the world are called to their judgment, scatter they will all over the face of the earth, running like hares till they come to the sea, and there they will perish."

" Ah, the love of God on the world! "

They went raking and raking, till they came to a great stiff hump of it that rolled over, and they could see sticking from the end of it two boots.

" O, what is it, in the name of God ? " asks Kilsheelan.

" Sorra and all, but I'd not like to look," says Tom Tool, and they called the girl to come see what was it.

" A dead man! " says Christine, in a thin voice with a great tremble coming on her, and she white as a tooth. " Unwind him now." They began to unwind him like a tailor with a bale of tweed, and at last they came to a man black in the face. Strangled he was. The girl let a great cry out of her. " Queen of heaven, 'tis my dad; choked he is, the long strands have choked him, my good pleasant dad! " and she went with a run to the house crying.

" What has he there in his hand ? " asked Kilsheelan.

" 'Tis a chopper," says he.

" Do you see what is on it, Tom Tool ? "

" Sure I see, and you see, what is on it; blood is on it, and murder is on it. Go fetch a peeler, and I'll wait while you bring him."

When his friend was gone for the police Tom Tool took a little squint around him and slid his hand into the dead man's pocket. But if he did he was nearly struck mad from his senses, for he pulled out a loose dead hand that had been chopped off as neat as the foot of a pig. He looked at the dead man's arms, and there was a hand to each; so he looked at the hand again. The fingers were covered with the rings of gold and diamonds. Covered!

" Glory be to God! " said Tom Tool, and he put his hand in another pocket and fetched a budget full of papers and banknotes.

" Glory be to God! " he said again, and put the hand and the budget back in the pockets, and turned his back and said prayers until the peelers came and took them all off to the court.

It was not long, two days or three, until an inquiry was held; grand it was and its judgment was good.

And the big-wig asked: " Where is the man that found the body ? "

" There are two of him," says the peeler.

" Swear 'em," says he, and Kilsheelan stepped up to a great murdering joker of a clerk, who gave him a book in his hand and roared at him: " I swear by Almighty God . . . "

" Yes," says Kilsheelan.

" Swear it," says the clerk.

" Indeed I do."

" You must repeat it," says the clerk.

" I will, sir."

" Well, repeat it then," says he.

" And what will I repeat ? "

So he told him again and he repeated it. Then the clerk goes on: " . . . that the evidence I give . . ."

" Yes," says Kilsheelan.

" Say those words, if you please."

" The words! Och, give me the head of 'em again ! "

So he told him again and he repeated it. Then the clerk goes on: " . . . shall be the truth . . ."

" It will," says Kilsheelan.

" . . . and nothing but the truth . . ."

" Yes, begod, indeed ! "

" Say ' nothing but the truth,' " roared the clerk.

" No ! " says Kilsheelan.

" Say ' nothing.' "

" All right," says Kilsheelan.

" Can't you say ' nothing but the truth ' ? "

" Yes," he says.

" Well, say it ! "

" I will, so," says he, " the scrapings of sense on it all! "

So they swore them both, and their evidence they gave.

" Very good," his lordship said, " a moſt important and opportune discovery, in the nick of time, by the tracing of God. There is a reward of fifty pounds offered for the finding of this property and jewels: fifty pounds you will get in due course."

They said they were obliged to him, though sorrow a one of them knew what he meant by a due course, nor where it was.

Then a lawyer man got the rights of the whole case; he was the cunningeſt man ever lived in the city of Cork; no one could match him, and he made it ſtraight and he made it clear.

Old Horan muſt have returned from his journey unbeknown on the night of the gale when the deed was done. Perhaps had made a poor profit on his toil, for there was little of his own coin found on his body. He saw the two drunks ſtaggering along the bay—he clove in the head of the one with a bit of pipe—he hit the other a good whack to ſtill or ſtiffen him—he got an axe from the yard—he shore off the Mexican's two hands, for the rings were grown tight and wouldn't be drawn from his fat fingers. Perhaps he dragged the captain home to his bed— you couldn't be sure of that—but put the hand in the captain's pocket he did, and then went to the paddock to bury the treasure. But a blaſt of wind whipped and wove some of the hemp ſtrand around his limbs, binding him sudden. He was all huffled and hogled and went mad with the fear struggling, the hemp rolling him and binding him till he was strangled or smothered.

And that is what happened him, believe it or no, but believe it you should. It was the tracing of God on him for his dark crime.

Within a week of it Peter Corcoran was away out of gaol, a stout walking man again, free in Ballygoveen. But on the day of his release he did not go near the ropewalker's house. The Horans were there waiting, and the two old silly men, but he did not go next or near them. The next day Kilsheelan said to her: " Strange it is my cousin not to seek you, and he a sneezer for gallantry."

" 'Tis no wonder at all," replied Christine, " and he with his picture in all the papers."

" But he had a right to have come now and you caring him in his black misfortune," said Tom Tool.

" Well, he will not come then," Christine said in her soft voice, " in regard of the red murder on the soul of my dad. And why should he put a mark on his family, and he the captain of a ship."

In the afternoon Tom Tool and the other went walking to try if they should see him, and they did see him at a hotel, but he was hurrying from it; he had a frieze coat on him and a bag in his hand.

" Well, who are you at all ? " asks Peter Corcoran.

" You are my cousin from Ameriky," says Kilsheelan.

" Is that so ? And I never heard it," says Peter. " What's your name ? "

The Man from Kilsheelan hung down his old head and couldn't answer him, but Tom Tool said: " Drifty he is, sir, he forgets his little name."

" Astray is he ? My mother said I've cousins in Roscommon, d'ye know 'em ? the Twingeings . . ."

" Twingeing! Owen Twingeing it is! " roared Kilsheelan. " 'Tis my name! 'Tis my name! 'Tis my name! " and he danced about squawking like a parrot in a frenzy.

" If it's Owen Twingeing you are, I'll bring you to my mother in Manhattan." The captain grabbed up his bag. " Haste now, come along out of it. I'm going from the cunning town this minute, bad sleep to it for ever and a month! There's a cart waiting to catch me the boat train to Queenstown. Will you go ? Now ? "

" Holy God contrive it," said Kilsheelan; his voice was wheezy as an old goat, and he made to go off with him. " Good-day to you, Tom Tool, you'll get all the reward and endure a rich life from this out, fortune on it all, a fortune on it all! "

And the two of them were gone in a twink.

Tom Tool went back to the Horans then; night was beginning to dusk and to darken. As he went up the ropewalk Christine came to him from her potato gardens and gave him signs, he to be quiet and follow her down to the strand. So he followed her down to the strand and told her all that happened, till she was vexed and full of tender words for the old fool.

" Aren't you the spit of misfortune ? It would daunt a saint, so it would, and scrape a tear from silky Satan's eye. Those two deluderers, they've but the

drainings of half a heart between 'em. And he not
willing to lift the feather of a thought on me ? I'd
not forget him till there's ten days in a week and
every one of 'em lucky. But . . . but . . . isn't Peter
Corcoran the nice name for a captain man, the very
pattern ? "

She gave him a little bundle into his hands.
" There's a loaf and a cut of meat. You'd beſt be
ſtirring from here."

" Yes," he said, and ſtood looking ſtupid, for his
mind was in a dream. The rock at one horn of the
bay had a red glow on it like the shawl on the neck
of a lady, but the other was black now. A man was
dragging a turf boat up the beach.

" Liſten, you," said Chriſtine. " There's two
upſtart men in the house now, seeking you and the
other. There's trouble and damage on the head of it.
From the asylum they are. To the police they have
been, to put an embargo on the reward, and sorra a
sixpence you'll receive of the fifty pounds of it: to
the expenses of the asylum it muſt go, they say. The
treachery ! Devil and all, the blood sweating on every
coin of it would rot the palm of a nigger. Do you
hear me at all ? "

She gave him a little shaking for he was ſtanding
ſtupid, gazing at the bay which was dying into
grave darkness except for the wash of its broken
waves.

" Do you hear me at all ? It's quit now you should,
my little old man, or they'll be taking you."

" Ah, yes, sure, I hear you, Chriſtine; thank you
kindly. Juſt looking and liſtening I was. I'll be

stirring from it now, and I'll get on and I'll go. Just looking and listening I was, just a wee look."

"Then good-bye to you, Mr. Tool," said Christine Horan, and turning from him she left him in the darkness and went running up the ropewalk to her home.

Tribute

TWO HONEST YOUNG MEN LIVED IN
Braddle, worked together at the spinning mills at
Braddle, and courted the same girl in the town of
Braddle, a girl named Patience who was poor and
pretty. One of them, Nathan Regent, who wore
cloth uppers to his best boots, was steady, silent, and
dignified, but Tony Vassall, the other, was such a
happy-go-lucky fellow that he soon carried the good
will of Patience in his heart, in his handsome face, in
his pocket at the end of his nickel watch chain, or
wherever the sign of requited love is carried by the
happy lover. The virtue of steadiness, you see, can
be measured only by the years, and this Tony had put
such a hurry into the tender bosom of Patience:
silence may very well be golden, but it is a currency
not easy to negotiate in the kingdom of courtship;
dignity is so much less than simple faith that it is
unable to move even one mountain, it charms the
hearts only of bank managers and bishops.

So Patience married Tony Vassall and Nathan
turned his attention to other things, among them to a
girl who had a neat little fortune—and Nathan
married that.

Braddle is a large gaunt hill covered with dull little
houses, and it has flowing from its side a stream
which feeds a gigantic and beneficent mill. Without
that mill—as everybody in Braddle knew, for it was
there that everybody in Braddle worked—the heart
of Braddle would cease to beat. Tony went on working at the mill. So did Nathan in a way, but he had

a cute ambitious wife, and what with her money and influence he was soon made a manager of one of the departments. Tony went on working at the mill. In a few more years Nathan's steadiness so increased his opportunities that he became joint manager of the whole works. Then his colleague died; he was appointed sole manager, and his wealth became so great that eventually Nathan and Nathan's wife bought the entire concern. Tony went on working at the mill. He now had two sons and a daughter, Nancy, as well as his wife Patience, so that even his possessions may be said to have increased although his position was no different from what it had been for twenty years.

The Regents, now living just outside Braddle, had one child, a daughter named Olive, of the same age as Nancy. She was very beautiful and had been educated at a school to which she rode on a bicycle until she was eighteen.

About that time, you must know, the country embarked upon a disastrous campaign, a war so calamitous that every sacrifice was demanded of Braddle. The Braddle mills were worn from their very bearings by their colossal efforts, increasing by day or by night, to provide what were called the sinews of war. Almost everybody in Braddle grew white and thin and sullen with the strain of constant labour. Not quite everybody, for the Regents received such a vast increase of wealth that their eyes sparkled; they scarcely knew what to do with it; their faces were neither white nor sullen.

" In times like these," declared Nathan's wife,

" we must help our country still more, still more we must help; let us lend our money to the country."

" Yes," said Nathan.

So they lent their money to their country. The country paid them tribute, and therefore, as the Regent wealth continued to flow in, they helped their country more and more; they even lent the tribute back to the country and received yet more tribute for that.

" In times like these," said the country, " we must have more men, more men we must have." And so Nathan went and sat upon a Tribunal; for, as everybody in Braddle knew, if the mills of Braddle ceased to grind, the heart of Braddle would cease to beat.

" What can we do to help our country ? " asked Tony Vassall of his master, " we have no money to lend."

" No ? " was the reply. " But you can give your strong son Dan."

Tony gave his son Dan to the country.

" Good-bye, dear son," said his father, and his brother and his sister Nancy said " Good-bye." His mother kissed him.

Dan was killed in battle; his sister Nancy took his place at the mill.

In a little while the neighbours said to Tony Vassall: " What a fine strong son is your young Albert Edward! "

And Tony gave his son Albert Edward to the country.

" Good-bye, dear son," said his father; his sister kissed him, his mother wept on his breast.

Albert Edward was killed in battle; his mother took his place at the mill.

But the war did not cease; though friend and foe alike were almost drowned in blood it seemed as powerful as eternity, and in time Tony Vassall too went to battle and was killed. The country gave Patience a widow's pension, as well as a touching inducement to marry again; she died of grief. Many people died in those days, it was not strange at all. Nathan and his wife got so rich that after the war they died of over-eating, and their daughter Olive came into a vast fortune and a Trustee.

The Trustee went on lending the Braddle money to the country, the country went on sending large sums of interest to Olive (which was the country's tribute to her because of her parents' unforgotten, and indeed unforgettable, kindness), while Braddle went on with its work of enabling the country to do this. For when the war came to an end the country told Braddle that those who had not given their lives must now turn to and really work, work harder than before the war, much, much harder, or the tribute could not be paid and the heart of Braddle would therefore cease to beat. Braddle folk saw that this was true, only too true, and they did as they were told.

The Vassall girl, Nancy, married a man who had done deeds of valour in the war. He was a mill hand like her father, and they had two sons, Daniel and Albert Edward. Olive married a grand man, though it is true he was not very grand to look at. He had a small sharp nose, but they did not matter very much because when you looked at him in profile his bouncing red cheeks quite hid the small sharp nose, as completely as two hills hide a little barn in a valley. Olive lived in a grand mansion with numerous servants who helped her to rear a little family of one, a girl named Mercy, who also had a small sharp nose and round red cheeks.

Every year after the survivors' return from the war Olive gave a supper to her workpeople and their families, hundreds of them; for six hours there would be feasting and toys, music and dancing. Every year Olive would make a little speech to them all, reminding them all of their duty to Braddle and Braddle's duty to the country, although, indeed, she did not remind them of the country's tribute to Olive. That was perhaps a theme unfitting to touch upon, it would have been boastful and quite unbecoming.

" These are grave times for our country," Olive would declare, year after year: " her responsibilities are enormous, we must all put our shoulders to the wheel."

Every year one of the workmen would make a little speech in reply, thanking Olive for enabling the heart of Braddle to continue its beats, calling down the spiritual blessings of heaven and the golden blessings of the world upon Olive's golden head. One year the honour of replying fell to the husband of Nancy, and he was more than usually eloquent for on that very day their two sons had commenced to doff bobbins at the mill. No one applauded louder than Nancy's little Dan or Nancy's Albert Edward, unless it was Nancy herself. Olive was always much moved on these occasions. She felt that she did not really know these people, that she would never know them; she wanted to go on seeing them, being with them, and living with rapture in their workaday world. But she did not do this.

" How beautiful it all is! " she would sigh to her daughter, Mercy, who accompanied her. " I am so happy. All these dear people are being cared for by us, just simply us. God's scheme of creation—you see—the Almighty—we are his agents—we must always remember that. It goes on for years, years upon years it goes on. It will go on, of course, yes, for ever; the heart of Braddle will not cease to beat. The old ones die, the young grow old, the children mature and marry and keep the mill going. When I am dead . . .''

" Mamma, mamma! "

" O yes, indeed, one day! Then *you* will have to look after all these things, Mercy, and you will talk to them—just like me. Yes, to own the mill is a grave and difficult thing, only those who own them know how grave and difficult; it calls forth all one's deepest and rarest qualities; but it is a divine position, a noble responsibility. And the people really love me—I think."

The Handsome Lady

TOWARDS THE CLOSE OF THE NINE-
teenth century the parish of Tull was a genial but
angular hamlet hung out on the north side of a
midland hill, with scarcely renown enough to get
itself marked on a map. Its felicities, whatever they
might be, lay some miles distant from a railway
station, and so were seldom regarded, being neither
boasted of by the inhabitants nor visited by strangers.

But here as elsewhere people were born and, as
unusual, unconspicuously born. John Pettigrove
made a note of them then, and when people came in
their turns to die Pettigrove made a note of that too,
for he was the district registrar. In between whiles,
like fish in a pond, they were immersed in labour until
the Divine Angler hooked them to the bank, and
then, as is the custom, they were conspicuously
buried and laboured presumably no more.

The registrar was perhaps the one person who had
love and praise for the simple place. He was born
and bred in Tull, he had never left Tull, and at forty
years of age was as firmly attached to it as the black
clock to the tower of Tull Church, which never
recorded anything but twenty minutes past four.
His wife Carrie, a delicate woman, was also satisfied
with Tull, but as she owned two or three small pieces
of house property there her fancy may not have been
entirely beyond suspicion; possession, as you might
say, being nine points of the prejudice just as it is of
the law. A year or two after their marriage Carrie
began to suffer from a complication of ailments that

139

turned her into a permanent invalid; she was seldom seen out of the house and under her misfortunes she peaked and pined, she was troublesome, there was no pleasing her. If Pettigrove went about unshaven she was vexed; it was unclean, it was lazy, disgusting; but when he once appeared with his moustache shaven off she was exceedingly angry; it was scandalous, it was shameful, maddening. There is no pleasing some women—what is a man to do? When he began to let it grow again and encouraged a beard she was more tyrannical than ever.

The grey church was small and looked shrunken, as if it had sagged; it seemed to stoop down upon the green yard, but the stones and mounds, the cypress and holly, the strangely faded blue of a door that led through the churchyard wall to the mansion of the vicar, were beautiful without pretence, and though as often as not the parson's goats used to graze among the graves and had been known to follow him into the nave, there was about the ground, the indulgent dimness under the trees, and the tower with its unmoving clock, the very delicacy of solitude. It inspired compassion and not cynicism as, peering as it were through the glass of antiquity, the stranger gazed upon its mortal register. In its peace, its beauty, and its age, all those pious records and hopes inscribed upon its stones, seemed not uttered in pride nor all in vain. But to speak truth the church's grace was partly the achievement of its lofty situation. A road climbing up from sloping fields turned abruptly and traversed the village, sidling up to the church; there, having apparently satisfied some itch of curiosity, it turned abruptly again and trundled back another way into that northern prospect of farms and forest that lay in the direction of Whitewater Copse, Hangman's Corner, and One O'clock.

It was that prospect which most delighted Pettigrove, for he was a simple-minded countryman full of ambling content. Not even the church allured him so much, for though it pleased him and was just at his own threshold, he never entered it at all. Once upon a time there had been talk of him joining the church choir, for he had a pleasant singing voice, but he would not go.

" It's flying in the face of Providence," cried his exasperated wife—her mind, too, was a falsetto one: " You've as strong a voice as anyone in Tull, in fact stronger, not that that is saying much, for Tull air don't seem good for songsters if you may judge by that choir. The air is too thick maybe, I can't say, it certainly oppresses my own chest, or perhaps it's too thin, I don't thrive on it myself; but you've the strength and it would do you credit; you'd be a credit to yourself and it would be a credit to me. But that won't move you! I can't tell what you'd be at; a drunken man 'ull get sober again, but a fool . . . well, there! "

John, unwilling to be a credit, would mumble an objection to being tied down to that sort of thing. That was just like him, no spontaneity, no tidiness in his mind. Whenever he addressed himself to any discussion he had, as you might say, to tuck up his intellectual sleeves, give a hitch to his argumentative trousers. So he went on singing, just when he had a

mind to it, old country songs, for he disliked what he
called " gimcrack ballads about buzzums and roses."

Pettigrove's occupation dealt with the extreme
features of existence, but he himself had no extreme
notions.   He was a good medium type of man
mentally and something more than that physically,
but nevertheless he was a disappointment to his wife
—he never gave her any opportunity to shine by his
reflected light. She had nurtured foolish ideas of him
first as a figure of romance, then of some social
importance; he ought to be a parish councillor or
develop eminence somehow in their way of life. But
John was nothing like this, he did not develop, or
shine, or offer counsel, he was just a big, solid, happy
man.   There were times when his childless wife
hated every ounce and sign of him, when his fair
clipped beard and hair, which she declared were the
colour of jute, and his stolidity, sickened her.

" I do my duty by him and, please God, I'll continue to do it.   I'm a humble woman and easily
satisfied.   An afflicted woman has no chance, no
chance at all," she said.   After twelve years of
wedded life Pettigrove sometimes vaguely wondered
what it would have been like not to have married
anybody.

One Michaelmas a small house belonging to Mrs.
Pettigrove was let to a widow from Eastbourne.
Mrs. Cronshaw was a fine upstanding woman, grace-
fully grave and, as the neighbours said, clean as a
pink.   For several evenings after she had taken
possession of the house Pettigrove, who was a very
handy sort of man, worked upon some alterations to

her garden, and at the end of the third or fourth evening she had invited him into her bower to sip a glass of some cordial, and she thanked him for his labours.

"Not at all, Mrs. Cronshaw." And he drank to her very good fortune. Just that and no more.

The next evening she did the same, and the very next evening to that again. And so it was not long before they spoke of themselves to each other, turn and turn about as you might say. She was the widow of an ironmonger who had died two years before, and the ironmonger's very astute brother had given her an annuity in exchange for her interest in the business. Without family and with few friends she had been lonely.

"But Tull is such a hearty place," she said. "It's beautiful. One might forget to be lonely."

"Be sure of that," commented Pettigrove. They had the light of two candles and a blazing fire. She grew kind and more communicative to him; a strangely, disturbingly attractive woman, dark, with an abundance of well-dressed hair and a figure of charm. She had carpet all over her floor; nobody else in Tull dreamed of such a thing. She did not cover her old dark table with a cloth as everybody else habitually did. The pictures on the wall were real, and the black-lined sofa had cushions on it of violet silk which she sometimes actually sat upon. There was a dainty dresser with china and things, a bureau, and a tall clock that told the exact time. But there was no music, music made her melancholy. In Pettigrove's home there were things like these but they were not the same. His bureau was jammed in a corner with flowerpots upon its top; his pictures comprised two photo prints of a public park in Swansea—his wife had bought them at an auction sale. Their dresser was a cumbersome thing with knobs and hooks and jars and bottles, and the tall clock never chimed the hours. The very armchairs at Mrs. Cronshaw's were wells of such solid comfort that it made him feel uncomfortable to use them.

"Ah, I should like to be sure of it!" she continued. "I have not found kindly people in the cities—they do not even seem to notice a fine day!— I have not found them anywhere, so why should they be in Tull? You are a wise man, tell me, is Tull the exception?"

"Yes, Mrs. Cronshaw. You must come and visit us whenever you've a mind to; have no fear of loneliness."

"Yes, I will come and visit you," she declared, "soon, I will."

"That's right, you must visit us."

"Yes, soon, I must."

But weeks passed over and the widow did not keep her promise although she only lived a furlong from his door. Pettigrove made no further invitation for he found excuses on many evenings to visit her. It was easy to see that she did not care for his wife, and he did not mind this for neither did he care for her now. The old wish that he had never been married crept back into his mind, a sly, unsavoury visitant; it was complicated by a thought that his wife might

not live long, a dark, shameful thought that nevertheless trembled into hope. So on many of the long
winter evenings, while his wife dozed in her bed, he
sat in the widow's room talking of things that were
strange and agreeable. She could neither understand
nor quite forgive his parochialism; this was sweet
flattery to him. He had scarcely ever set foot outside
a ten-mile radius of Tull, but he was an intelligent
man, and all her discourse was of things he could
perfectly understand! For the first time in his life
Pettigrove found himself lamenting the dullness of
existence. He tried to suppress this tendency, but
words would come and he was distressed. He had
always been in love with things that lasted, that had
stability, that gave him a recognition and guidance,
but now his feelings were flickering like grass in a gale.

"How strange that is," she said, when he told
her this, "we seem to have exchanged our feelings.
I am happy here, but I know that dark thought, yes,
that life is a dull journey on which the mind searches
for variety, unvarying variety."

"But what for?" he cried.

"It is constantly seeking change."

"But for why? It seems like treachery to life."

"It may be so, but if you seek, you find."

"What?"

"Whatever you are seeking."

"What am I seeking?"

"Not to know that is the blackest treachery to life.
We are growing old," she added inconsequently,
stretching her hands to the fire. She wore black silk
mittens.

" Perhaps that's it," he allowed, with a laugh. " Childhood's best."

" Surely not," she protested.

" Ah, but I was gay enough then. I'm not a religious man, you know—and perhaps that's the reason—but however—I can remember things of great joy and pleasure then."

And it seemed from his recollections that not the least pleasant and persistent was his memory of the chapel, a Baptist hall long since closed and decayed, to which his mother had sent him on Sunday afternoons. It was a plain, tough, little tabernacle, with benches of deal, plain deal, very hard, covered with a clear varnish that smelled pleasant. The platform and its railing, the teacher's desk, the pulpit were all of deal, the plainest deal, very hard and all covered with the clear varnish that smelled very pleasant. And somehow the creed and the teacher and the attendants were like that too, all plain and hard, covered with a varnish that was pleasant. But there was a way in which the afternoon sun beamed through the cheap windows that lit up for young Pettigrove an everlasting light. There were hymns with tunes that he hoped would be sung in Paradise. The texts, the stories, the admonitions of the teachers, were vivid and evidently beautiful in his memory. Best of all was the privilege of borrowing a book at the end of school time—*Pilgrim's Progress* or *Uncle Tom's Cabin*.

For a while his recollections restored him to cheerfulness, but his dullness soon overcame him again.

" I have been content all my life. Never was a

146

man more content. And now! It's treachery if
you like. My faith's gone, content gone, for
why ? "

He rose to go, and as he paused at the door to bid
her good-night she took his hand and softly and
tenderly said: " Why are you depressed? Don't
be so. Life is not dull, it is only momentarily
unkind."

" Ah, I'll get used to it."

" John Pettigrove, you must never get used to
dullness, I forbid you."

" But I thought Tull was beautiful," he said as he
paused upon the doorsill. " I thought Tull was
beautiful . . ."

" Until I came ? " It was so softly uttered and
she closed the door so quickly upon him. They
called " Good-night, good-night " to each other
through the door.

He went away through the village, his mind streaming with strange emotions. He exulted, and yet he
feared for himself and for the widow, but he could not
summon from the depths of his mind what it was he
feared. He passed a woman in the darkness who,
perhaps mistaking him for another, said " Good-
night, my love."

The next morning he sat in the kitchen after breakfast. It wanted but a few days to Christmas. There
was no frost in the air; the wind roared, but the day,
though grey, was not gloomy; only the man was
gloomy.

" Nothing ever happens," he murmured. " True,
but what would you want to happen ? "

147

Out in the scullery a village girl was washing
dishes; as she rattled the ware she hummed a song.
From his back window Pettigrove could see a barn
in a field, two broken gates, a pile of logs, faggots, and
a single pollarded willow whose head was strangled
under a hat of ivy. Beside a barley stack was a goose
with a crooked neck; it stood sulking. High aloft
in the sky thousands of blown rooks wrangled like
lost men. And Pettigrove vowed he would go no
more to the widow—not for a while. Something
inside him kept asking, Why not? And he as quickly
replied to himself: "You know, you know. You'll
find it all in God-a-mighty's own commandments.
Stick to them, you can't do more—at least, you
might, but what would be the good?"

So that evening he went along to the Christmas
lottery held in a vast barn, dimly lit and smelling of
vermin. A rope hung over each of its two giant
beams, dangling smoky lanterns. There was a crowd
of men and boys inspecting the prizes in the gloomy
corners, a pig sulking in a pen of hurdles, sacks of
wheat, live hens in coops, a row of dead hares hung
on the rail of a wagon. Amid silence a man plunged
his hand into a corn measure and drew forth a
numbered ticket; another man drew from a similar
measure a blank ticket or a prize ticket. Each time
a prize was drawn a hum of interest spread through
the onlookers, but when the chief prize, the fat pig,
was drawn against number seventy-nine there was
agitation, excitement even.

"Who be it?" cried several. "Who be number
seventy-nine for the fat pig?"

A man consulted a list and said doubtfully: " Miss Subey Jones—who be she ? "

No one seemed to know until a husky alto voice from a corner piped: " I know her. She's from Shottsford way, over by Squire Marchand's."

" Oh," murmured the disappointed men; the husky voice continued: " Day afore yesterday she hung herself."

For a few seconds there was a pained silence, until a powerful voice cried: " It's a mortal shame, chaps."

The ceremony proceeded until all the tickets were drawn and all the prizes won and distributed. The cackling hens were seized from the pens by their legs and handed upside down to their new owners. The pig was bundled squealing into a sack. Bags of wheat were shouldered and the white-bellied hares were held up to the light. Everybody was animated and chattered loudly.

" I had number thirty in the big chance and I won nothing. And I had number thirty-one in the little chance and I won a duck. Number thirty-one was my number, and number thirty in the big draw; I won nothing in that, but in the little draw I won a duck. Well, there's flesh for you."

Some of those who had won hens held them out to a white-faced youth who smoked a large rank pipe; he took each fowl quietly by the neck and twisted it till it died. A few small feathers stuck to his hands or wavered to the floor, and even after the bird was dead and carried away it continued slowly and vaguely to flap its big wings and scatter its lorn feathers.

Pettigrove spent most of the next day in the forest

plantation south of Tull Great Wood, where a few chain of soil had been cultivated and reserved for seedlings, trees of larch and pine no bigger than potted geraniums, groves of oaks with stems slender as a cockerel's leg and most of the stiff brown leaves still clinging to the famished twigs; or sycamores, thin but tall, flourishing in a mat of their own dropped foliage that was the colour of butter fringed with blood and stained with black gouts like a child's copy-book. It was a toy forest, dense enough for the lair of a beast, and dim enough for an anchorite's meditations, but a dog could leap over it, and a boy could stand amid its growth and look like Gulliver in Lilliput.

"May I go into the wood?" a voice called to Pettigrove. Looking sharply up he saw Mrs. Cronshaw, clad in a long dark blue cloak with a fur necklet, a grey velvet hat trimmed with a pigeon's wing confining her luxuriant hair.

"Ah, you may," he said, stalking to her side, "but you'd best not, 'tis a heavy marshy soil within and the ways are stabbled by the hunters' horses. Better keep out till summer comes, then 'tis dry and pleasant-like."

She sat down awkwardly on a heap of faggots, her feet turned slightly inwards, but her cheeks were dainty pink in the cold air. What a smart lady! He stood telling her things about the wood, its birds and foxes; deep in the heart of it all was a lovely open space covered with the greenest grass and a hawthorn tree in the middle of that. It bloomed in spring with heavy creamy blossom. No, he had never seen any fairies there. Come to that, he did not expect to, he had never thought of it.

"But there are fairies, you know," cried the widow. "O yes, in old times, I mean very old times, before the Romans, in fact before Abraham, Isaac, and Jacob then, the Mother of the earth had a big family, thousands, something like the old woman who lived in a shoe she was. And one day God sent word to say he was coming to visit her. Well, then! She was so excited—the Mother of the earth—that she made a great to do you may be sure, and after she had made her house sparkle with cleanliness and had baked a great big pie she began to wash her children. All of a sudden she heard the trumpets blow—God was just a-coming! So as she hadn't got time to finish them all, she hid those unwashed ones away out of sight, and bade them to remain there and make no noise or she would be angry and punish them. But you can't conceal anything from the King of All and He knew of those hidden children, and he caused them to be hidden from mortal eyes for ever, and they are the fairies, O yes!"

"No, nothing can be concealed," Pettigrove admitted in his slow grave fashion, "murder will out, as they say, but that's a tough morsel if you're going to swallow it all."

"But I like to believe in those things I wish were true."

"Ah, so, yes," said Pettigrove.

It was an afternoon of damp squally blusters, uncheering, with slaty sky; the air itself seemed slaty, and though it had every opportunity and invitation to fall, the rain, with strange perversity, held off. In the oddest corners of the sky, north and east, a miraculous glow could be seen, as if the sun in a moment of aberration had determined to set just then and just there. The wind made a long noise in the sky, the smell of earth rose about them, of timber and of dead leaves; except for rooks, or a wren cockering itself in a bush, no birds were to be seen.

Letting his spade fall Pettigrove sat down beside the widow and kissed her. She blushed red as a cherry and he got up quickly.

" I ought not to ha' done it, I ought not to ha' done that, Mrs. Cronshaw! "

"Caroline!" said she, smiling the correction at him.

" Is that your name ? " He sat down by her again. " Why, it is the same as my wife's."

And Caroline said " Humph! You're a strange man, but you are wise and good. Tell me, does she understand you ? "

" What is there to understand ? We are wed and we are faithful to each other, I can take my oath on that to God or man."

" Yes, yes, but what is faith—without love between you ? You see ? You have long since broken your vows to love and cherish, understand that, you have broken them in half."

She had picked up a stick and was drawing patterns of cubes and stars in the soil.

" But what is to be done, Caroline ? Life is good, but there is good living and there is bad living, there is fire and there is water. It is strange what the Almighty permits to happen."

A slow-speaking man; scrupulous of thought and speech he weighed each idea before its delivery as carefully as a tobacconist weighs an ounce of to-bacco.

"Have some cake?" said Caroline, drawing a package from a pocket. "Will you have a piece . . . John?"

She seemed to be on the point of laughing aloud at him. He took the fragment of cake but he did not eat it as she did. He held it between finger and thumb and stared at it.

"It's strange how a man let's his tongue wag now and again as if he'd got the universe stuck on the end of a common fork."

"Or at the end of a knitting needle, yes, I know," laughed Caroline, brushing the crumbs from her lap. Then she bent her head, patted her lips, and regurgitated with a gesture of apology—just like a lady. "But what are you saying? If there is love between you there is faithfulness, if there is no love there is no fidelity."

He bit a mouthful off the cake at last.

"Maybe true, but you must have respect for the beliefs of others . . ."

"How can you if they don't fit in with your own?"

"Or there is sorrow." He bolted the rest of his cake. "O you are right, I daresay, Caroline, no doubt; it's right, I know, but is it reasonable?"

"There are afflictions," she said, "which time will cure, so they don't matter; but there are others which time only aggravates, so what can we do? I daresay it's different with a man, but a woman, you know, grasps at what she wants. That sounds reasonable, but you don't think it's right?"

In the cold whistling sky a patch of sunset had now begun to settle in its proper quarter, but as frigid and unconvincing as a stage fireplace. Pettigrove sat with his great hands clasped between his knees. Perhaps she grew tired of watching the back of him; she rose to go, but she said gently enough: "Come in to-night, I want to tell you something."

"I will, Caroline."

Later, when he reached home, he found two little nieces had arrived, children of some relatives who lived a dozen miles away. A passing farmer had dropped them at Tull; their parents were coming a day later to spend Christmas with the Pettigroves.

They sat up in his wife's room after tea, for Carrie left her bed only for an hour or two at noon. She dozed against her pillows, a brown shawl covering her shoulders, while the two children played by the hearth. Pettigrove sat silent, gazing in the fire.

"What a racket you are making, Polly and Jane!" quavered Carrie.

The little girls thereupon ceased their sporting and took a picture book to the hearthrug where they examined it in awed silence by the firelight. After some minutes the invalid called out: "Don't make such a noise turning over all them leaves."

Polly made a grimace and little Jane said: "We are looking at the pictures."

"Well," snapped Mrs. Pettigrove, "why can't you keep to the one page!"

John sat by the fire vowing to himself that he

would not go along to the widow, and in the very act of vowing he got up and began putting on his coat.

"Are you going out, John?"

"There's a window catch to put right along at Mrs. Cronshaw's," he said. At other times it had been a pump to mend, a door latch to adjust, or a jamb to ease.

"I never knew things to go like it before—I can't understand it," his wife commented. "What with windows and doors and pumps and bannisters anyone would think the house had got the rot. It's done for the purpose, or my name's not what it is."

"It won't take long," he said as he went.

The wind had fallen away, but the sky, though clearer, had a dull opaque mean appearance, and the risen moon, without glow, without refulgence, was like a brass-headed nail stuck in a kitchen wall.

The yellow blind at the widow's cot was drawn down and the candles within cast upon the blind a slanting image of the birdcage hanging at the window; a fat dapper bird appeared to be snoozing upon its rod; a tiny square was probably a lump of sugar; the glass well must have been half full of water, it glistened and twinkled on the blind. The shadowy bird shifted one foot, then the other, and just opened its beak as Pettigrove tapped at the door.

They did not converse very easily, there was constraint between them, Pettigrove's simple mind had a twinge of guilt.

"Will you take lime juice or cocoa?" asked the widow, and he said: "Cocoa."

" Little or large ? "

And he said: " Large."

While they sat sipping the cocoa Caroline began: " Well, I am going away, you know. No, not for good, just a short while, for Christmas only, or very little longer. I must go."

She nestled her blue shawl more snugly round her shoulders. A cough seemed to trouble her. " There are things you can't put on one side for ever . . ."

" Even if they don't fit in with your own ideas! " he said slyly.

" Yes, even then."

He put down his cup and took both her hands in his own. " How long ? "

" Not long, not very long, not long enough . . ."

" Enough for what ? " He broke up her hesitation. " For me to forget you ? No, no, not in the fifty-two weeks of the whole world of time."

" I did want to stay here," she said, " and see all the funny things country people do now." She was rather vague about those funny things. " Carols, mumming, visiting; go to church on Christmas morning, though how I should get past those dreadful goats, I don't know; why are they always in the churchyard ? "

" Teasy creatures they are! Followed parson into service one Sunday, indeed, ah! one of 'em did. Jumped up in his pulpit, too, so 'tis said. But when are you coming back ? "

She told him it was a little uncertain, she was not sure, she could not say, it was a little uncertain.

" In a week, maybe ? "

Yes, a week; but perhaps it would be longer, she could not say, it was uncertain.

" So. Well, all right then, I shall watch for you."

" Yes, watch for me."

They gave each other good wishes and said good-bye in the little dark porch. The shadowy bird on the blind stood up and shrugged itself. Pettigrove's stay had scarcely lasted an hour, but in that time the moon had gone, the sky had cleared, and in its ravishing darkness the stars almost crackled, so fierce was their mysterious perturbation. The village man felt Caroline's arms about him and her lips against his mouth as she whispered a " God bless you." He turned away home, dazed, entranced, he did not heed the stars. In the darkness a knacker's cart trotted past him with a dim lantern swinging at its tail and the driver bawling a song. In the keen air the odour from the dead horse sickened him.

Pettigrove passed Christmas gaily enough with his kindred, and even his wife indulged in brief gaieties. Her cousin was one of those men full of affable disagreements; an attitude rather than an activity of mind. He had a curious face resembling an owl's except in its colour (which was pink) and in its tiny black moustache curling downwards like a dark ring under his nose. If Pettigrove remarked upon a fine sunset the cousin scoffed, scoffed benignantly; there was a sunset every day, wasn't there?—common as grass, weren't they? As for the farming hereabouts, nothing particular in it was there? The scenery was, well, it was just scenery, a few hills, a few woods, plenty of grass fields. No special suitability of soil for any crop; corn would be just average, wasn't that so? And the roots, well, on his farm at home he could show mangolds as big as young porkers, forty to the cartload, or thereabouts. There weren't no farmers round here making a fortune, he'd be bound, and as for their birds, he should think they lived on rook pie.

Pettigrove submitted that none of the Tull farmers looked much the worse for farming.

" Well, come," said the other, " I hear your work-houses be middling full. Now an old neighbour of mine, old Frank Stinsgrove, was a man as *could* farm, any mortal thing. He wouldn't have looked at this land, not at a crown an acre, and he was a man as *could* farm, any mortal thing, oranges and lemons if he'd a mind to it. What a head that man had, God bless, his brain was stuffed! Full!! He'd declare black was white, and what's more he could prove it. I like a man like that."

The cousin's wife was a vast woman, shaped like a cottage loaf. For some reason she clung to her stays: it could not be to disguise or curb her bulk, for they merely put a gloss upon it. You could only view her as a dimension, think of her as a circumference, and wonder grimly what she looked like when she prepared for the bath. She devoured turkey and pig griskin with such audible voracity that her husband declared that he would soon be compelled to wear corks in his earholes at meal times, yes, the same as they did in the artillery. She was quite unperturbed by this even when little Jane giggled, and she avowed that good food was a great enjoyment to her.

158

" O 'tis a good thing and a grand thing, but take
that child now," said her father. Resting his elbow
on the table he indicated with his fork the diminutive
Jane; upon the fork hung a portion of meat large
enough to half-sole a lady's shoe. " She's just the
reverse, she eats as soft as a fly, a spillikin a day, and
not a mite more; no, very dainty is our Jane."
Here he swallowed the meat and treated four promis-
ing potatoes with very great savagery. " Do you
know our Jane is going to marry a house-painter,
yah, a house-painter, or is it a coach-painter ? 'Tis
smooth and gentle work, she says, not like rough
farmers or chaps that knock things pretty hard,
smiths and carpenters, you know. O Lord! eight
years old, would you believe it ? The spillikin!
John, this griskin's a lovely bit of meat."

" Beautiful meat," chanted his wife, " like a pig
we killed a month ago. That was a nice pig, fat and
contented as you'd find any pig, 'twould have been a
shame to keep him alive any longer. It dressed so
well, a picture it was, the kidneys shun like gold."

" That reminds me of poor old Frank Stinsgrove,"
said her husband. " He'd a mint of money, a very
wealthy man, but he didn't like parting with it.
He'd got oldish and afraid of his death, must have a
doctor calling to examine him every so often. Didn't
mind spending a fortune on doctors, but every other
way he'd skin a flint. And there was nought wrong
with him, 'cept age. So his daughter ups and says
to him one day—You are wasting your money on all
these doctors, father, they do you no good, what you
must have is nice, dainty, nourishing food. Now

what about some of these new laid eggs? How
much are they fetching now? old Frank says. A
penny farthing, says she. A penny farthing! I
cannot afford it. And there was that man with a
mint of money, a mint, could have bought Bucking-
ham Palace—you understand me—and yet he must
go on with his porridge and his mustard plasters and
his syrup of squills, until at last a smartish doctor
really did find something the matter with him, in his
kidneys. They operated, mark you, and they say—
but I never quite had the rights of it—they say they
gave him a new kidney made of wax; a new wax
kidney, ah, and I believe it was successful, only he
had not to get himself into any kind of a heat, of
course, nor sit too close to the fire. 'Stonishing what
they doctors can do with your innards. But of course
he was too old, soon died. Left a fortune, a mint of
money, could have bought the crown of England.
Staunch old chap, you know."

Throughout the holidays John sang his customary
ballads, "The Bicester Ram," "The Unquiet
Grave," and dozens of others. After songs there
would be things to eat. Then a game of cards, and
after that things to eat. Then a walk to the inn, to
the church, to a farm, or to a friend's where, in all
jollity, there would be things to eat and drink. They
went to a meet of the hounds, a most successful
outing for it gave them ravening appetites. In short,
as the cousin's wife said when bidding farewell, it was
a time of great enjoyment.

And Pettigrove said so too. He believed it, and
yet was glad to be quit of his friends in order to

contemplate the serene dawn that was to come at any
hour now. By New Year's Day Mrs. Cronshaw had
not returned, but the big countryman was patient,
his mind, though not at rest, was confident. The
days passed as invisibly as warriors in a hostile
country, and almost before he had begun to despair
February came, a haggard month to follow a frosty
January. Mist clung to the earth as tightly as the
dense grey fur on the back of a cat, ice began to
uncongeal, adjacent lands became indistinct, and
distant fields could not be seen at all. The banks of
the roads and the squat hedges were heavily dewed.
The cries of invisible rooks, the bleat of unseen sheep,
made yet more gloomy the contours of motionless
trees wherefrom the slightest movement of a bird
fetched a splatter of drops to the road, cold and uncheering.

All this inclemency crowded into the heart of the
waiting man, a distress without a gleam of anger or
doubt, but only a fond anxiety. Other anxieties
came upon him which, without lessening his melancholy, somewhat diverted it: his wife suffered a
sudden grave decline in health, and on calling in the
doctor Pettigrove was made aware of her approaching
end. Torn between a strange recovered fondness for
his sinking wife and the romantic adventure with the
widow, which, to his mind at such a juncture, wore
the sourest aspect of infidelity, Pettigrove dwelt in
remorse and grief until the night of St. Valentine's
Day, when he received a letter. It came from a coast
town in Norfolk, from a hospital; Caroline, too, was
ill. She made light of her illness, but it was clear to

him now that this and this alone was the urgent reason of her retreat from Tull at Christmas. It was old tubercular trouble (that was consumption, wasn't it?) which had driven her into sanatoriums on several occasions in recent years. She was getting better now, she wrote, but it would be months before she would be allowed to return. It had been rather a bad attack, so sudden. Now she had no other thought or desire in the world but to be back at Tull with her friend, and in time to see that fairy may tree at bloom in the wood—he had promised to show it to her— they would often go together, wouldn't they—and she signed herself his, " with the deepest affection."

He did not remember any promise to show her the tree, but he sat down straightway and wrote her a letter of love, incoherently disclosed and obscurely worded for any eyes but hers. He did not mention his wife; he had suddenly forgotten her. He sealed the letter and put it aside to be posted on the morrow. Then he crept back to his wife's room and continued his sick vigil.

But in that dim room, lit by one small candle, he did not heed the invalid. His mind, feverishly alert, was devoted to thoughts of that other who also lay sick, and who had intimidated him. He had feared her, feared for himself. He had behaved like a lost wanderer who at night, deep in a forest, had come upon the embers of a fire left mysteriously glowing, and had crept up to it frightened, without stick or stone: if only he had conquered his fear he might have lain down and rested by its strange comfort. But now he was sure of her love, sure of his own, he

162

was secure, he would lay down and rest. She would come with all the sweetness of her passion and the valour of her frailty, stretching smooth, quiet wings over his lost soul.

Then he began to be aware of a soft, insistent noise, tapping, tapping, tapping, that seemed to come from the front door below. To assure himself he listened intently, and soon it became almost the only sound in the world, clear but soft, sharp and thin, as if struck with the finger nails only, tap, tap, tap, quickly on the door. When the noise ceased he got up and groped stealthily down his narrow crooked staircase. At the bottom he waited in an uncanny pause until just beyond him he heard the gentle urgency again, tap, tap, and he flung open the door. There was enough gloomy light to reveal the empti- ness of the porch; there was nothing there, nothing to be seen, but he could distinctly hear the sound of feet being vigorously shuffled on the doormat below him, as if the shoes of some light-foot visitor were being carefully cleaned before entry. Then it stopped. Beyond that—nothing. Pettigrove was afraid, he dared not cross the startling threshold, he shot back the door, bolted it in a fluster, and blundered away up the stairs.

And there was now darkness, the candle in his wife's room having spent itself, but as a glow from the fire embers remained he did not hasten to light another candle. Instead, he fastened the bedroom door also, and stood filled with wondering uneasiness, dreading to hear the tap, tap, tap come again, just there, behind him. He listened for it with stopped breath, but he could hear nothing, not the faintest scruple of sound, not the beat of his own heart, not a flutter from the fire, not a rustle of feet, not a breath— no! not even a breathing! He rushed to the bed and struck a match: that was a dead face. . . . Under the violence of his sharpening shock he sank upon the bed beside dead Carrie and a faint crepuscular agony began to gleam over the pensive darkness of his mind, with a promise of mad moonlight to follow.

Two days later a stranger came to the Pettigrove's door, a short brusque, sharp-talking man with iron-grey hair and iron-rimmed spectacles. He was an ironmonger.

" Mr. Pettigrove ? My name is Cronshaw, of Eastbourne, rather painful errand, my sister-in-law, Mrs. Cronshaw, tenant of yours, I believe."

Pettigrove stiffened into antagonism: what the devil was all this ? " Come in," he remarked grimly.

" Thank you," said Cronshaw, following Pettigrove into the parlour where, with many sighs and much circumstance, he doffed his overcoat and stood his umbrella in a corner. " Had to walk from the station, no conveyances; that's pretty stiff, miles and miles."

" Have a drop of wine ? " invited Pettigrove.

" Thank you," said the visitor.

" It's dandelion."

" Very kind of you, I'm sure." Cronshaw drew a chair up to the fireplace, though the fire had not been lit, and the grate was full of ashes, and asked if he might smoke. Pettigrove did not mind; he poured out a glass of the yellow wine while Cronshaw lit his pipe. The room smelled stuffy, heavy noises came from overhead as if men were moving furniture. The stranger swallowed a few drops of the wine, coughed, and said: " My sister-in-law is dead, I'm sorry to say. You had not heard, I suppose ? "

" Dead! " whispered Pettigrove. " Mrs. Cronshaw! No, no, I had not, I had not heard that, I did not know. Mrs. Cronshaw dead—is it true ? "

" Ah," said the stranger with a laboured sigh. " Two nights ago in a hospital at Mundesley. I've just come on from there. It was very sudden, O, frightfully sudden, but it was not unexpected, poor woman, it's been off and on with her for years. She was very much attached to this village, I suppose, and we're going to bury her here, it was her last request. That's what I want to do now. I want to arrange about the burial and the disposal of her things and to give up possession of your house. I'm very sorry for that."

" I'm uncommon grieved to hear this," said Pettigrove. " She was a handsome lady."

" O yes," the ironmonger took out his pocket-book and prepared to write in it.

" A handsome lady," continued the countryman tremulously, " handsome, handsome."

At that moment someone came heavily down the stairs and knocked at the parlour door.

" Come in," cried Pettigrove. A man with red face and white hair shuffled into the room; he was dressed in a black suit that had been made for a man not only bigger, but probably different in other ways.

165

" We shall have to shift her down here now," he
began. " I was sure we should, the coffin's too big
to get round that awkward crook in these stairs when
it's loaded. In fact, 'tis impossible. Better have her
down now afore we put her in, or there'll be an accident on the day as sure as judgment." The man,
then noticing Cronshaw, said: " Good-morning, sir,
you'll excuse me."

The ironmonger stared at him with horror, and
then put his notebook away.

" Yes, yes, then," mumbled Pettigrove. " I'll
come up in a few minutes."

The man went out and Cronshaw jumped up and
said: " You'll pardon me, Mr. Pettigrove, I had no
idea that you had had a bereavement too."

" My wife," said Pettigrove dully, " two nights
ago."

" Two nights ago! I am very sorry, most sorry,"
stammered the other, picking up his umbrella and
hat. " I'll go away. What a sad coincidence! "

" There's no call to do that; what's got to be
done must be done."

" I'll not detain you long then, just a few details:
I am most sorry, very sorry, it's extraordinary."

He took out his notebook again—it had red edges
and a fat elastic band—and after conferring with
Pettigrove for some time the stranger went off to see
the vicar, saying, as he shook hands: " I shall of
course see you again when it is all over. How
bewildering it is, and what a shock it is; from one
day to another. and then nothing; and the day after
to-morrow they'll be buried beside one another. I

am very sorry, most sorry. I shall of course come and see you again when it is all over."

After he had gone Pettigrove walked about the room murmuring: " She was a lady, a handsome lady," and then, still murmuring, he stumbled up the stairs to the undertakers. His wife lay on the bed in a white gown. He enveloped her stiff thin body in a blanket and carried it downstairs to the parlour; the others, with much difficulty, carried down the coffin and when they had fixed it upon some trestles they unwrapped Carrie from the blankets and laid her in it.

Caroline and Carrie were buried on the same day in adjoining graves, buried by the same men, and as the ironmonger was prevented by some other misfortune from attending the obsequies there were no other mourners than Pettigrove. The workshop sign of the Tull carpenter bore the following notice:

☞ COMPLETE UNDERTAKER   Small Hearse Kept.

and therefore it was he who ushered the handsome lady from the station on that bitter day. Frost was so heavy that the umbrage of pine and fir looked woolly, thick grey swabs. Horses stood miserably in the frozen fields, breathing into any friendly bush. Rooks pecked industriously at the tough pastures, but wiser fowls, unlike the fabulous good child, could be neither seen nor heard. And all day someone was grinding corn at the millhouse; the engine was old and kept on emitting explosions that shook the neighbourhood like a dreadful bomb. Pettigrove,

167

who had not provided himself with a black overcoat and therefore wore none at all, shivered so intensely during the ceremony that the keen edge of his grief was dulled, and indeed from that time onwards his grief, whatever its source, seemed deprived of all keenness: it just dulled him with a permanent dullness.

He caused to be placed on his wife's grave a headstone, quite small, not a yard high, inscribed to

CAROLINE
The beloved wife
of
John Pettigrove

Some days after its erection he was astonished to find the headstone had fallen flat on its face. It was very strange, but after all it was a small matter, a simple affair, so in the dusk he himself took a spade and set it up again. A day or two later it had fallen once more. He was now inclined to some suspicion, he fancied that mischievous boys had done it; he would complain to the vicar. But Pettigrove was an easy-going man, he did not complain; he replaced the stone, setting it more deeply in the earth and padding the turf more firmly around it.

When it fell the third time he was astonished and deeply moved, but he was no longer in doubt, and as he once more made a good upheaval by the grave in the dusk he said in his mind, and he felt too in his heart, that he understood.

" It will not fall again," he said, and he was right: it did not.

Pettigrove himself lived for another score of years, during which the monotony of his life was but mildly varied; he just went on registering births and deaths and rearing little oaks and pines, firs and sycamores. Sentimental deference to the oft-repeated wish of his wife led him to join the church choir and sing its anthems and hymns with a secular blitheness that was at least mellifluous. Moreover, after a year or two, he *did* become a parish councillor and in a modest way was something of a " shining light."

" If I were you," observed an old countryman to him, " and I had my way, I know what I would do: I would live in a little house and have a quiet life, and I wouldn't care the toss of a ha'penny for nothing and nobody! "

In the time of May, always, Pettigrove would wander in Tull Great Wood as far as the hidden pleasaunce where the hawthorn so whitely bloomed. None but he knew of that, or remembered it, and when its dying petals were heaped upon the grass he gathered handfuls to keep in his pocket till they rotted. Sometimes he thought he would leave Tull and see something of the world; he often thought of that, but it seemed as if time had stabilized and contracted round his heart and he did not go. At last, after twenty years of widowhood, he died and was buried, and this was the manner of that.

Two men were digging his grave on the morning of the interment, a summer's day so everlasting beautiful that it was incredible anyone should be dead. The two men, an ancient named Jethro and a younger whom he called Mark, went to sit in the cool porch for a brief rest. The work on the grave had been very much delayed, but now the old headstone was laid on one side, and most of the earth that had covered his wife's body was heaped in untidy mounds upon the turf close by. Otherwise there was no change in the yard or the trees that grew so high, the grass that grew so greenly, the dark brick wall, or the door of fugitive blue; there was even a dappled goat quietly cropping. A woman came into the porch, remarked upon the grand day, and then passed into the church to her task of tidying up for the ceremony. Jethro took a swig of drink from a bottle and handed it to his mate.

" You don't remember old Fan as used to clean the church, do you ? No, 'twas 'fore you come about these parts. She was a smartish old gal. Bother me if one of they goats didn't follow her into the darn church one day, ah, and wouldn't be drove out on it, neither, no, and she chasing of it from here to there and one place and another but out it would not go, that goat. And at last it act-u-ally marched up into the pulpit and putt its two forelegs on the holy book and said ' Baa-a-a! ' " Here Jethro gave a prolonged imitation of a goat's cry. " Well, old Fan had been a bit skeered but she was so overcome by that bit of piety that, darn me, if she didn't sit down and play the organ for it! "

Mark received this narration with a lack-lustre air and at once the two men resumed their work. Meanwhile a man ascended the church tower; other men had gone into the home of the dead man. Soon the vicar came hurrying through the blue door in the wall and the bell gave forth its first solemn toll.

"Hey, Jethro," called Mark from the grave. "What d'you say's the name of this chap?"

"Pettigrove. Hurry up, now."

Mark, after bending down, whispered from the grave: "What was his wife's name?"

"Why, man alive, that 'ud be Pettigrove, too."

The bell in the tower gave another profoundly solemn beat.

"What's the name on that headstone?" asked Mark.

"Caroline Pettigrove. What be you thinking on?"

"We're in the wrong hole, Jethro; come and see for yourself, the plate on this old coffin says Caroline Cronshaw, see for yourself, we're in the wrong hole."

Again the bell voiced its melancholy admonition.

Jethro descended the short ladder and stood in the grave with Mark just as the cortège entered the church by the door on the opposite side of the yard. He knelt down and rubbed with his own fingers the dulled inscription on the mouldering coffin; there was no doubt about it, Caroline Cronshaw lay there.

"Well, may I go to glory," slowly said the old man. It may have occurred to Mark that this was an extravagantly remote destination to prescribe; at any rate he said: "There ain't no time, now, come on."

"Who the devil be she? However come that wrong headstone to be putt on this wrong grave?" quavered the kneeling man.

"Are you coming out?" growled Mark, standing

171

with one foot on the ladder, " or ain't you ? They'll be chucking him on top of you in a couple o' minutes. There's no time, I tell you."

" 'Tis a strange come-up as ever I see," said the old man; striking one wall of the grave with his hand: " that's where we should be, Mark, next door, but there's no time to change it and it must go as it is, Mark. Well, it's fate; what is to be must be whether it's good or right and you can't odds it, you darn't go against it, or you be wrong." They stood in the grave muttering together. " Not a word, Mark, mind you! " At last they shovelled some earth back upon the tell-tale name-plate, climbed out of the grave, drew up the ladder, and stood with bent heads as the coffin was borne from the church towards them. It was lowered into the grave, and at the " earth to earth " Jethro, with a flirt of his spade dropped in a handful of sticky marl, another at " ashes to ashes," and again at the " dust to dust." Finally, when they were alone together again, they covered in the old lovers, dumping the earth tightly and everlastingly about them, and reset the headstone, Jethro remarking as they did so: " That headstone, well, 'tis a mystery, Mark! And I can't bottom it, I can't bottom it at all, 'tis a mystery."

And indeed, how should it not be, for the secret had long since been forgotten by its originator.

The Fancy Dress Ball

THERE WAS A YOUNG FELLOW NAMED Bugloss. He wore cufflinks made of agate with studs to match, but was otherwise an agreeable person who suffered much from a remarkable diffidence, one of nature's minor inconsistencies having been to endow him with a mute desire for romantic adventure and an entire incapacity to inaugurate any such thing.

It was in architecture that he found his way of life, quite a profitable and genteel way; for while other hands and heads devised the mere details of drainage, of window and wall, staircase, cupboard, and floor, in fact each mechanical thing down to the hooks and bells in every room, he it was who painted those entrancing draughts of elevation and the general prospect (with a few enigmatic but graceful trees, clouds in the offing, and a tiny postman plodding sideways up the carriage drive) which lured the fond fly into the architectural parlour. It must be confessed that he himself lived in rooms over the shop of a hairdresser, whose window displayed the elegantly coiffed head and bust of a wax lady suffering either from an acute attack of jaundice or the effects of a succession of late nights: next door was an establishment dealing exclusively, but not exhaustingly, in mangles and perambulators. In Bugloss's room there were two bell handles with wires looking very handy and complete, yet whenever he desired the attendance of the maid he had (*a*) to take a silver whistle from his pocket; (*b*) to open the door; and (*c*) to blow it smartly in the passage.

His exceeding shyness was humiliating to himself and annoying to people of friendly disposition, it could not have been more preposterous had he been condemned to wear a false nose; he might have gone (he may even now be going) to his grave without once looking into a woman's eyes. What a pity! His own eyes were worth looking at; he was really a nice young man, tall and slender with light fluffy hair, who if he couldn't hide his amiable light under a bushel certainly behaved as if it wasn't there. Things were so until one day he chanced to read with envious pleasure but a good deal of scepticism a book called *Anatol* by a Viennese writer; almost immediately the fascinating possibilities of romantic infidelity were confirmed by a quarrel which began in the hairdresser's house between the young hairdresser and his wife, Monsieur and Madame Rabignol, and lasted for a week in the course of which Bugloss learned that the hairdresser was indulging in precisely one of those intrigues with an unknown lady living somewhere near by; Madame Rabignol, charming but virulent, protested a thousand times that it must be a base woman who walked the streets at night, and that Monsieur Rabignol was a low pig. The fair temptress, it appeared, was given to the use of a toilet unguent with the beguiling misdescription of " Vanishing Face Cream "; that was an unfortunate circumstance, because the wife of the hairdresser, a very cute woman, on her husband's return from an evening's absence, invariably kissed him and smelt him.

" Evil communications," saith St. Paul (borrowing

the phrase from Menander), " corrupt good manners," and his notion muſt have something of truth
in it, for these domeſtic revelations produced an
unusual ſtir in the Bugloss bosom—he bought a
ticket for a popular fancy dress ball and made a
mighty resolve to discard his pusillanimous self with
one grand geſture and there and then take the plunge.
At a fancy dress ball you could do that; everyone
made a fool of himself more or less; and Bugloss
determined to plunge into whatever there was to
plunge in. This was desperately unwise, but you are
not to suppose that he harboured any looseness or
want of principle; he was good and modeſt, and
virtuous as any young man could possibly be; he
only hoped, at the very leaſt, to look some fair girl
deep in the eyes. So he designed an oriental coſtume,
simple to make (being loose-fitting), and having
bought quantities of purple and crimson fabric he
wrapped them up and sent the office-boy with his
design, materials, measurements, and inſtruction to
a dressmaker in the neighbourhood, whom he wisely
thought would make a better job of it than a tailor.
When the coſtume was finished he was delighted;
it was magnificent, resplendent, artiſtic, and the
dressmaker's charge was moderate.

On the night of the ball, a warm Auguſt night with
soft thrilling air and a sky of sombre velvet, he drove
in a closed cab. Dancing was in the open, the lawns
of a mansion were lent for the occasion, and Bugloss
went rather late to escape notice—nearly eleven o'clock
—but in the cab his timorousness conspiring againſt
him had deepened to palpitating dejeċtion; he was

afraid again, the grand gesture was forgotten, and his attire was fantastically guarded from the public eye. From his window he had watched the arrival of the cab and had slunk down to it secretly—not a word to the Rabignols!—in a bowler hat and a mackintosh that reached to his feet; his fancy shoes were concealed under a pair of goloshes, the bright tasselled cap was in his pocket.

Heavens! It was too painful. This was no plunge, this miserable sink or swim—it was delirium, hell—what a stupid man he had been to come—it was no go, it was useless—and he was about to order the cabman to turn back home when the cab stopped at the gates of the mansion, the door was flung open and a big policeman almost dragged him out upon the carpeted pavement. A knot of jocular bystanders caused him to scurry into the grounds where three officials—good, bad, and indifferent—examined his ticket and directed him onwards. But the cloak rooms were right across the grounds, the great lawn was simply a bath of illumination, the band played in the centre and the dancers, madly arrayed, were waltzing madly. Bugloss, desiring only some far corner of darkness to flee into, saw on all sides shadowy trees, dim shrubs, and walks that led to utter gloom— thank God!—and there was a black moonless sky, though even that seemed positively to drip with stars.

At this moment the big policeman, following after him, said: " What about this cab, sir ?"

" What—yes—this cab! " repeated Bugloss, and to his agonized imagination every eye in the grounds became ironically fixed upon him alone; even the music ceased, and there resounded a flutter of coruscating amiability.

" D'ye want him to wait ? " the policeman was grinning—" He ain't got any orders."

" O, O dear, how much, what's his fare ? I don't want him again and—gracious! I haven't a cent on me—what, what—O, please tell him to call at my house to-morrow. Pay him then I will. Please! "

" Righto, my lord! " said the big policeman, saluting—he was a regular joker that fellow. Then Bugloss, trembling in every limb, almost leapt towards one of the dark walks, away from those grinning eyes. The shrubs and trees concealed him, though even here an odd paper lantern or two consorted with a few coloured bulbs of light. Shortly he began his observations.

The cloak rooms, he found, could be approached only by crossing the lawn. In a mackintosh, goloshes, and a bowler hat, that was too terrific an ordeal; the trembling Israelite during that affrighting passage of the Red Sea had all the incitements of escape and the comfort of friends, but this more violent ordeal led into captivity, and Bugloss was alone. What was to be done ? The music began again and it was agreeable, the illuminations were lustrous and pretty, the dancers gay, but Bugloss was neither agreeable nor gay, and his prettiness was not yet on the surface. He was in a highly wrought condition, he was limp, and he remained in what seclusion he could find in the garden, peering like a sinner at some assembly of the blest. At last he snatched off his goloshes and stuffed them in his pocket. " So far," he murmured,

M

" so good. I will hide the mackintosh among the
bushes, I can't face that dressing room." Juſt then
the band gave a heightened blare, drum and cymbals
were rapidly beaten and the music ceased amid
clapping and polite halloing. " Dash it, I muſt wait
till the next dance," said Bugloss, " and, O lord,
there's a lot of them coming this way." He turned to
retreat into deeper darkness when suddenly, near the
musicians, he saw a fascinating girl, a dainty but
ſtartling figure skimming across the lawn as if to
overtake a friend. Why—yes—she had a wig of
bright green hair, green; a short-waiſted cherry silk
jacket and harlequin pantaloons, full at the hips but
narrowing to the ankles, where white ſtockings
slipped into a pair of gilded leather shoes with heels
of scarlet. Delicately charming were her face and
figure, entrancing were her movements, and she
tinkled all over with hidden bells.

" Sweet God, what beauty ! " thought Bugloss,
" this is She, the Woman to know, I muſt, I muſt . . .
but how ? "

She disappeared. For the moment he could not
rid himself of the bowler hat and mackintosh, so
many couples roamed in the dark glades; wherever
he went he could see the glow of cigarettes, generally
in twos, and there were whispering or silent couples
ſtanding about in unexpeᴄted places. Retiring to the
darkeſt corner he had previously found he was about
to discard his mackintosh when he was ſtartled by a
cry at his elbow: " Lena, where are you, what's
that ? " and a girl scuttled away, calling " Lena!
Lena! " Her terror dismayed him, the little shock

itself brought the sweat to his brow, but the music beginning again drew all the stragglers back to the lawn. There, from his gloomy retreat, he beheld the green-haired beauty in the arms of a pirate king who was adorned with an admiral's hat and a dangerous moustache. "If," thought Bugloss, still in his mufti, "I couldn't have discovered a better get-up than that fellow, I'd have stayed away. There's no picture in it, it's just silly, I couldn't wear a thing like that, I couldn't wear it, I'd have perished rather than come." And indeed there was an absence of imagination about all the male adornment; many of the ladies were right enough, but some were horrors, and most of the men were horrors; there was justification for Bugloss's subsequent reflection: "I'll show them, · a little later on, what can be done when an artist takes the thing in hand; now after this dance is over . . . ." etc., etc."

Two lovers startled him by beginning to quarrel. They were passing among the trees behind him and talking quite loudly, both with a slight foreign accent. "But I shall not let you go, Johannes," said the lady with a fierce little cry. Bugloss turned and could just discern a lady costumed as a vivandière; her companion was in the uniform of a Danish soldier.

"If you forced me to stop I would kill you," retorted the man.

"O, you would kill me!"

"If you forced me to stop."

"You would kill me . . . so!"

"Yes, I would kill you."

"But you have told me that if I *can* keep you here

in England I may do it. You know. If I can. You know that, Johannes!"

Bugloss was persuaded that he had heard her voice before, though he could not recognize the speaker. "Be quiet, you are a fool," the man said. That was all Bugloss heard. It was brutal enough. If only a woman, any woman, had wanted *him* like that!

He wandered about during other dances. The green-haired girl was always with that idiotic pirate, and it made things very difficult, because although Bugloss had fallen desperately in love with her he could not, simply could not, march up and drag her away from her companion. He could not as yet even venture from his ambush among the trees, and they never wandered in the gloom—they were always dancing together or eating together. He, Bugloss, had no interest in any other woman there, no spark of interest whatsoever. That being so, why go to all the fuss of discarding the mackintosh and making an exhibition of himself? Why go bothering among that crowd, he was not a dancer at all, he didn't want to go! But still . . . by and by perhaps . . . when that lovely treasure was not so extraordinarily engaged. Sweet God! she was just . . . well, but he could not stand much more of that infernal pirate's antics with her. Withdrawing his tantalized gaze he sat down in darkness behind a clump of yew trimmed in the shape of some fat animal that resembled a tall hippopotamus. Here he lit his tenth cigarette. At once a dizziness assailed him, he began to see scarlet splashes in the gloom, to feel as if he were being lacerated with tiny pins. Throwing the cigarette away he stretched himself at full length under the bush. Scarcely had he done so when he became aware that two others were sitting down on the other side of it, the same foreign couple, the vivandière and her threatening cavalier.

" Listen to me, Hélène," the man was saying in a soft consoling voice, " you shall trust to me and come away. Together we will go. But here I cannot stay. It is fate. You love, eh ? Come then, we will go to Copenhagen, I will take you to my country. Now, Hélène ! "

The lady made no reply; Bugloss felt that she must be crying. The Dane continued to woo and the Frenchwoman to murmur back to him: " Is it not so, Johannes ? " " No, Hélène, no." But at last he cried angrily: " Pah! Then stop with your bandit, that pig! Pah! "and chattering angrily in his strange language he sprang up and stalked away. Hélène rose too and followed him beseechingly into the gloom: " No, no, Johannes, no ! "

Bugloss got up from the grass; his dizziness was gone. He knew that voice, it seemed impossible, but he knew her, and he had half a mind to rush home: but being without his watch and unable to discover what o'clock it was, he did not care to walk out into the streets with the chance of being guyed by any half-drunken sparks passing late home. He would wait, he was sure it was past midnight now, there would be a partial exodus soon, and he would go off unnoticed in the crowd. There was no more possibility now of him shedding his coat and joining the revellers than there was of that beauteous girl flying into his arms; his inhibition possessed him with tenfold power, he was an imbecile. Sad, pitiful, wretched, outcast! Through the screen of foliage the music floated with exquisite faintness, luminous cadenzas from a gleaming but guarded Eldorado whose light was music, whose music was all a promise and a mockery; he was a miserable prisoner pent in his own unbearable but unbreakable shackles and dressed up like a doll in a pantomime! Many people had come in their ordinary clothes; why, O why had he put on this maddening paralysing raiment? Why had he come at all?

Some of the lights had begun to fade; at one end of the lawn most of the small lamps had guttered out, leaving a line of a dozen chairs in comparative obscurity. Weary of standing, he slunk to the corner chair and sat down with a sigh. Just beside him was a weeping ash that he supposed only looked happy when it rained, and opposite was a poplar straining so hard to brush the heavens that he fancied it would be creaking in every limb. By and by an elderly decorous lady, accompanied by two girls not so decorous—the one arrayed as a Puritan maiden and the other as a Scout mistress—came and sat near him, but he did not move. They did not perceive the moody Bugloss. The elderly lady spoke: " Do go and fetch her here; no, when this waltz is over. She is very rude, but I want to see her. I can't understand why she avoids us, and how she is getting on is a mystery to everybody. Bring her here."

The puritan maiden and the scout mistress, embracing each other, skipped away to the refreshment booth. Glorious people sat about there drinking wine as if they disliked it, sipping ices as if it were a penance, and eating remarkable food or doing some other reasonable things, but Bugloss dared not join them although he was very hungry. It was not hunger he wanted to avert, but an impending tragedy.

The hypersensitive creature sees in the common mass of his fellows only something that seeks to deny him, and either in fear of that antagonism or in the knowledge of his own imperfections he isolates and envelopes the real issue of his being—much as an oyster does with the irritant grain in its beard; only the outcome is seldom a pearl and not always as useful as a fish. Bugloss was still wholly enveloped, and his predicament gave a melancholy tone to his thoughts. He sat hunched in his chair until the dance ended and the two girls came back, bringing with them the lovely green-haired one!

" Hello, aunt," she cried merrily enough, " why aren't you in costume ? Like my get-up ? "

Without a word the elderly lady kissed her, and all sat down within a few feet of Bugloss. It thrilled him to hear her voice; at least he would be able to recognize that when she turned back again to daylight's cool civilities.

" Did you know that I had blossomed out in business ? " she was saying. Bugloss thought it a beautiful voice.

" I heard of it," said her aunt, whom you may figure as a lady with a fan, eyeglasses, and the repellant profile of a bird of prey, " about half an hour ago. I wish I had heard of it before."

" I am a full-blown modiste."

" Yes, you might have told me."

" But I have told you."

" You might have told me before."

" But I haven't seen you before, aunt."

" No, we haven't seen you. How is this business, Claire, is it thriving, making money ? "

" O, we get along, aunt," said the radiant niece in a tone of almost perverse amiability. " I have several assistants. Do you know, we made seven of the costumes for this ball—seven—one of them for a man."

" I thought ladies only made for ladies."

" So did I, but this order just dropped in upon us very mysteriously, and we did it, from top to toe, a most gorgeous arrangement, all crimson and purple and silver and citron, but I haven't seen anybody wearing it yet. I wonder if you have ? I'm so disappointed. It's a sultan, or a nabob, or a nankipoo of some kind, I am certain it was for this ball. I was so anxious to see it worn. I had made up my mind to dance at least half the dances with the wearer, it was so lovely. Have you seen such a costume here ? "

" No," said the aunt grimly, " I have not, but I have noticed the pirate king—did you make his costume too ? I hope not! "

" O no, aunt," laughed Claire, " isn't he a fright? "

" Who is he ? "

" That ? O, a friend of mine, a business friend."

" He seems fond of you."

" I have known him some time. Yes, I like him.

184

Don't you like my pirate king?" asked Claire, turning to her two cousins.

The cousins both thought he was splendid.

(" Good God! " groaned Bugloss.)

" I don't," declared auntie. " Do you know him very well, has he any intentions? An orphan girl living by herself—you have your way to make in the world—I am not presuming to criticize, my dear Claire, but is it wise? Who is he? "

" Yes, aunt," said Claire. Bugloss could hear the tinkle of her bells as she moved a little restlessly.

" Are his intentions honourable? I should think they were otherwise."

Claire did not reply immediately. It looked as if the musicians were about to resume. There was a rattle of plates and things over at the booth. Then she said reflectively: " I don't think he has any—what you call honourable intentions."

" Not! Is he a bad man? "

" O no, I don't mean that, aunt, no."

" But what do you mean then, you're a strange girl, what *could* his intentions be? "

" He hasn't any intentions at all."

" Not one way or the other? "

Claire seemed vaguely to hover over the significance of this. She said calmly enough: " Not in any way. He's my hairdresser, a Frenchman, and so clever. He made this beautiful wig and gave it me. What do you think of my beautiful wig, isn't it sweet? "

There was a note of exasperation in the elder woman's voice: " Why don't you get married, girl? "

" I'd rather work," said Claire, " and besides, he's already married."

The music did begin, and a gentleman garbed as a druid came to claim auntie for a dance. The three girls were left alone.

" Did he *really* give you that wig ? " asked the puritan maiden.

" Yes, isn't it bonny ? I love it." She shook the dangling curls about her face. " He's frightfully clever with hair. French! You know his saloon probably, Rabignol's in the High Street. His wife is here, you must have seen her too—a French soldier woman—what do you call them ? She hates me. She's with a Danish captain. He *is* a Dane, but he is really an ice merchant. He thinks she adores him."

" O Claire! " cried the two shocked cousins.

" But she doesn't," said Claire. " Sakes, I'm beginning to shiver; come along."

They all romped back towards the orchestra. Bugloss shivered too and was glad—yes, glad—that she had gone. The tragedy had floated satisfactorily out of his hands, thank the fates; it was Rabignol's affair. Damn Rabignol! Curse Rabignol! the bandit, the pig! He hoped that Madame Rabignol *would* elope with Johannes. He hoped the green-haired girl—frail and lovely thing—would behave well; and he hoped finally and frenziedly that Rabignol himself would be choked by the common hangman. Bugloss then wanted to yawn, but somehow he could not. He put on his rubber goloshes again. With unwonted audacity he stalked off firmly, even a little fiercely, across the lawn in his mackintosh and bowler hat, passing round the fringe of the dancers but looking neither to the right nor to the left, then out of the gates into the dark empty streets and so home. There, feeling rather like a Cromwell made of chutney, he disarrayed himself and crept into bed yawning and murmuring to himself: "So that's a fancy dress ball! Sweet God, but I'm glad I went! And I could have shown them something, I could have. Say what you like, but mine was the finest costume at the show; there's no doubt about that, it was, it was! And I'm very glad I went."

The Cat, the Dog, and the bad old Dame

THE CHEMIST HAD CERTAIN ODD notions that were an agreeable reflex of his name, which was Oddfellow—Herbert Oddfellow. Our man was odd about diet. It was believed that he lived without cookery, that he browsed, as it were, upon fruit and salads. Ironically enough he earned a considerable income by the sale of nostrums for indigestion. At any hour of the day you were likely to find him devouring apples, nibbling artichokes, or sucking an orange, and your inquiry for a dose of bismuth or some such aid would cause by an obscure process a sardonic grin to assemble upon his face. You would scarcely have expected to find a lot of indigestion in the working-class neighbourhood where his pharmacy flourished, but it was there, certainly; he was quite cynical about it—his business throve abundantly upon dietary disorders.

There were four big ornamental carboys in his shop windows—red, violet, green, and yellow; incidentally he sold peppermint drops and poisons, and at forty years of age he was reputed to be the happiest, as he was certainly the healthiest, man in the county. This was not merely because he was unmarried . . . but there, I declare this tale is not about Oddfellow himself, but about his lethal chamber.

You must know that the sacrificial exactions of the war did not spare cats and dogs. They, too, were immolated—but painlessly—scores of them, at Oddfellow's. He was unhappy about that part of his business, very much so; he loved animals, perhaps

rather more than people, for, naturally, what he
ministered to in his pharmacy was largely human
misery or human affectation. Evil cruel things—the
bolt of a gaol, the lime of the bird-snarer, the butcher's
axe—maddened him.

In the small garden at the back of the dispensary
the interments were carried out by Horace the errand
boy, a juvenile with snub nose and short, tough hair,
who always wore ragged puttees. He delighted in
such obsequies, and had even instituted some cere-
monial orgies. But at last these lethal commissions
were so numerous that the burial-ground began to
resemble the habitat of some vast, inappeasable mole,
and thereupon Oddfellow had to stipulate for sorrowing owners to conduct the interments themselves in
cemeteries of their own. Even this provision did
not quell the inflow of these easily disposable
victims.

Mr. Franks brought him a magnificent cat to be
destroyed. (Shortly afterwards Franks was conveyed
to the lunatic asylum, an institution which still
nurtures him in despotic durance.) Pending the
return of Horace, who was disbursing remedial
shrapnel to the neighbourhood, the cat, tied to a rail
in the shop, sat dozing in the sunlight.

" What a beautiful cat! " exclaimed a lady caller,
stroking its purring majesty. The lady herself was
beautiful. Oddfellow explained that its demise was
imminent—nothing the matter with it—owner didn't
want it.

" How cruel, you sweet thing, how cruel! " pronounced the lady, who really was very beautiful. " I

would love to have it. Why shouldn't I have it . . .
if its owner doesn't want it ? I wonder. May I ? "

Manlike was Oddfellow, beautiful was the lady;
the lady took the cat away. Twenty-four hours later
the shop counter was stormed by the detestable
Franks, incipient insanity already manifest in him.
He carried the selfsame cat under his arm—it had
returned to its old home. Franks assailed the
abashed chemist with language that at its mildest
was abusive and libellous. His chief complaint
seemed to repose upon the circumstance of having
paid for the cat's destruction, whereupon Oddfellow
who, like an Irishman, never walked into an argument—he simply bounced in—threw down the fee
upon the counter and urged Mr. Franks to take his
cat, and his money, and himself away as speedily as
might be. This reprehensible behaviour did by no
means allay the tension; the madman-designate
paraded many further signs of his impending doom.

" Take your cat away, I tell you," shouted Oddfellow, " take it away. I wouldn't destroy it for a
thousand pounds! "

" You won't, oh ? "

" Put an end to you with pleasure! "

" Yes ? "

" Make you a present of a dose of poison whenever
you like to come and take it! "

" Yes ? "

" I will! "

Franks went away with his tom-cat.

" O . . . my . . . lord! " ejaculated the chemist, that
being his favourite evocation; " I'll do no more of

190

this cat-and-dog business. I shall not do any more; no, I shall not. I do not like it at all."

But in the afternoon his assistant, who had not been informed of this resolve, accepted two more victims for the lethal chamber, another tom-cat and a collie dog.

"O ... my ... lord!" groaned the chemist distractedly; but there was no help for it, and, calling his boy Horace, they carried the cat into the store-room. The lethal box was in a corner; all round were shelves of costly drugs. The place did not smell of death; it smelt of paint, oils, volatile spirits, tubs of white lead, and packing-cases that contained scented soap or feeding-bottles. As Oddfellow prepared his syringe, a sporting friend named Jerry peeped in to watch the proceedings.

"Shut the door!" cried little Horace. "I can't hold him. ... He's off!"

Sure enough the cat, sensing its danger, had burst from his arms and sprung to one of the shelves. Immediately phials of drugs began to fall and smash upon the floor, and as the cat rushed and scurried from their grasp disaster was heaped upon disaster; the green, glowing eyes, the rigid teeth, that seemed to grow as large as a tiger's, confounded them, and the havoc deterred them; they da. ed not approach the spitting fury, it was a wild beast again, and a bold one.

"O ... my ... lord!" said Oddfellow, also swearing softly, for bottles continued to slip from shelf to floor. "What's to be done?"

"Open the door—let the flaming thing go," said Jerry.

"No fear," replied the chemist, "I've had enough of these dead cats turning up like Banquo's ghost—just enough."

Horace intervened. "My father's got a gun, sir; shall I run round home and get it?"

Jerry's eyes began to gleam, the costly phials kept dropping to the floor—the chemist distractedly agreed—the boy Horace ran home and fetched a rook rifle. But his prowess was so poor, his aim so disastrous—he shot a hole through a barrel of linseed oil and received a powerful squirt of it in his eye—that Jerry deprived him of the weapon. Even then several rounds had to be fired, a carboy of acid was cracked, a window smashed, a lamp blown to pieces, before poor tom was finally subdued. Oddfellow had gone into the shop. He could not bring himself to witness the dismal slaughter. Every repercussion sent a pang of pity to his heart, and when at last the bleeding body of the cat was laid in the yard to await removal by its owner he almost vomited and he almost wept; if he had not sniffed the bunch of early primroses in his buttonhole he would surely have done one or the other.

"Now the dog," whispered the chemist. The collie was very subdued, good dog, he gave no trouble at all, good dog, he was hustled into the big box, good dog, and quietly chloroformed. Later on, a countryman with his cart called for the body. The old woman who owned it was going to make a hearthrug with the skin. It was enveloped in a sack; the countryman carried it out on his shoulder like a butcher carrying the carcase of a sheep and flung it into the cart. The callousness of this struck Mr. Oddfellow so profoundly that he announced there and then, positively and finally, that he would undertake no more business of that kind, and doubly to insure this the lethal box was taken into the yard and chopped up.

Now, the poor old woman who owned the dog called next day at the chemist's shop. Behind her walked the very collie. For a moment or two Oddfellow feared that he was to be haunted by the walking ghost of cats and dogs for evermore. Said the old woman: "Please, sir, you must do him again; he's woke up!"

She described at great length the dog's strange revival. It stood humbly enough in the background, a little drowsy, but not at all uneasy.

"No," cried Oddfellow firmly; "can't do it—destroyed my tackle. You take him home, ma'am; he's all right. Dog that's been through that ought to live a long life. Take him home again, ma'am," he urged, "he's all right."

The woman was old; she was feeble and poor; she was not able to keep him now, he was such a big dog. Wasn't it hard enough to get him food, things were so dear, and now there was the licence money due! She hadn't got it; she never would have it; she really couldn't afford it.

"You take him, sir, and keep him, sir."

"No, I can't keep a dog—no room."

"Have him, sir," she pleaded; "you'll be kind to him."

"No, no; . . . but . . . if it's only his licence . . .

I'll tell you what. I'll pay for his licence rather than destroy him."

Putting his hand into the till, he laid three half-crowns before her. The old woman stared at the chemist, but she stared still more at the money. Then, thanking him with quaint, confused dignity, she gathered it up, but again stood gazing meditatively at the three big coins, now lying, so unexpectedly, in her thin palm.

" Good dog," said the chemist, giving him a final pat. " Good dog! "

Then the poor old woman, with tears in her eyes, turned out of Mr. Oddfellow's shop and, followed by her dog, walked off to a quarter of the town where there was another chemist who kept a lethal chamber.

The Wife of Ted Wickham

PERHAPS IT IS A MERCY WE CAN'T see ourselves as others see us. Molly Wickham was a remarkable pretty woman in days gone by; maybe she is wiser since she has aged, but when she was young she was foolish. She never seemed to realize it, but I wasn't deceived.

So said the cattle-dealer, a healthy looking man, massive, morose, and bordering on fifty. He did not say it to anybody in particular, for it was said—it was to himself he said it—privately, musingly, as if to soothe the still embittered recollection of a beauty that was foolish, a fondness that was vain.

Ted Wickham himself was silly, too, when he married her. Must have been extraordinarily touched to marry a little soft, religious, teetotal party like her, and him a great sporting cock of a man, just come into a public-house business that his aunt had left him, "The Half Moon," up on the Bath Road. He always ate like an elephant, but she'd only the appetite of a scorpion. And what was worse, he was a true blood conservative while all her family were a set of radicals that you couldn't talk sense to: if you only so much as mentioned the name of Gladstone they would turn their eyes up to the ceiling as if he was a saint in glory. Blood is thicker than water, I know, but it's unnatural stuff to drink so much of. Grant their name was. They christened her Pamela, and as if that wasn't cruel enough they messed her initials up by giving her the middle name of Isabel.

But she was a handsome creature, on the small side

195

but sound as a roach and sweet as an apple tree in bloom. Pretty enough to convert Ted, and I thought she would convert him, but she was a cussed woman —never did what you would expect of her—and so she didn't even try. She gave up religion herself, gave it up altogether and went to church no more. That was against her inclination, but of course it was only right, for Ted never could have put up with that. Wedlock's one thing and religion's two: that's odd and even: a little is all very well if it don't go a long ways. Parson Twamley kept calling on her for a year or two afterwards, trying to persuade her to return to the fold—he couldn't have called oftener if she had owed him a hundred pound—but she would not hear of it, she would not go. He was not much of a parson, not one to wake anybody up, but he had a good delivery, and when he'd the luck to get hold of a sermon of any sense his delivery was very good, very good indeed. She would say: " No, sir, my feelings arn't changed one bit, but I won't come to church any more, I've my private reasons." And the parson would glare across at old Ted as if he were a Belze-boob, for Ted always sat and listened to the parson chattering to her. Never said a word himself, always kept his pipe stuck in his jaw. Ted never persuaded her in the least, just left it to her, and she would come round to his manner of thinking in the end, for though he never actually said it, she always knew what his way of thinking was. A strange thing, it takes a real woman to do that, silly or no! At election times she would plaster the place all over with tory bills, do it with her own hands!

Still, there's no stability in meekness of that sort, a weathervane can only go with wind and weather, and there was no sense in her giving in to Ted as she did, not in the long run, for he couldn't help but despise her. A man wants something or other to whet the edge of his life on; and he did despise her, I know.

But she was a fine creature in her way, only her way wasn't his. A beautiful woman, too, well-limbered up, with lovely hair, but always a very proper sort, a milksop—Ted told me once that he had never seen her naked. Well, can you wonder at the man? And always badgering him to do things that could not be done at the time. To have " The Half Moon " painted, or enlarged, or insured: she'd keep on badgering him, and he could not make her see that any god's amount of money spent on paint wouldn't improve the taste of liquor.

" I can see as far into a quart pot as the King of England," he says, " and I know that if this bar was four times as big as 'tis a quart wouldn't hold a drop more then than it does now."

" No, of course," she says.

" Nor a drop less neither," says Ted. He showed her that all the money expended on improvements and insurance and such things were so much off something else. Ted was a generous chap—liked to see plenty of everything, even though he had to give some of it away. But you can't make some women see some things.

" Not a roof to our heads, nor a floor to our feet, nor a pound to turn round on if a fire broke out," Molly would say.

" But why should a fire break out ? " he'd ask her.
" There never has been a fire here, there never ought
to be a fire here, and what's more, there never will be
a fire here, so why should there be a fire ? "

And of course she let him have his own way, and
they never had a fire there while he was alive, though
I don't know that any great harm would have been
done anyways, for after a few years trade began to
slacken off, and the place got dull, and what with the
taxes it was not much more than a bread and cheese
business. Still, there's no matter of that: a man
don't ask for a bed of roses: a world without some
disturbance or anxiety would be like a duckpond
where the ducks sleep all day and are carried off at
night by the foxes.

Molly was like that in many things, not really
contrary, but no tact. After Ted died she kept on at
" The Half Moon " for a year or two by herself, and
regular as clockwork every month Pollock, the insurance manager, would drop in and try for to persuade
her to insure the house or the stock or the furniture,
any mortal thing. Well, believe you, when she had
only got herself to please in the matter that woman
wouldn't have anything to say to that insurance—she
never did insure, and never would.

" I wouldn't run such a risk; upon my soul it's
flying in the face of possibilities, Mrs. Wickham "—
he was a palavering chap, that Pollock; a tall fellow
with sandy hair, and he always stunk of liniment for
he had asthma on the chest—" A very grave risk, it
is indeed," he would say, " the Meazer's family
was burnt clean out of hearth and home last St.

Valentine's day, and if they hadn't taken up a policy what would have become of those Meazers?"

"I dunno," Molly says—that was the name Ted give her—"I dunno, and I'm sorry for unfortunate people, but I've my private reasons."

She was always talking about her private reasons, and they must have been devilish private, for not a soul on God's earth ever set eyes on them.

"Well, Mrs. Wickham," says Pollock, "they'd have been a tidy ways up Queer Street, and ruin's a long-lasting affair," Pollock says. He was a rare palavering chap, and he used to talk about Gladstone, too, for he knew her family history; but that didn't move her, and she did not insure.

"Yes, I quite agree," she says, "but I've my private reasons."

Sheer female cussedness! But where her own husband couldn't persuade her Pollock had no chance at all. And then, of course, two years after Ted died she did go and have a fire there. "The Half Moon" was burnt clean out, rafter and railings, and she had to give it up and shift into the little bullseye business where she is now, selling bullseyes to infants and ginger beer to boy scholars on bicycles. And what does it all amount to? Why, it don't keep her in hairpins. She had the most beautiful hair once. But that's telling the story back foremost.

Ted was a smart chap, a particular friend of mine (so was Molly), and he could have made something of himself and of his business, perhaps, if it hadn't been for her. He was a sportsman to the backbone; cricket, shooting, fishing, always game for a bit of life, any mortal thing—what was there he couldn't do? And a perfect demon with women, I've never seen the like. If there was a woman for miles around as he couldn't come at, then you could bet a crown no one else could. He had the gift. Well, when one woman ain't enough for a man, twenty ain't too many. He and me were in a tight corner together more than once, but he never went back on a friend, his word was his Bible oath. And there was he all the while tied up to this soft wife of his, who never once let on she knew of it at all, though she knowed much. And never would she cast the blink of her eyes—splendid eyes they were, too—on any willing stranger, nor even a friend, say, like myself; it was all Ted this and Ted that, though I was just her own age and Ted was twelve years ahead of us both. She didn't know her own value, wouldn't take her opportunities, hadn't the sense, as I say, though she had got everything else. Ah, she was a woman to be looking at once, and none so bad now; she wears well.

But she was too pious and proper, it aggravated him, but Ted never once laid a finger on her and never uttered one word of reproach though he despised her; never grudged her a thing in reason when things were going well with him. It's God Almighty's own true gospel—they never had a quarrel in all the twelve years they was wed, and I don't believe they ever had an angry word, but how he kept his hands off her I don't know. I couldn't have done it, but I was never married—I was too independent for that work. He'd contradict her sometimes, for she *would* talk, and Ted was one of your silent sorts, but *she*—she would talk for ever more. She was so artful that she used to invent all manners of tomfoolery on purpose to make him contradict her; believe you, she did, even on his death-bed.

I used to go and sit with him when he was going, poor Ted, for I knew he was done for; and on the day he died, she said to him—and I was there and I heard it: " Is there anything you would like me to do, dear ? " And he said, " No." He was almost at his last gasp, he had strained his heart, but she was for ever on at him, even then, an unresting woman. It was in May, I remember it, a grand bright after-noon outside, but the room itself was dreadful, it didn't seem to be afternoon at all; it was unbearable for a strong man to be dying in such fine weather, and the carts going by, and though we were a watching him, it seemed more as if something was watching us.

And she says to him again: " Isn't there anything you would like me to do ? "

Ted says to her: " Ah! I'd like to hear you give one downright good damn curse. Swear, my dear! "

" At what ? " she says.

" Me, if you like."

" What for ? " she says. I can see her now, staring at him.

" For my sins."

" What sins ? " she says.

Now did you ever hear anything like that ? What sins! After a while she began at him once more.

" Ted, if anything happens to you I'll never marry again."

" Do what you like," says he.

" I'll not do that," she says, and she put her arms round him, " for you'd not rest quiet in your grave, would you, Ted ? "

" Leave me alone," he says, for he was a very crusty sick man, very crusty, poor Ted, but could you wonder ? " You leave me alone and I'll rest sure enough."

" You can be certain," she cries, " that I'd never, never do that, I'd never look at another man after you, Ted, never; I promise it solemnly."

" Don't bother me, don't bother at all." And poor Ted give a grunt and turned over on his side to get away from her.

At that moment some gruel boiled over on the hob —gruel and brandy was all he could take. She turned to look after it, and just then old Ted gave a breath and was gone, dead. She turned like a flash, with the steaming pot in her hand, bewildered for a moment. She saw he had gone. Then she put the pot back gently on the fender, walked over to the window and pulled down the blind. Never dropped a tear, not one tear.

Well, that was the end of Ted. We buried him, one or two of us. There was an insurance on his life for fifty pounds, but Ted had long before mortgaged the policy and so there was next to nothing for her. But what else could the man do ? (Molly always swore the bank defrauded her!) She put a death notice in the paper, how he was dead, and the date, and what he died of: " after a long illness, nobly and patiently borne." Of course, that was sarcasm, she never meant one word of it, for he was a terror to nurse, the worst that ever was; a strong man on his back is like a wasp in a bottle. But every year, when the day comes round—and it's ten years now since he died—she puts a memorial notice in the same paper about her loving faithful husband and the long illness nobly and patiently borne!

And then, as I said, the insurance man and the parson began to call again on that foolish woman, but she would not alter her ways for any of them. Not one bit. The things she had once enjoyed before her marriage, the things she had wanted her own husband to do but were all against his grain, these she could nohow bring herself to do when he was dead and gone and she was alone and free to do them. What a farce human nature can be! There was an Italian hawker came along with rings in his ears and a coloured cart full of these little statues of Cupid, and churches with spires a yard long and red glass in them, and heads of some of the great people like the Queen and General Gordon.

" Have you got a head of Lord Beaconsfield ? " Molly asks him.

He goes and searches in his cart and brings her out a beautiful head on a stand, all white and new, and charges her half a crown for it. Few days later the parson calls on the job of persuading her to return to his flock now that she was free to go once more. But no. She says: " I can never change now, sir, it may be all wrong of me, but what my man thought

203

was good enough for me, and I somehow cling to that. It's all wrong, I suppose, and you can't understand it, sir, but it's all my life."

Well, Twamley chumbled over an argument or two, but he couldn't move her; there's no mortal man could ever more that woman except Ted—and he didn't give a damn.

" Well," says parson, " I have hopes, Mrs. Wickham, that you will come to see the matter in a new light, a little later on perhaps. In fact, I'm sure you will, for look, there's that bust," he says, and he points to it on the mantelpiece. I thought you and he were all against Gladstone, but now you've got his bust upon your shelf; it's a new one, I see."

" No, no, that isn't Gladstone," cried Molly, all of a tremble, " that isn't Gladstone, it's Lord Beaconsfield! "

" Indeed, but pardon me, Mrs. Wickham, that is certainly a bust of Mr. Gladstone."

So it was. This Italian chap had deceived the silly creature and palmed her off with any bust that come handy, and it happened to be Gladstone. She went white to the teeth, and gave a sort of scream, and dashed the little bust in a hundred pieces on the hearth in front of the minister there. O, he had a very vexing time with her.

That was years ago. And then came the fire, and then the bullseye shop. For ten years now I've prayed that woman to marry me, and she just tells me: No. She says she pledged her solemn word to Ted as he lay a-dying that she would not wed again. It was his last wish—she says. But it's a lie, a lie, for I heard them both. Such a lie! She's a mad woman, but fond of him still in her way, I suppose. She liked to see Ted make a fool of himself, liked him better so. Perhaps that's what she don't see in me. And what I see in her—I can't imagine. But it's a something, something in her that sways me now just as it swayed me then, and I doubt but it will sway me for ever.

Tanil

A GREAT WHILE AGO A MAN IN A stripéd jacket went travelling almost to the verge of the world, and there he came upon a region of green fertility, quiet sounds, and sharp colour; save for one tiny green mound it was all smooth and even, as level as the moon's face, so flat that you could see the sky rising up out of the end of everything like a blue dim cliff. He passed into a city very populous and powerful, and entered the shop of a man who sold birds in traps of wicker, birds of rare kinds, the flame-winged antillomeneus and kriffs with green eyes.

" Sir," said he to the hawker of birds, " this should be a city of great occasions, it has the smell of opulence. But it is all unknown to me, I have not heard the story of its arts and policy, or of its people and their governors. What annalists have you recording all its magnificence and glory, or what poets to tell if its record be just ? "

The hawker of birds replied: " There are tales and the tellers of tales."

" I have not heard of these," said the other, " tell me, tell me."

The bird man drew finger and thumb downwards from the bridge of his long nose to its extremity, and sliding the finger across his pliant nostrils said: " I will tell you." They both sat down upon a coffer of wheat. " I will tell you," repeated the bird man, and he asked the other if he had heard of the tomb in which none could lie, nor die, nor mortify.

" No," said he.

" Or of the oracle that destroys its interpreter ? "

" No," answered the man in the stripéd jacket, and a talking bird in a cage screamed: " No, no, no, no! " The traveller whistled caressingly to the bird, tapping his finger nail along the rods of its cage, while the bird man continued: " Or of Fax, Mint, and Bombassor, the three faithful brothers ? "

" No," replied he again.

" They had a sister of beauty, of beauty indeed, beyond imagination. (*Soo-eet*! *soo-eet*! chirped the oracular bird.) It smote even the hearts of kings like a reaping hook among grass, and her favour was a ransom from death itself, as I will tell you."

" Friend," said he of the stripéd jacket, " tell me of that woman."

" I will tell you," answered the other; and he told him, and this was the way of it.

* * * * *

There was once a king of this country, mighty with riches and homage, with tribute from his enemies— for he was a great warrior—and the favour of many excellent queens. His ancestors were numberless as the hairs of his black beard; so ancient was his lineage that he may have sprung from divinity itself, but he had a heart of brass, his bowels were of lead, and at times he was afflicted with madness.

One day he called for his captain of the guard, Tanil, a valiant, debonair man of much courtesy, and delivered to him his commands.

Tanil took a company of the guard and they

marched to that green hill on the plain—it is but a league away. At the foot of the hill they crossed a stream; beyond that was a white dwelling and a garden; at the gate of the garden was a stumbling stone; a flock grazed on the hill. The soldiers threw down the stone and, coming into the vineyard, they hacked down the vines until they heard a voice call to them. They saw at the door of the white dwelling a woman so beautiful that the weapons slid from their hands at the wonder of it. " Friends, friends! " said she. Tanil told her the King's bidding, how they must destroy the vineyard, the dwelling, and the flock, and turn Fax, Mint, and Bombassor, with the foster sister Flaune, out from the kingdom of Cumac.

" You have denied the King tribute," said he.

" We are wanderers from the eastern world," Flaune answered. " Is not the mountain a free mountain ? Does not this stream divide it from Cumac's country ? "

She took Tanil into the white dwelling and gave a pitcher of wine to his men.

" Sir," said she to Tanil, " I will go to your King. Take me to your King."

And when Tanil agreed to do this she sent a message secretly to her brothers to drive the flock away into a hiding-place. So while Flaune was gone a-journeying to the palace with Tanil's troup, Fax, Mint, and Bombassor set back the stumbling stone and took away the sheep.

The King was resting in his palace garden, throwing crumbs into the lake, and beans to his peacocks, but when Flaune was brought to him he rose and bowed himself to the pavement at her feet. The woman said nothing, she walked to and fro before him, and he was content to let his gaze rest upon her. The carp under the fountain watched them, the rose drooped on its envious briar, the heart of King Cumac was like a tree full of chirping birds.

Tanil confessed his fault; might the King be merciful and forgive him! but the lady had taken their trespass with a soft temper and policy that had overcome both his loyalty and his mind. It was unpardonable, but it was not guilt, it was infirmity, she had bewitched him. Cumac grinned and nodded. He bade Tanil return to the vineyard and restore the vines, bade him requite the brothers and confirm them in those pastures for ever. But as to this Flaune he would not let her go.

She paces before him, or she dips her palm into the fountain, spilling its drops upon the ground; she smiles and she is silent.

Cumac gave her into the care of his groom of the women, Yali, the sister of Tanil, and thereafter, every day and many a day, the King courted and coveted Flaune. But he could not take her; her pride, her cunning words, and her lustre bore her like an anchored boat upon the tide of his purpose. At one moment full of pride and gloom, and in the next full of humility and love, he would bring gifts and praises.

" I will cover you," he whispered, " with green garnets and jargoons. A collar of onyx and ruby, that is for you; breastknots of beryl, and rings for the finger, wrist, and ear. Take them, take them! For you I would tear the moon asunder."

But all her desire was only to return to the green mountain and her brothers and the flock by the stumbling stone. The King was merged in anger and in grief.

"Do not so," he pleaded, "I have given freedom to your men; will you not give freedom to me?"

"What freedom, Cumac?" she asked him.

And he said: "Love."

"How may the bound give freedom?"

"With the gift of love."

"The spirit of the gift lies only in the giver." Her voice was mournful and low.

He was confused and cast down. "You humble me with words, but words are nothing, beautiful one. Put on your collar of onyx, and fasten your breast-knots of beryl. Have I not griefs, fierce griefs, that crash upon my brain, and frenzies that shoot in fire! Does not your voice—that rest-recovering lure—allay them, your presence numb them! I cannot let you go, I cannot let you go."

"He who woos and does not win," so said Flaune, "wins what he does not woo for."

"Though I beg but a rose," murmured the King, "do you offer me a sword?"

"Time's sword is laid at the breast of every rose."

"But I am your lowly servant," he cried. "You have that which all secretly seek and denyingly long for; it is seen without sight and affirmed without speech."

"What is the thing you seek and long for?"

"Purity," said he.

"Purity!" She seemed to muse upon it as a

theme of mystery. "If you found purity, what would you match it with?"

"My sins!" he cried again. "Would you waste purity on purity, or mingle sin with sin?"

"Cumac," said the wise woman, with no pride then but only pity, "you seek to conquer that which strikes the conqueror dead."

Then, indeed, for a while he was mute, and then for a while he talked of his sickness and his frenzy. "Are there not charms," he asked, "or magic herbs, to find and bind these demons?"

There was no charm—she told him—but the mind, and no magic but in the tranquillity of freedom.

"I do not know this," he sighed, "it will never be known."

The unknown—she told him—was better than the known.

"Alas, then," sighed the King again, "I shall never discover it."

"It is everywhere," said Flaune, "but it is like a sweet herb that withers in the ground. All may gather it—and it is not gathered. All may see it—and it is not seen. All destroy it—and it never dies . . ."

"Shall I be a little wind," laughed Cumac, "and gush among this grass?"

"It is the wind's way among the roses. It has horns of bright brass and quiet harps of silver. Its golden boats flash in every tossing bay."

Cumac laughed again, but still he would not let her go. "The fox has many tricks, the cat but one," he said, and caused her ankles to be fastened with two jewelled links tied with a hopple of gold. But in a day he struck them from her with his own hands, and hung the hopple upon her lustrous neck.

And still he would not let her go; so Yali and Tanil connived to send news to the brothers, and in a little time Bombassor came to her aid.

Bombassor was a dancer without blemish, in beauty or movement either. He came into the palace to Cumac who did not know him, and the King's household came to the beaten gongs to witness the art of Bombassor. Yali brought Flaune a harp of ivory, and to its music Bombassor caracoled and spun before the delighted King. Then Flaune (who spoke as a stranger to him) asked Bombassor if he would dance with her, and he said they would take the dance of " The Flying Phœnix." The King was enchanted; he vowed he would grant any wish of Bombassor's, any wish; yes, he would cut the moon in half did he desire it. " I will dance for your pledge," said Bombassor.

It seemed to the King then as if a little whirling wind made of flame, and a music that was perfume, gyred and rose before him: the tapped gongs, the tinkle of harp, the surprise of Flaune's swaying and reeling, now coy, now passionate, the lure of her wooing arms, the rhythm of her flying feet, the chanting of the onlookers, and the flashing buoyance of Bombassor, so thrilled and distracted him that he shouted like an eager boy.

But when Bombassor desired Cumac to give him the maiden Flaune, the King was astonished. " No,

no," he said, " but give him an urn full of diamonds,"
and Bombassor was given an urn full of diamonds.
He let it fall at the King's feet, and the gems clattered
upon the pavement like a heap of peas. " Give him
Yali, then," Cumac shouted. Yali was a nymph of
splendour, but Bombassor called aloud, " No, a
pledge is a pledge! "

Then the King's joy went from him and, like a
star falling, left darkness and terror.

" Take," he cried, " an axe to his head and pitch it
to the crows."

And so was Bombassor destroyed, while the King
continued ignorantly to woo his sister. Silent and
proud was she, silent and proud, but her beauty began
to droop until Yali and Tanil, perceiving this, connived again to send to her brothers, and in a little
time Mint came. To race on foot he was fleeter than
any of Cumac's champions; they strove with him,
but he was like the unreturning wind, and although
they cunningly moved the bounds of the course, and
threw thorns and rocks under his feet, he defeated
them all, and the King jeered at his own champions.
Then Mint called for an antelope to be set in the
midst of the plain and cried: " Who will catch this
for the King ? " All were amazed and Cumac said:
" Whoever will do it I will give him whatever a King
may give, though I crack the moon for it."

The men let go the hind and it swooped away,
Mint pursuing. Fast and far they sped until no
man's gaze could discern them, but in a while Mint
returned bearing the breathing hind upon his back.
" Take off his shoes," cried the King, " and fill them

with gold." But when this was done Mint spilled
the gold back at the King's feet.

"Give me," said he, "this maiden Flaune."

The King grinned and refused him.

"Was it not in the bond?" asked Mint.

"Ay," replied Cumac, "but choose again."

"Is this then a King's bond?" sneered Mint.

"It was a living bond," said the King, "but death
can sever it. Let this dog be riven in sunder and his
bowels spilled to the foxes." Mint died on the
moment, and Cumac continued ignorantly to woo his
sister.

Then Flaune conferred with Tanil and with Yali
about a means of escape. Tanil feared to be about
this, but he loved Flaune, and his sister Yali persuaded
him. He showed them a great door in the back of the
palace, a concealed issue through the city wall, from
which Flaune might go in a darkness could but the
door be opened. But it had not been opened for a
hundred years, and they feared the hinges would
shriek and the wards grind in the lock and so discover them.

"Let us bring oil to-morrow," they said, "and
oil it."

In the morning they brought oil to the hinge and
brushed it with drops from a cock's feather. The
hinge gave up its squeak but yet it groaned. They
filled Yali's thimble that was made of tortoise horn
and poured this upon it. The hinge gave up its groan
but yet it sighed. They filled the eggshell of a goose
with oil and poured upon the hinge until it was silent.
Then they turned to the lock, which, as they threw

back the wards, cried clack, clack. Tanil lapped the great key with ointment, but still the lock clattered. He filled his mouth with oil and spat into the hole, but still it clinked. Then Flaune caught a grasshopper which she dipped in oil and cast into the lock. After that the lock was silent too.

On the mid of night Tanil ushered Flaune to the great door, and it opened in peace. She said " Farewell " to him tenderly, and vanished away into the darkness, and so to the green mountain. As he stooped, watching her until his eyes could see no more, the door suddenly closed and locked against him, leaving him outside the wall. Lights came, and an outcry and a voice roaring: " Tanil is fled with the King's mistress. Turn out the guard." Tanil knew it to be the voice of a jealous captain, and, filled with consternation, he too turned and fled away into the night; not towards the mountains, but to the sea, hoping to catch a ship that would deliver him.

Throughout the night he was going, striving or sleeping, and it was stark noon before he came to the shore and passed over the strait in a ship conveying merchants to a fair where no one knew him and all were friendly. He hobnobbed with the merchants for several days, feeding and sleeping in the booths until the morning of the sixth day, and on that day a crier came into the fair ringing and bawling, bawling and ringing, and what he cried was this:

That King Cumac, Lord of the Forty Kingdoms, Prince of the Moon, and Chieftain under God, laid a ban upon all who should aid or relieve his treacherous servant Tanil, who had conspired against the King and fled. Furthermore it was to be known that Yali, the sister of Tanil, was taken as hostage for him, that if he failed to redeem her and deliver up his own body Yali herself was doomed to perish at sunset of the seventh day after his flight.

Tanil scarcely waited to hear the conclusion, for he had but one day more and he could suffer not his sister Yali to die. He turned from the fair and ran to the sea. As he ran he slipped upon a rock and was stunned, but a good wife restored him and soon he reached the harbour. Here none of the sailors would convey him over the strait, for they were bound to the merchantmen who intended not to sail that day. Having so little time to reckon Tanil offered them bribes (but in vain), and threats (but they would not), and he was in torment and anguish until he came to an old man who said he would take him within the hour if the wind held and the tide turned. But if the wind failed, although the tide should ebb never so kindly, yet he would not go: and even should the tide ebb strongly, yet if the wind wavered from its quarter he would not go: and if by mysterious caprice (for all was in the hands of God and a great wonder) the tide itself should not turn, then the wind might blow a dainty squall but he would not be able to undertake him. Upon this they agreed, and Tanil and the old sailor sat down in the little ship to play at checkers. Alas, fortune was against Tanil, he could not conquer the sailor, so he made to pay down his loss.

" Friend," said the sailor, " a game is but a game, put up your purse."

Tanil would not put back the money and the sailor said: " Let us then play on, friend; double or quits." They played on, and again Tanil loſt, and, as before, tendered his money. " Nay," said the sailor, " a game is but a paſtime, put back your money." But Tanil laid it in a heap upon one of the thwarts. The old sailor sighed and said: " Come, you are now at the turn of fortune; is not an egg made of water and a ſtone of fire: let us play once more; double or quits." And so continually, until it was long paſt noon ere they began to sail in a course for Cumac's shore, two leagues over the ſtrait. Now they had accomplished about three parts of this voyage when the wind slackened away like a wisp of smoke; slowly they drifted onwards until at eve the boat lay becalmed, and as yet some way out from the land. " Friend," said the old sailor, laying out the checkers again, " let us tempt the winds of fortune." But, full of grief at having squandered the precious hours, Tanil leaped into the sea and swam towards the shore. Soon the tide checked and was changed, and a current washed him far down the ſtrait until the fading of day; then he was caſt upon a crooking cape of sand in such darkness of night and such weariness of mind and body that he could not rise. He lay there for a while consumed with languor and hunger until the peace refreshed him; the winds of night were lulled and the waves; but though there were ſtars in the sky they could not guide him.

" Alas," he groaned, " darkness and the oddness of the coaſt deceive me. Whether I venture to the right hand or the left, how shall I make my way ?

How little is man's power; the fox and the hare may wander deceitfully but undeterred, yet here in this darkness I go groping like a worm laid upon a rock. Yali, my sister, how shall I preserve you?"

He went wandering across a hill away from the sea until he stumbled upon a hurdle, and fell; and where he fell he lay still, sleeping.

Not until the dawn did Tanil wake; then he lay shivering in bonds, with a company of sheep watchers that stood by and mocked at him. Their shadows were long, a hundred-fold, for day was but newly dawned.

Their master was not yet risen from his bed, but the watchers carried Tanil to the door of his house and called to him.

"Master, we have caught a robber of the flock, lying by the fold and feigning sleep."

Now the sleepy master lay with a new bride, and he would not stir.

"Come, master, we have taken a robber," they cried again. And still he did not move, but the bride rose and came to the window.

"What sheep has he stole?"

They answered her: "None, for we swaddled him; behold!"

She looked down at Tanil with her pleasant eyes, and bade the men unbind him.

"Who guards now the sheep from robbers and wolves?" she called. They were all silent, and some made to go off. She bade them mend their ways, and went back to her lover. When the thongs were loosened from Tanil he begged them to give him a little food for he was empty and weak, but they scolded him and went hastily away. Their shadows were long, a hundred-fold.

Tanil travelled on wings. Yali was to die at fall of night. He hastened like a lover, but sickness and hunger overcame him; at noon he lay down in a cool cavern to recover. No other travellers came by him and no homes were near, for he was passing across the fringe of a desert to shorten his journey, and the highway crooked round far to the eastward. Nothing that man could eat was there to sustain him, but he slept. When he rose his legs weakened and he limped onwards like a slow beggar whose life lies all behind him. Again he sank down, again he could not keep from sleeping. The sun was setting when he awoke, the coloured towers of his city shone only a league away. Then in his heart despair leaped and maddened him—Yali had died while he tarried.

Searching through a thicket for some place where he could hang himself he came upon a river, and saw, close to the shore, a small ship standing slowly down towards the straits from which he had come. Under her slack sail a man was playing on a pipe; with him was a monkey gazing sorrowfully from the deck at the great glow in the sky.

"Shipman," cried Tanil, "will you give me bread, I am at an end?"

The man with a smile of malice held up from the deck a dish of fruits and said: "Take. I have done."

But the hungry man could not reach it. "Throw it to me," he cried, following the ship. But the sailor had no mind to throw it upon the shore; he went leaning against his mast, piping an air, while the monkey peered at him and gabbled. Tanil plunged into the river and swam beneath the ship's keel. Taking a knife from his girdle he was for mounting by a little hawser, but the man beflogged him with a cudgel until he fell back into the water. There he would have died but that a large barque presently catched him up on board and recovered him.

The ship carried Tanil from the river past the straits and so to the great sea, where for the space of a year he was borne in absence, willy-nilly, while the ship voyaged among the archipelagos, coasted grim seaboards, or lay against strange wharves docking her cargo of oil. Faithfully he laboured for wages under this ship's captain, being a man of pith and limb, valiant in storm, and enamoured of the uncouth work: the haul of anchor, and men singing; setting, reefing, furling, and men singing; the watch, the sleep, the song; the treading of unknown waters, the crying gust, the change to glassy endless calm, and the change again from green day to black night and the bending of the harsh sheet in a starry squall, the crumpling of far thunder, the rattle of halyard and block, the howl of cordage. Grand it was in some bright tempest to watch the lubber wave slide greenly to the bows and crack in showers of flying diamonds, but best of all was the long crunch in from the vast gulfs, and the wafture to some blue bay sighing below a white dock and the homes of men.

Forgotten was Yali his loved sister, but that proud living Flaune who had brought Yali to her death, she was not forgotten. He sailed the seas and he sailed the seas, but she was ever a soft recalling wonder in his breast, the sound of a bell of glass beaten by a spirit.

After a year of hazards the ship by chance docked in that harbour where Tanil had heard the crier crying of Yali and her doom. Looking about him he espied an old sailor sitting in his boat playing a game of checkers with a young man. The crier bawled in the market place, but he had no news for Tanil. Standing again amid the merchants and the kind coloured sweetness of streets and people, this bliss of home so welled up in his breast that he hastened back to the ship. "Master," he said, "give me my wages, and let me go." The shipman gave him his wages, and he went back to the town.

But only nine days did he linger there, for joy, like truth, lives in the bottom of a well, and he cast in his wages. Then he went off with a hunter to trap leopards in a forest. A month they were gone, and they trapped the leopards and sold them, and then, having parted from the hunter, Tanil roved back to the port to spend his gains among the women of the town. Often his soul invited him to return to that city of Cumac, but death awaited him there and he did not go. Now he was come to poverty, but he was blithe, and evil could not chain him. "Surely," said Tanil, "life is a hope unquenched and a tree of longing. There is none so poor but he can love himself." With a stolen net he used to catch fish and live. Then he lost the net at dicing. So he went to bake loaves for certain scholars, but they were un-monied men and he desisted, and went wandering from village to village snaring birds, or living like the wild dogs, until a friendly warrior enlisted him to convoy a caravan across the desert to the great lakes. When he came again to the harbour town two years had withered since he had flown from Cumac's city.

He went to lodge at the inn, and as he paced in the evening along the wharf a man accosted him, called him by name, and would not let him go, and then Tanil knew it was Fax, the brother of that Flaune. His heart rocked in his breast when he took Fax to the inn and related all his adventure. "Tell me the tidings of our city, what comes or goes there, what lives or dies." And Fax replied: "I have wandered in the world searching after you from that time. I bring a greeting from my sister Flaune," he said, " and from your sister Yali, my beloved."

The wonder then, the joy and shame of Tanil, cannot be told: he threw himself down and wept, and begged Fax to tell him of the miracle: "For," said he, " my mind has misused me in this."

"Know then," proceeded Fax, "that after the unlocking of the door my sister flees in darkness to the green mountain. I go watching and lurking, and learn that the King is in jealous madness, for your enemy spreads a slander and Cumac is deceived. He believes that my sister's love has been cozened by you. Yali is caught fast in his net. My heart quivers in fear of his bloody intent, and I say to Flaune: 'What shall follow if Tanil return not?' And she smiles and says ever: 'He will return.' And again I say: 'He tarries. What if he be dead?' And she smiles and says ever: 'He is not dead.' But you come not, your steps are turned from us, no one has seen you, you are like a hare that has fallen into a pit, and you do not come. Then in that last hour Flaune goes to Cumac. He raves of deceit and treachery. 'It is my sin,' my sister pleads, 'the blame is mine. Spare but this Yali and I will wash out the blame.' 'Ay, you will wash it out with words!' 'I will pay the debt in kind,' says my sister Flaune, 'if Tanil does not return.' But the cunning King will not yield up Yali unless my sister yield in love to him. So thus it stands even now, but whether they live in peace and love I do not know. I only know that Yali lives and serves her in the palace there. But they wait, and I too wait. Now the thread is ravelled to its end; I have lived only to seek you. My flock is lost, perished; my vineyard fades, but I came seeking."

"Brother," cried Tanil in grief, "all shall be as before. Yali shall rest in your bosom."

At dawn then they sailed over the straits and landed, and having bargained with a wine carrier for two asses they rode off in the direction of the city. Tanil's heart was filled with joy and love, his voice carolled, his mind hummed like a homing bee. "Surely," he said, "life is a hope unquenched, a tree of longing. It yields its branches into a little world of summer. The asp and the dragon appear, but the tree buds, the enriching bough cherishes its leaves, and, lo, the fruit hangs."

But the heart of Fax was very grave within him. "For," thought he, "this man will surely die. Yet I would rather this than lose the love of Yali, and though they slay him I will bring him there."

So they rode along upon the asses, and a great bird on high followed them and hovered on its wings.

" What bird is that ? " asked the one. And the other, screening his eyes and peering upwards, said: " A vulture."

When King Cumac heard that they were come he ordered them to be bound, and they were bound, and the guard clustered around them. Tanil saw that his enemy was now captain of the men, and that the King was sour and distraught.

" You come! " cried Cumac, " why do you come ? "

They told him it was to redeem the bond and make quittance.

" Bonds and quittances! What bond can lie between a King and faithless subjects ? "

Said Fax: " It lies between the King and my sister Flaune."

" How if I kill you both ? "

" The bond will hold," said Fax.

" Come, is a bond everlasting then, shall nothing break it ? "

" Neither everlasting, nor to be broken."

" What then ? "

" It shall be fulfilled."

" Can nothing amend it ? "

" Nothing," said Fax.

" Nothing ? Nothing ? Fools! " laughed the King, " the woman is happy, and desires not to leave me! "

Tanil stood bowed in silence and shame, and Cumac turned upon him. " What says this rude passionate beaſt!" The King's anger rose like a blaſt among oaks. "Has he no talk of bonds, this toad that crawled into my heart and drank my living blood? Has he nothing to reſtore? or gives he and takes he at the will of the wind?"

"I have a life to give," said Tanil.

"To give! You have a life to lose!"

"Take it, Cumac," said he.

The King sprang up and seized Tanil by the beard, rocking him, and shouting through his gritting teeth: "Ay, bonds should be kept—should they not?—in truth and truſt—should they not?"

Then he flung from him and went wailing in misery, swinging his hands, and raging to and fro, up and down.

"Did she not come to me, come to me? Was it not agreed? Bonds and again bonds! Yet when I woo her she denies me ſtill. O, honeſty in petticoats is a saint with a devil's claw. The bitter virginal thing turned her wild heart to this piece of cloven honour. Bonds, more bonds! Spare me these supple bonds! O, you spread cunning nets, but what fowler ever thrived in his own snare? Did she not come to me? Was it not agreed?"

Suddenly he ſtopped and made a sign through a casement. "Is all ready?"

"Ay," cried a voice.

"Now I will make an end," said King Cumac. "Prop them againſt the casements." They carried Tanil to a casement on his right hand, and Fax to a casement on his left hand. Tanil saw Flaune ſtanding in the palace garden amid a troop of Ethiopians, each with a green turban and red shoes and a tunic coloured like a stone, but she half-clad with only black pantaloons, and her long dark locks flowing. And Fax saw Yali in fetters amid another troop of black soldiers.

Again a sigh from the King; two great swords flashed, and Tanil, at one casement, saw the head of Flaune turn over backwards and topple to the ground, her body falling after with a great swathe of shorn tresses floating over it. Fax at the other casement saw Yali die, screaming a long cry that it seemed would never end. Tanil swayed at the casement.

Then Cumac turned with a moan of grief, his madness all gone. " The bond is ended. I have done. I say I have done." He seemed to wake as from sleep, and, seeing the two captive men, he asked: " Why did they come ? What brought them here ? Take them away, the bond is ended, I say I have done. There shall be no more bonds given in the world. But take them out of the city gate and unbind them and cast them both loose; then clap fast the gate again. No more death, I would not have them die; let them wander in the live world, and dog each other for ever. Tanil, you rotten core of constancy, Fax brought you here and so Flaune, bitter and beautiful, dies. But Fax still lives—do you not see him ?—I give Fax to you: may he die daily for ever. Fax, blundering jackal, you spoke of bonds. The bond is met, and so Yali is dead, but Tanil still lives: I give you Tanil as an offering, but not of peace. May he die daily for ever."

So the guard took Fax and Tanil out of the city, struck off their shackles, and left them there together.

*   *   *   *   *

The bird man finished; there was a silence; the other yawned. " Did you hear this ? " asked the bird man. And the man in the striped jacket replied: " Ay, with both ears, and so may God bless you." So saying, he rose and went out singing.

The Devil in the Churchyard

"HENRY TURLEY WAS ONE OF those awkward old chaps as had more money than he knowed what to do wi'. Shadrach we called him, the silly man. He had worked for it, worked hard for it, but when he was old he ſtuck to his fortune and wouldn't spend a sixpence of it on his comforts. What a silly man!"

The thatcher, who was thus talking of Henry Turley (long since dead and gone) in the "Black Cat" of Starncombe, was himself perhaps fifty years old. Already there was a crank of age or of dampness or of mere cuſtom in moſt of his limbs, but he was bluff and gruff and hale enough, with a bluffness of manner that could only offend a fool—and fools never liſtened to him.

"Shadrach—that's what we called him—was a good man wi' cattle, a maſterpiece; he would ſtrip a cow as clean as a tooth and you never knowed a cow have a bad quarter as Henry Turley ever milked. And when he was buried he was buried with all that money in his coffin, holding it in his hand, I reckon. He had plenty of relations—you wouldn't know 'em, it is thirty years ago I be speaking oſ—but it was all down in black and white so's no one could touch it. A lot of people in these parts had a right to some of it, Jim Scarrott for one, and Issy Hawker a bit, Mrs. Keelson, poor woman, ought to have had a bit, and his own brother, Mark Turley; but he left it in the will as all his fortune was to be buried in the coffin along of him. 'Twas cruel, but so it is and so it will

228

be, for whenever such people has a shilling to give away they goes and claps it on some fat pig's haunches. The foolishness! Sixty pounds it was, in a canister, and he held it in his hand."

" I don't believe a word of it," said a mild-faced man sitting in the corner. " Henry Turley never did a deed like that."

" What ? " growled the thatcher with unusual ferocity.

" Coorse I'm not disputing what you're saying, but he never did such a thing in his life."

" Then you calls me a liar ? "

" Certainly not. O no, don't misunderstand me, but Henry Turley never did any such thing, I can't believe it of him."

" Huh! I be telling you facts, and facts be true one way or another. Now you waunts to call over me, you waunts to know the rights of everything and the wrongs of nothing."

" Well," said the mild-faced man, pushing his pot toward the teller of tales, " I might believe it to-morrow, but it's a bit of a twister now, this minute! "

" Ah, that's all right then "—the thatcher was completely mollified. " Well the worst part of the case was his brother Mark. Shadrach served him shameful, treated him like a dog. (Good health!) Ah, like a dog. Mark was older nor him, about seventy, and he lived by himself in a little house out by the hanging pust, not much of a cottage, it warn't —just wattle and daub wi' a thetch o' straa'—but the lease was running out ('twas a lifehold affair) and unless he bought this little house for fifty pound he'd got to go out of it. Well, old Mark hadn't got no fifty pounds, he was ate up wi' rheumatics and only did just a little light labour in the woods, they might as well a' asked him for the King's crown, so he said to his master: Would he lend him the fifty pounds ?

" ' No, I can't do that,' his master says.

" ' You can reduct it from my wages,' Mark says.

" ' Nor I can't do that neither,' says his master, ' but there's your brother Henry, he's worth a power o' money, ask him.' So Mark asks Shadrach to lend him the fifty pounds, so's he could buy this little house. ' No,' says Henry, ' I can't.' Nor he wouldn't. Well—old Mark says to him: ' I doan wish you no harm Henry,' he says, ' but I hope as how you'll die in a ditch.' (Good health!) And sure enough he did. That was his own brother, he were strooken wi' the sun and died in a ditch, Henry did, and when he was buried his fortune was buried with him, in a little canister, holding it in his hand, I reckons. And a lot of good that was to him! He hadn't been buried a month when two bad parties putt their heads together. Levi Carter, one was, he was the sexton, a man that was half a loony as I always thought. O yes, he had got all his wits about him, somewheres, only they didn't often get much of a quorum, still he got them—somewheres. T'other was a chap by the name of Impey, lived in Slack the shoemaker's house down by the old traveller's garden. He wasn't much of a mucher, helped in the fieldwork and did shepherding at odd times. And these two chaps made up their minds to goo and collar Henry

Turley's fortune out of his coffin one night and share it between theirselves. 'Twas crime, ye know, might a been prison for life, but this Impey was a bad lot—he'd the manners of a pig, pooh! filthy!—and I expects he persuaded old Levi on to do it. Bad as body-snatchen, coorse 'twas!

"So they goos together one dark night, 'long in November it was, and well you knows, all of you, as well as I, that nobody can't ever see over our churchyard wall by day let alone on a dark night. You all knows that, don't you?" asserted the thatcher, who appeared to lay some stress upon this point in his narrative. There were murmurs of acquiescence by all except the mild-faced man, and the thatcher continued: "'Twere about nine o'clock when they dug out the earth. 'Twarn't a very hard job, for Henry was only just a little way down. He was buried on top of his old woman, and she was on top of her two daughters. But when they got down to the coffin Impey didn't much care for that part of the job, he felt a little bit sick, so he gives the hammer and the screwdriver to Levi and he says: 'Levi,' he says, 'are you game to make a good job o' this?'

"'Yes, I be,' says old Levi.

"'Well, then,' Impey says, 'yous'll have my smock on now while I just creeps off to old Wannaker's sheep and collars one of they fat lambs over by the 'lotments.'

"'You're not going to leave me here,' says Carter, 'what be I going to do?'

"'You go on and finish this 'ere job, Levi,' he says, 'you get the money and put back all the earth and don't ſtir out of the yard afore I comes or I'll have yer blood.'

" ' No,' says Carter, ' you maun do that.'

" ' I 'ull do that,' Impey says, ' he've got some smartish lambs I can tell 'ee, fat as snails.'

" ' No,' says Carter, ' I waun't have no truck wi' that, tain't right.'

" ' You will,' says Impey, ' and I 'ull get the sheep. Here's my smock. I'll meet 'ee here again in ten minutes. I'll have that lamb if I 'as to cut his blaſted head off.' And he rooshed away before Levi could ſtop him. So Carter putts on the smock and finishes the job. He got the money and putt the earth back on poor Henry and tidied it up, and then he went and sat in the church poorch waiting for this Impey to come back. Juſt as he did that an oldish man passed by the gate. He was coming to this very place for a drop o' drink and he sees old Levi's white figure sitting in the church poorch and it frittened him so that he took to his heels and tore along to this very room we be sittin' in now—only 'twas thirty years ago.

" ' What in the name of God's the matter wi' you ? ' they says to him, for he'd a face like chalk and his lips was blue as a whetſtone. ' Have you seen a gooſt ? '

" ' Yes,' he says, ' I have seen a gooſt, juſt now then.'

" ' A gooſt ? ' they says, ' a gooſt ? You an't seen no gooſt.'

" ' I seen a gooſt.'

" ' Where a' you seen a gooſt ? '

" So he telled 'em he seen a goost sitting up in the church poorch.

" ' I shan't have that,' says old Mark Turley, for he was a setting here.

" ' I tell you 'twas then,' says the man.

" ' Can't be nothing worse'n I be myself,' Mark says.

" ' I say as 'tis,' the man said, and he was vexed too. ' Goo and see for yourself.'

" ' I would goo too and all,' said old Mark, ' if only I could walk it, but my rheumatucks be that scrematious I can't walk it. Goosts! There's ne'er a mortal man as ever see'd a goost. I'd go, my lad, if my legs 'ud stand it.' And there was a lot of talk like that until a young sailor spoke up—Irish he was, his name was Pat Crowe, he was on furlough. I dunno what he was a-doing in this part of the world, but there he was and he says to Mark: ' If you be game enough, I be, and I'll carry you up to the churchyard on my back.' A great stropping feller he was. ' You will?' says Mark. ' That I will,' he says. ' Well I be game for 'ee,' says Mark, and so they ups him on to the sailor's shoulders like a sack o' corn and away they goos, but not another one there was man enough to goo with them.

" They went slogging up to the churchyard gate all right, but when they got to staggering along 'tween the gravestones Mark thought he could see a something white sitting in the poorch, but the sailor couldn't see anything at all with that lump on his shoulders.

" ' What's that there?' Mark whispers in Pat's

233

ear. And Pat Crowe whispers back, just for joking:
'Old Nick in his nightshirt.'

" ' Steady now,' Mark whispers, ' go steady Pat,
it's getting up and coming.' Pat only gives a bit of a
chuckle and says: 'Ah, that's him, that's just like
him.'

" Then Levi calls out from the poorch soft like:
You got him then! Is he a fat 'un ? '

" ' Holy God,' cried the sailor, ' it *is* the devil! '
and he chucks poor Mark over his back at Levi's
feet and runs for his mortal life. He was the most
frittened of the lot 'cos he hadn't believed in anything
at all—but there it was. And just as he gets to the
gate he sees someone else coming along in the dark
carrying a something on its shoulder—it was Impey
wi' the sheep. ' Powers above,' cried Pat Crowe,
' it's the Day of Judgment come for sartin! ' And he
went roaring the news up street like a madman, and
Impey went off somewheres too—but I dunno where
Impey went.

" Well, poor old Mark laid on the ground, he
were a game old cock, but he could hardly speak, he
was strook dazzled. And Levi was frittened out of
his life in the darkness and couldn't make anythink
out of nothink. He just creeps along to Mark and
whispers: ' Who be that ? Who be that ? ' And
old Mark looks up very timid, for he thought his
last hour was on him, and he says: ' Be that you,
Satan ? ' Drackly Levi heard that all in a onexpected
voice he jumped quicker en my neighbour's flea.
He gave a yell bigger nor Pat Crowe and he bolted
too. But as he went he dropped the little tin canister

and old Mark picked it up. And he shook the canister, and he heerd money in it, and then something began to dawn on him, for he knowed how his brother's fortune had been buried.

"'I rede it, I rede it,' he says, 'that was Levi Carter, the dirty thief! I rede it, I rede it,' he says. And he putt the tin can in his pocket and hopped off home as if he never knowed what rheumatucks was at all. And when he opened that canister there was the sixty golden sovereigns in that canister. Sixty golden sovereigns! 'Bad things 'ull be worse afore they're better,' says Mark, 'but they never won't be any better than this.' And so he stuck to the money in the canister, and that's how he bought his cottage arter all. 'Twarn't much of a house, just wattle and daub, wi' a thetch o' straa', but 'twas what he fancied, and there he ended his days like an old Christian man. (Good health!)"

Huxley Rustem

HUXLEY RUSTEM SETTLED HIM-
self patiently upon the hairdresser's waiting
bench to probe the speculation that jumped
grasshopper-like into the field of his inquisitorial
mind: Why does a man become a barber? Well,
what *is* it that persuades a man, not by the mere
compulsion of destiny, but by the sweet reasonable-
ness of inclination, to dedicate his activities to the
excision of other people's pimples and the discom-
fiture of their hairy growths? He had glanced
through the two papers, *Punch* and *John Bull*,
handed him by the boy in buttons, and now, awaiting
his turn, posed himself with this inquiry. There
was a girl at it, too, at the end of the saloon. She
seemed to have picked him out from the crowd of
men there; he caught her staring, an attractive girl.
It seemed insoluble; misfortunate people may, indeed must, by the pressure of circumstances, become
sewermen, butchers, scavengers, and even clergy-
men, but the impulse to barbery was, he felt, quite
indelicately ironic. How that girl stared at him
—if she was not very careful she would be clip-
ping the fellow's ear—did she think she knew him?
He rather hoped she would have to attend to him;
would he be lucky enough? Huxley tried to estimate
the chances by observing the half-dozen toilets in
progress, but his calculations did not encourage the
hope at all. It was very charming for an agreeable
woman, a stranger, too, to do that kind of service
for you. He remembered that, after his marriage

five years ago, he had tried to persuade his wife to lather and shave him, "juſt for a lark, you know," but she was adamant, didn't see the joke at all! Well, well, he decided that the word barber derived in some ironic way from the words barbarism or barbarity, expressing, unconsciously perhaps, contempt on the part of the barber for a world that could only offer him this impoſture for a man's sacred will to order and aɛtivity. Yet it didn't seem so bad for women— that splendid young creature there at the end of the saloon! The boy in buttons approached, and Huxley Ruſtem was ushered to that vacant chair at the end; the splendid young thing had placed a wrapper about him—she had almoſt "cuddled" it round his neck— and ſtood demurely preparing to do execution upon his poll, turning her eyes mischievously upon his bright-hued socks, which, by a notable coincidence, were the same colour as her own handsome hose. Huxley had a feeling that she had cunningly arranged the succession of turns in order to secure him to her chair—which shows that he was ſtill young and very impressionable. Such a feeling is one of the cuſtomary assumptions of vanity, the natural and prized, but much-denied, possession of all agreeable people. Huxley, as the girl had already noted, and now saw more vividly in the mirror fronting them, *was* agreeable, was attraɛtive. (My dear reader, both you and Huxley Ruſtem are right, the dainty barbaress *had* laid her nets for this particular viɛtim.)

"How would you like it cut, sir?" she asked, placing a hand upon each of his shoulders, and peering round at him with enamouring eyes.

" Oh, with a pair of scissors, don't you think ? " he replied at a venture, for he was not often waggish. But it was a very successful sally, the girl chuckled with rapture, loose fringes of her hair tickled his cheek, and he caught puffs of her sweet-scented breath. She was gold-haired, not very tall, and had pleasant turns about her neck and face and wrists that almost fascinated him. When they had agreed upon the range and extent of his shearing, the girl proceeded to the accomplishment of the task in complete silence, almost with gravity. Huxley began wondering how many hundreds and thousands of crops were squeezed annually by the delicious fingers, how many polls denuded by those competent shears. Very sad. Once a year, he supposed, she would go holidaying for a week or ten days; she would go to Bournemouth for the bathing or for whatever purpose it is people go to Bournemouth, Barmouth, or Blackpool. He determined to come in again the day after to-morrow and be shaved by her.

At the conclusion of the rite she brushed his coat collar very meticulously, tiptoeing a little, and remarked in a bright manner upon the weather, which was also bright. Then she went back to shave what Huxley described to himself as a " red-faced old cockalorum," whom he at once disliked very thoroughly. She had given him a check with a fee marked upon it; he took this down the stairs and paid his dues to " a bald-headed old god-like monster " —Huxley felt sure he was—who sat in the shop below, surrounded by fringe-nets, stuffings, moustache wax, creams, toothbrushes, and sponges.

Two days later Huxley Ruftem repeated his visit, but not all the intrigue of the girl nor his own man-œuvring could effeét the happy arrangement again, although he sat for a long time feeling sure that there was no other eftablishment of its kind in which the elements of celerity were so unreservedly abandoned, and the flunkeyism so peculiarly viscous. The many mirrors, of course, multiplied the objeéts of his faétitious contempt; those male barbers were small vain beings of disagreeable outline to whom the doom of shaving tens of thousands of chins for ever and ever afforded a white-faced languid happiness. Huxley was exasperated—his personality always ran so easily to exasperation—by the care with which the wrinkled face of a sportive old gent of sixty was being massaged with fteaming cloths. He wore pretty brown button boots and large check trousers; there was ftill a vain wisp or two of white hair left upon his tight round skull and his indescribably silly old face. In the outcome our hero had perforce to be shaved by a youth of the laft revolting assiduity, who caressed his chin with ftrong, excoriating palms.

In the ensuing weeks Huxley Ruftem became a regular visitor to the saloon, but he suffered repeated disappointments. He was disconsolate; it was moft baffling; not once did he secure the bliss of her attentions. He felt himself a fool; some men could do these things as easily as they grew whiskers, but Ruftem was not one of them, for the traditions of virtue and sweet conduét were very firmly rooted in him; he was like a mouse living in a large white empty bath which, if it was unscaleable, was clean,

239

and if it was rather blank was never terrifying. It is easy, so very easy, to be virtuous when you can't be anything else. But still he very much desired to take the fair barber out to dinner, say, just for an hour or two in a quiet place where one eats and chats and listens to the pleasant shrilling of restaurant violins. He would be able to amuse her with tales and recitals of his experiences and she would constantly exclaim "Really!" as if entranced—as she probably would be. In his imagined hour her conversational exchanges never developed beyond that, yet it was enough to thrill him with a mild happiness. An egoist is a mystic without a god, but seldom ever without a goddess. It was bliss to adore her, but very heaven for her to be adoring him. To be just to Huxley Rustem that was all he meant, but try as he would he could never make up the happy occasion. It was a most discomfiting experience. It is true that he saw her in the street on three or four occasions, but each time he was accompanied by his wife, and each time he was guilty of a vain pretence, his behaviour to his companion being extremely casual —as if she were just an acquaintance instead of being an important alliance. But no one could possibly have mistaken the lady for anything but Huxley's very own wife, and the little barber was provocatively demure at these encounters. Once, however, he was alone, and she passed, ogling him in a very frank way. But she did not understand egoists like Rustem. He was impervious to any such direct challenge; he thought it a little silly, coarse even. Had she been shy and diffident, allowing him to be masterful instead of confusing him, he would have fluttered easily into her flame.

So the affair remained, and would have remained for ever but that, by the grace of fortune, he found himself one day at last actually sitting again in front of the charming girl, who was not less aware of the attraction than he himself. She was nervous and actually with her shears clipped a part of his ear. Huxley was rather glad of that, it eased the situation, but on his departure he committed the rash act for which he never afterwards forgave himself. Her fingers were touching his as she gave him the pay check, when he took suddenly from his pocket a silver coin and pressed it into her hand, smiling. It was as if he had struck her a blow. He was shocked at the surprised resentment in the fierce glance she flung him. She tossed the coin into a tray for catching tobacco ash and cigarette ends. He realized at once the enormity of the affront; his vulgar act had smashed the delicate little coil between them. Vague and almost frivolous as it was, she had prized it. Poor as it was, it could yet deeply humiliate him. But it was a blunder that could never be retrieved, and he turned quickly and sadly out of the saloon, feeling the awful sting of his own contempt. Crass fool that he was, didn't he realize that even barbers had their altitudes ? Did he think he could buy a jewel like that, as he bought a packet of tobacco, with a miserable shilling ? Perhaps Huxley Rustem was unduly sensitive about it, but he could never again bring himself to enter the saloon and meet that wounded gaze. He only recovered his balance when, a fortnight later, he encountered her in the street wearing the weeds of a widow! Then he felt almost as indignant as if she had indeed deceived him!

Big Game

OLD SQUANCE WAS THE UNDER-taker, but in the balmy, healthy, equable air of Tamborough undertaking was not a thriving trade; its opportunities were but an ornamental adjunct to his more vital occupation of builder. Even so those old splendid stone-built cottages never needed repairs, or if they did Squance didn't do them. Storms wouldn't visit Tamborough, fires didn't occur, the hand of decay was, if anything, more deliberate than the hand of time itself, and no new-comer, loving the old houses so much, ever wanted to build a new one: so Mrs. Squance had to sell hard-looking bullseyes and stiff-looking fruit in a hard, stiff-looking shop. Also knitting needles and, in their time of the year, garden seeds. Squance was a meek person whom you would never have credited with heroic tendencies; nevertheless, with no more romantic background than a coffin or two, a score of scaffold poles, and sundry hods and shovels, he had acquired in a queer, but still not unusual, way the repute of a lion-slayer. Mrs. Squance was not so meek, she was not meek at all, she was ambitious—but vainly so. Her ambitions secured their fulfilment only in her nocturnal dreams, but in that sphere they were indeed triumphant and she was satisfied. The most frequent setting of her uncon-scious imagination happened to be a tiny modern flat in which she and old Ben seemed to be living in harmony and luxury. It was a delightful flat, very high up—that was the proper situation for a flat,

mind you, just under the roof—with stairs curling
down, and down, and down till it made you giddy to
think of them. The kitchen, well, really Mrs.
Squance could expatiate endlessly on that and the
tiny corner place with two wash-basins in it and room
enough to install a bath if you went in for that kind
of thing. Best of all was the sitting-room in front,
looking into a street so very far below that Mrs.
Squance declared she felt as if she had been sitting
in a balloon. Here Mrs. Squance, so she dreamed,
would sit and browse. She didn't have to look at
ordinary things like trees and mud and other people's
windows. That was what made it so nice, Mrs.
Squance declared. She had instead a vista of roofs
and chimneys, beautiful telephone standards, and
clouds. The people, too, who walked far down
beneath were always unrecognizable; a multitude of
hat crowns seemed to collect her gaze, linked with
queer movements, right, left, right, left, of knees and
boots, though sometimes she would be lucky enough
to observe a very fat man, just a glimpse perhaps of
his watch-guard lying like a chain of oceanic islands
across a scholastic globe. In the way of dreams she
knew the street by the name of Lather Lane. It was
cobbled with granite setts. There was a barber's
shop at one corner and a depot for foreign potatoes
and bananas at another. That flat was so constantly
the subject of her dream visitations that she came to
invest it with a romantic reality, to regard it as an
ultimate real possession lying fortuitously somewhere,
at no very great remove, in some quarter she might
actually, any day now, luckily stumble across.

And it was in that very flat she beheld Mr. Squance's heroism. It seemed to be morning in her dream, early; it must have been early. She and Squance were at breakfast when what should walk deliberately and astoundingly into the room but a lion. Mrs. Squance, never having seen a lion before, took it to be a sheepdog, and she shouted, " Go out, you dirty thing! " waving a threatening hand towards it. But the animal did not go out; it pranced up to Mrs. Squance in a genial way, seized her admonishing hand and playfully tried to bite it off. Really! Mr. Squance had risen to his startled feet shouting " Lion! lion! " and then Mrs. Squance realized that she had to contend with a monster that kept swelling bigger and bigger before her very eyes, until it seemed that it would never be able to go out of that door again. It had a tremendous head and mane, with whiskers on its snout as stiff as knitting needles, and claws like tenpenny nails; but its tail was the awfullest thing, long and very flexible, with a bush of hair at the end just like a mop, which it wagged about, smashing all sorts of things.

" Ben," said Mrs. Squance, " 'ave you a pistol ? "

" No, I 'ave not," said Ben.

" Then we're done," she had declared. " Oh, no, we ain't, though! You 'old 'im, Ben, and I'll go and get a pistol; 'old 'im! "

Ben valiantly seized the lion by its mane and tail, but it did not care for such treatment; it began to snarl and swish about the room, dragging poor Ben as if he had been just a piece of rabbit pie.

" 'Old 'im! 'old 'im! " exhorted Mrs. Squance, as

she popped on her bonnet and shawl. "You 'old 'im!"

"All right," breathed Ben, as she ran off and began the descent of the long narrow staircase. Almost at the bottom she met a piano coming upwards. It was not a very large piano, but it was large enough to prevent her from descending any further. It was resting upon the backs of two men, one in front, whose entirely bald, perspiring, projecting head reminded her of the head of a tortoise, and one who followed him unseen. They crawled on all fours, while the piano was balanced by a man who pulled it in front and another who pushed it from behind.

"Dear me!" exclaimed Mrs. Squance. "I 'ope you won't be long."

They made no reply; the piano continued to advance, the bald man swaying his head still more like a tortoise. She began to retire before them, and continued retiring step by step until she became irritated and demanded to know the owner of that piano. The men seemed to be dumb, so she skipped up to the second floor to make enquiries, knocking at the first door with her left hand—the right one still hurting her very much. It was exasperating. Someone had just painted and varnished the doors, and she was compelled to tap very lightly instead of giving the big bang the occasion required. Consequently no one heard her, while her hand became covered with a glutinous evil liquid. She ran up to the third floor. Here the doors were all right, but although she set up a vigorous cannonade again no one heard her, at least, no one replied except some gruff voice that kept repeating " Gone, no address! Gone, no address! " She opened the doors, but there seemed to be no one about, although each room had every appearance of recent occupation: fires alight, breakfast things recently used, and in the bedrooms the disordered beds. She was now extremely annoyed. She opened all the doors quickly until she came to the last room, which was occupied by the old clergyman who kept ducks there and fed them on macaroni cheese. It was just as she feared; the ducks were waiting, they flocked quacking upon the passage and stairs before she could prevent them.

" I'm sure," screamed Mrs. Squance, in her dreadful rage, " it's that lion responsible for all this! "

She wasted no more time upon the matter. She rapidly descended the stairs again, treading upon innumerable indignant ducks, until she came to the piano. Here she said not a word, but, brushing the leading man aside, placed her foot roughly upon the slippery head of the first crawling man and scrambled over the top of the instrument, jumping thence upon the back part of the hindmost man, who turned his feet comically inwards, and wore round his loins a belt as large as the belly-band of a waggon horse.

She proceeded breathlessly until she came to the last flight, where, behold! the stairs had all been smashed in by those awkward pianists, and she stood on the dreadful verge of a drop into a cellar full of darkness and disgusting smells. But she was able to leap upon the banister-rail which was intact, and slide splendidly to the ground floor. An unusual sight awaited her. Mrs. Squance did not remember

247

ever to have seen such a thing before, but there in the
hall a marvellous eustacia tree was growing out of the
floor. She was not surprised at the presence of a
tree in that unwonted situation. She had not
noticed it before, but it did not seem out of place.
Why shouldn't trees grow where they liked ? They
always did. Mrs. Squance invariably took life as she
found it, even in dreams. While she was surveying
the beautiful proportions of the eustacia tree, the
richness of its leaves, and its fine aroma a small bird,
without warning or apology, alighted upon her right
hand—which she carried against her chest as if it
were in a sling, though it wasn't—and laid an egg on
it. It *was* so annoying, she did not know what to do
with it; she was afraid of smashing it. She rushed
from the building, and entered the butcher's shop a
few doors away. The shop was crowded with
customers, and the butcher perspired and joked with
geniality, as is the immemorial custom with butchers.
His boy, a mere tot of five or six years of age, observed
to Mrs. Squance that it was " a lovely day, ma'am,"
and she replied that it was splendid. So it was.
People were buying the most extraordinarily fleshly
fare, the smelt of an ox, a rib of suet, a fillet of liver,
and one little girl purchased nineteen lambs' tongues,
which she took away secretly in a portmanteau.

" Now Mrs. Squance, what can I do for you ? "
enquired the butcher. Without comment she handed
him the egg of the bird. He cast it into the till as if it
were a crown piece. " And the next thing, ma'am ? "

" 'Ave you got such a thing as a pistol, Mr.
Verryspice ? "

Mr. Verryspice had, he had got two, and drawing them from the belt wherefrom dangled his sharpener, he laid two remarkable pieces of ordnance before her. In her renewed agitation she would have snatched up one of the pistols, but Mr. Verryspice prevented her.

"No, no, ma'am, I shall have to get permission for you to use it first."

"But I really must 'ave it immediate . . ."

"Yes ? " said the butcher.

" . . . for my husband."

"I see," he replied sympathetically. "Well, come along then and I'll get an interim permission at once." Seizing a tall silk hat from its hook and placing it firmly upon his head he led her from his establishment.

"Singular that the trams are all so full this morning," commented Mrs. Squance as they awaited a conveyance.

"Most unusual, ma'am," replied Mr. Verryspice. But at last they persuaded a bathchair man to give them a lift to their destination, where they arrived a little indecorously perhaps, for the top-hatted butcher was sitting as unconcernedly and as upright as a wax figure upon Mrs. Squance's knees. The office they sought lay somewhere in a vast cavernous building full of stairs and corridors, long, exhausting, hollow corridors like the Underground railway, and on every floor and turning were signposts of the turnpike variety with directions:

"To the Bedel of St. Thomas's Basket, 3 miles."

"Registrar of Numismatics and Obligations, $2\frac{1}{4}$."

Along one of these passages they plunged, and after some aggravating hindrances, including a demand from a humpty-backed clerk for a packet of No. 19 egg-eyed sharps, and five pennyworth of cachous which she found in her bosom, the permission was secured, and the butcher thereupon handed the weapon to Mrs. Squance.

" What did you say you wanted it for ? " he asked.

Mrs. Squance's gratitude was great, but her indignation was deep and disdained reply. She seized the pistol and began to run home. Rather a stout lady, too, and the exercise embarrassed her. Her hair fetched loose, her stockings slipped down, and her strange, hurrying figure, brandishing a pistol, soon attracted the notice of policemen and a certain young greengrocer with a tray of onions, who trotted in her wake until she threatened them all with the firearm.

Breathlessly at last she mounted the tremendous staircase. Happily in the interval the damage had been repaired, the tree chopped down, piano delivered, and ducks recaptured. She reached her rooms only in time to hear a great crash of glass from within. Old Ben was strutting about with a triumphant air.

" I done 'im—I done 'im," he called. " You can come in now; I've just chucked 'im through the window! " And sure enough he had. The sash looked as if it had been blown out by a cannon-ball. Mrs. Squance peered out, and there, far down at the front door, curled up as if asleep, lay the lion. At that moment the milkman arrived, with that dissonant clatter peculiar to milkmen. He dashed down his cans close by the nose of the lion, which apparently he had not seen. The scared animal leaped up in its terror, and darting down an alley was seen no more.

So far this narrative, devoid as it is of moral grandeur and literary grace, has subjected the reader's comprehension to no scientific rigours; but he who reads on will discern its cunning import—a psychological outcome with the profoundest implications. Listen. Mrs. Squance awoke that morning in her own hard-looking little house of one floor, with the hard-looking shop, startled to find the window of their room actually smashed, and inexplicable pains in her right hand. She related these circumstances in after years with so many symptoms of truth and propriety that she herself at last vividly believed in the figure of old Ben as a lion-slayer. " Saved my life when I was 'tacked by a lion! " she would say to her awed grandchildren, and she would proceed to regale them with a narration which, I regret to say, had only the remotest likeness to the foregoing story.

The Poor Man

ONE OF THE COMMONEST SIGHTS IN the vale was a certain man on a bicycle carrying a bag full of newspapers. He was as much a sound as a sight, for what distinguished him from all other men to be encountered there on bicycles was not his appearance, though that was noticeable; it was his sweet tenor voice, heard as he rode along singing each morning from Cobbs Mill, through Kezzal Predy Peter, Thasper, and Buzzlebury, and so on to Trinkel and Nunčton. All sorts of things he sang, ballads, chanties, bits of glees, airs from operas, hymns, and sacred anthems—he was leader of Thasper church choir—but he seemed to observe some sort of rotation in their rendering. In the forepart of the week it was hymns and anthems; on Wednesday he usually turned to modestly secular tunes; he was rolling on Thursday and Friday through a gamut of love songs and ballads undoubtedly secular and not necessarily modest, while on Saturday—particularly at eve, spent in the tap of " The White Hart "— his programme was entirely ribald and often a little improper. But always on Sunday he was the most decorous of men, no questionable liquor passed his lips, and his comportment was a credit to the church, a model even for soberer men.

Dan Pavey was about thirty-five years old, of medium height and of medium appearance except as to his hat (a hard black bowler which seemed never to belong to him, though he had worn it for years) and as to his nose. It was an ugly nose, big as a

baby's elbow; he had been born thus, it had not
been broken or maltreated, though it might have
engaged in some pre-natal conflict when it was
malleable, since when nature had healed, but had not
restored it. But there was ever a soft smile that
covered his ugliness, which made it genial and said,
or seemed to say: Don't make a fool of me, I am a
friendly man, this is really my hat, and as for my
nose—God made it so.

The six hamlets which he supplied with newspapers lie along the Icknield Vale close under the
ridge of woody hills, and the inhabitants adjacent to
the woods fell the beech timber and, in their own
homes, turn it into rungs or stretchers for chair
manufacturers who, somewhere out of sight beyond
the hills, endlessly make chair, and nothing but chair.
Sometimes in a wood itself there may be seen a shanty
built of faggots in which sits a man turning pieces of
chair on a treadle lathe. Tall, hollow, and greenly
dim are the woods, very solemn places, and they
survey the six little towns as a man might look at six
tiny pebbles lying on a green rug at his feet.

One August morning the newspaper man was
riding back to Thasper. The day was sparkling like
a diamond, but he was not singing, he was thinking
of Scroope, the new rector of Thasper parish, and
the thought of Scroope annoyed him. It was not
only the tone of the sermon he had preached on
Sunday, " The poor we have always with us," though
that was in bad taste from a man reputed rich and
with a heart—people said—as hard as a door-knocker;
it was something more vital, a congenital difference

between them as profound as it was disagreeable. The Rev. Faudel Scroope was wealthy, he seemed to have complete confidence in his ability to remain so, and he was the kind of man with whom Dan Pavey would never be able to agree. As for Mrs. Scroope, gloom pattered upon him in a strong sighing shower at the least thought of her.

At Larkspur Lane he came suddenly upon the rector talking to an oldish man, Eli Bond, who was hacking away at a hedge. Scroope never wore a hat, he had a curly bush of dull hair. Though his face was shaven clean it remained a regular plantation of ridges and wrinkles; there was a stoop in his shoulders, a lurch in his gait, and he had a voice that howled.

"Just a moment, Pavey," he bellowed, and Dan dismounted.

"All those years," the parson went on talking to the hedger; "all those years, dear me!"

"I were born in Thasper sixty-six year ago, come the twenty-third of October, sir, the same day—but two years before—as Lady Hesseltine eloped with Rudolf Moxley. I was reared here and I worked here sin' I were six year old. Twelve children I have had (though five on 'em come to naught and two be in the army) and I never knowed what was to be out of work for one single day in all that sixty year. Never. I can't thank my blessed master enough for it."

"Isn't that splendidly feudal," murmured the priest, "who is your good master?"

The old man solemnly touched his hat and said: "God."

" O, I see, yes, yes," cried the Rev. Scroope.
" Well, good health and constant, and good work
and plenty of it, are glorious things. The man who
has never done a day's work is a dog, and the man
who deceives his master is a dog too."

" I never donn that, sir."

" And you've had happy days in Thasper, I'm
sure ? "

" Right-a-many, sir."

" Splendid. Well ... um ... what a heavy rain we
had in the night."

" Ah, that *was* heavy! At five o'clock this morning I daren't let my ducks out—they'd a bin drown-
ded, sir."

" Ha, now, now, now! " warbled the rector as he
turned away with Dan.

" Capital old fellow, happy and contented. I wish
there were more of the same breed. I wish ..."
The parson sighed pleasantly as he and Dan walked
on together until they came to the village street
where swallows were darting and flashing very low.
A small boy stood about, trying to catch them in his
hands as they swooped close to him. Dan's own dog
pranced up to his master for a greeting. It was black,
somewhat like a greyhound, but stouter. Its tail
curled right over its back and it was cocky as a
bird, for it was young; it could fight like a tiger
and run like the wind—many a hare had had proof
of that.

Said Mr. Scroope, eyeing the dog: " Is there
much poaching goes on here ? "

" Poaching, sir ? "

255

"I am told there is. I hope it isn't true for I have rented most of the shooting myself."

"I never heard tell of it, sir. Years ago, maybe. The Buzzlebury chaps one time were rare hands at taking a few birds, so I've heard, but I shouldn't think there's an onlicensed gun for miles around."

"I'm not thinking so much of guns. Farmer Prescott had his warren netted by someone last week and lost fifty or sixty rabbits. There's scarcely a hare to be seen, and I find wires wherever I go. It's a crime like anything else, you know," Scroope's voice was loud and strident, "and I shall deal very severely with poaching of any kind. O yes, you have to, you know, Pavey. O yes. There was a man in my last parish was a poacher, cunning scoundrel of the worst type, never did a stroke of work, and *he* had a dog, it wasn't unlike your dog—this *is* your dog, isn't it? You haven't got your name on its collar, you should have your name on a dog's collar—well, he had a perfect brute of a dog, carried off my pheasants by the dozen; as for hares, he exterminated them. Man never did anything else, but we laid him by the heels and in the end I shot the dog myself."

"Shot it?" said Dan. "No, I couldn't tell a poacher if I was to see one. I know no more about 'em than a bone in the earth."

"We shall be," continued Scroope, "very severe with them. Let me see—are you singing the Purcell on Sunday evening?"

"*He Shall Feed His Flock*—sir—*like a Shepherd.*"

"Splendid! *Good*-day, Pavey."

Dan, followed by his bounding, barking dog,

256

pedalled home to a little cottage that seemed to sag under the burden of its own thatch; it had eaves a yard wide, and birds' nests in the roof at least ten years old. Here Dan lived with his mother, Meg Pavey, for he had never married. She kept an absurd little shop for the sale of sweets, vinegar, boot buttons and such things, and was a very excellent old dame, but as naïve as she was vague. If you went in to her counter for a newspaper and banged down a half-crown she would as likely as not give you change for sixpence—until you mentioned the discrepancy, when she would smilingly give you back your half-crown again.

Dan passed into the back room where Meg was preparing dinner, threw off his bag, and sat down without speaking. His mother was making a heavy succession of journeys between the table and a larder.

" Mrs. Scroope's been here," said Meg, bringing a loaf to the table.

" What did *she* want ? "

" She wanted to reprimand me."

" And what have *you* been doing ? "

Meg was in the larder again. " 'Tis not me, 'tis you."

" What do you mean, mother ? "

" She's been a-hinting," here Meg pushed a dish of potatoes to the right of the bread, and a salt-cellar to the left of the yawning remains of a rabbit pie, " about your not being a teetotal. She says the boozing do give the choir a bad name and I was to persuade you to give it up."

" I should like to persuade her it was time she is dead. I don't go for to take any pattern from that rich trash. Are we the grass under their feet ? And can you tell me why parsons' wives are always so much more awful than the parsons themselves ? I never shall understand that if I lives a thousand years. Name o' God, what next ? "

" Well, 'tis as she says. Drink is no good to any man, and she can't say as I ain't reprimanded you."

" Name o' God," he replied, " do you think I booze just for the sake o' the booze, because I like booze ? No man does that. He drinks so that he shan't be thought a fool, or rank himself better than his mates—though he knows in his heart he might be if he weren't so poor or so timid. Not that one would mind to be poor if it warn't preached to him that he must be contented. How can the poor be contented as long as there's the rich to serve ? The rich we have always with *us*, that's *our* responsibility, we are the grass under their feet. Why should we be proud of that ? When a man's poor the only thing left him is hope—for something better: and that's called envy. If you don't like your riches you can always give it up, but poverty you can't desert, nor it won't desert you."

" It's no good flying in the face of everything like that, Dan, it's folly."

" If I had my way I'd be an independent man and live by myself a hundred miles from anywheres or anybody. But that's madness, that's madness, the world don't expect you to go on like that, so I do as

258

other folks do, not because I want to, but because I a'nt the pluck to be different. You taught me a good deal, mother, but you never taught me courage and I wasn't born with any, so I drinks with a lot of fools who drink with me for much the same reason, I expect. It's the same with other things besides drink."

His indignation lasted throughout the afternoon as he sat in the shed in his yard turning out his usual quantity of chair. He sang not one note, he but muttered and mumbled over all his anger. Towards evening he recovered his amiability and began to sing with a gusto that astonished even his mother. He went out into the dusk humming like a bee, taking his dog with him. In the morning the Rev. Scroope found a dead hare tied by the neck to his own door-knocker, and at night (it being Saturday) Dan Pavey was merrier than ever in "The White Hart." If he was not drunk he was what Thasper calls "tightish," and had never before sung so many of those ribald songs (mostly of his own composition) for which he was noted.

A few evenings later Dan attended a meeting of the Church Men's Guild. A group of very mute country-men sat in the village hall and were goaded into speech by the rector.

"Thasper," declared Mr. Scroope, "has a great name for its singing. All over the six hamlets there is surprising musical genius. There's the Buzzle-bury band—it is a capital band."

"It is that," interrupted a maroon-faced butcher from Buzzlebury, "it can play as well at nine o'clock in the morning as it can at nine o'clock at night, and that's a good band as can do it."

"Now I want our choir to compete at the county musical festival next year. Thasper is going to show those highly trained choristers what a native choir is capable of. Yes, and I'm sure our friend Pavey can win the tenor solo competition. Let us all put our backs into it and work agreeably and consistently. Those are the two main springs of good human conduct—consistency and agreeability. The consistent man will always attain his legitimate ends, always. I remember a man in my last parish, Tom Turkem, known and loved throughout the county; he was not only the best cricketer in our village, he was the best for miles around. He revelled in cricket, and cricket only; he played cricket and lived for cricket. The years went on and he got old, but he never dreamed of giving up cricket. His bowling average got larger every year and his batting average got smaller, but he still went on, consistent as ever. His order of going in dropped down to No. 6 and he seldom bowled; then he got down to No. 8 and never bowled. For a season or two the once famous Tom Turkem was really the last man in! After that he became umpire, then scorer, and then he died. He had got a little money, very little, just enough to live comfortably on. No, he never married. He was a very happy, hearty, hale old man. So you see? Now there is a cricket club at Buzzlebury, and one at Trinkel. Why not a cricket club at Thasper? Shall we do that? . . . Good!"

The parson went on outlining his projects, and

although it was plain to Dan that the Rev. Scroope had very little, if any, compassion for the weaknesses natural to mortal flesh, and attached an extravagant value to the virtues of decency, sobriety, consistency, and, above all, loyalty to all sorts of incomprehensible notions, yet his intentions were undeniably agreeable and the Guild was consistently grateful.

" One thing, Pavey," said Scroope when the meeting had dispersed, " one thing I will not tolerate in this parish, and that is gambling."

" Gambling ? I have never gambled in my life, sir. I couldn't tell you hardly the difference between spades and clubs."

" I am speaking of horse-racing, Pavey."

" Now that's a thing I never see in my life, Mr. Scroope."

" Ah, you need not go to the races to bet on horses; the slips of paper and money can be collected by men who are agents for racing bookmakers. And that is going on all round the six hamlets, and the man who does the collecting, even if he does not bet himself, is a social and moral danger, he is a criminal, he is against the law. Whoever he is," said the vicar, moderating his voice, but confidently beaming and patting Dan's shoulder, " I shall stamp him out mercilessly. *Good*-night, Pavey."

Dan went away with murder in his heart. Timid strangers here and there had fancied that a man with such a misshapen face would be capable of committing a crime, not a mere peccadillo—you wouldn't take notice of that, of course—but a solid substantial misdemeanour like murder. And it was true, he *was* capable of murder—just as everybody else is, or ought to be. But he was also capable of curbing that distressing tendency in the usual way, and in point of fact he never did commit a murder.

These rectorial denunciations troubled the air but momentarily, and he still sang gaily and beautifully on his daily ride from Cobbs Mill along the little roads to Trinkel and Nuncton. The hanging richness of the long woods yellowing on the fringe of autumn, the long solemn hills themselves, cold sunlight, coloured berries in briary loops, the brown small leaves of hawthorn that had begun to drop from the hedge and flutter in the road like dying moths, teams of horses sturdily ploughing, sheepfolds already thatched into little nooks where the ewes could lie—Dan said—as warm as a pudding: these things filled him with tiny ecstasies too incoherent for him to transcribe—he could only sing.

On Bonfire Night the lads of the village lit a great fire on the space opposite " The White Hart." Snow was falling; it was not freezing weather, but the snow lay in a soft thin mat upon the road. Dan was returning on his bicycle from a long journey and the light from the bonfire was cheering. It lit up the courtyard of the inn genially and curiously, for the recumbent hart upon the balcony had a pad of snow upon its wooden nose, which somehow made it look like a camel, in spite of the huddled snow on its back which gave it the resemblance of a sheep. A few boys stood with bemused wrinkled faces before the roaring warmth. Dan dismounted very carefully opposite the blaze, for a tiny boy rode on the back of the bicycle, wrapped up and tied to the frame by a long scarf; very small, very silent, about five years old. A red wool wrap was bound round his head and ears and chin, and a green scarf encircled his neck and waist, almost hiding his jacket; gaiters of grey wool were drawn up over his knickerbockers. Dan lifted him down and stood him in the road, but he was so cumbered with clothing that he could scarcely walk. He was shy; he may have thought it ridiculous; he moved a few paces and turned to stare at his footmarks in the snow.

" Cold ? " asked Dan.

The child shook its head solemnly at him and then put one hand in Dan's and gazed at the fire that was bringing a brightness into the longlashed dark eyes and tenderly flushing the pale face.

" Hungry ? "

The child did not reply. It only silently smiled when the boys brought him a lighted stick from the faggots. Dan caught him up into his arms and pushed the cycle across the way into his own home.

Plump Meg had just shredded up two or three red cabbages and rammed them into a crock with a shower of peppercorns and some terrible knots of ginger. There was a bright fire and a sharp odour of vinegar—always some strange pleasant smell in Meg Pavey's home—she had covered the top of the crock with a shield of brown paper, pinioned that with string, licked a label: " Cabege Novenbr 5t," and smoothed it on the crock, when the latch lifted and Dan carried in his little tiny boy.

" Here he is, mother."

Where Dan stood him, there the child remained; he did not seem to see Mother Pavey, his glance had happened to fall on the big crock with the white label—and he kept it there.

" Whoever's that ? " asked the astonished Meg with her arms akimbo as Dan began to unwrap the child.

" That's mine," said her son, brushing a few flakes of snow from the curls on its forehead.

" Yours! How long have it been yours ? "

" Since 'twas born. No, let him alone, I'll undo him, he's full up wi' pins and hooks. I'll undo him."

Meg stood apart while Dan unravelled his off-spring.

" But it is not your child, surely, Dan ? "

" Ay, I've brought him home for keeps, mother. He can sleep wi' me."

" Who's its mother ? "

" 'Tis no matter about that. Dan Cupid did it."

" You're making a mock of me. Who is his mother ? Where is she ? You're fooling, Dan, you're fooling! "

" I'm making no mock of anyone. There, there's a bonny grandson for you! "

Meg gathered the child into her arms, peering into its face, perhaps to find some answer to the riddle, perhaps to divine a familiar likeness. But there was nothing in its soft smooth features that at all resembled her rugged Dan's.

" Who are you ? What's your little name ? "

The child whispered: " Martin."

" It's a pretty, pretty thing, Dan."

" Ah! " said her son, " that's his mother. We were rare fond of each other—once. Now she's wedd'n another chap and I've took the boy, for it's best that way. He's five year old. Don't ask me about her, it's *our* secret and always has been. It was a good secret and a grand secret, and it was well kept. That's her ring."

The child's thumb had a ring upon it, a golden ring with a small green stone. The thumb was crooked, and he clasped the ring safely.

For a while Meg asked no more questions about the child. She pressed it tenderly to her bosom.

But the long-kept secret, as Dan soon discovered, began to bristle with complications. The boy was his, of course it was his—he seemed to rejoice in his paternity of the quiet, pretty, illegitimate creature. As if that brazen turpitude was not enough to confound him he was taken a week later in the act of receiving betting commissions and heavily fined in the police court, although it was quite true that he himself did not bet, and was merely a collecting agent for a bookmaker who remained discreetly in the background and who promptly paid his fine.

There was naturally a great racket in the vestry about these things—there is no more rhadamanthine formation than that which can mount the ornamental forehead of a deacon—and Dan was bidden to an interview at the " Scroopery." After some hesitation he visited it.

" Ah, Pavey," said the rector, not at all minatory but very subdued and unhappy. " So the blow has fallen, in spite of my warning. I am more sorry than I can express, for it means an end to a very long connection. It is very difficult and very disagreeable for me to deal with the situation, but there is no help for it now, you must understand that. I offer no judgment upon these unfortunate events, no judgment at all, but I can find no way of avoiding my clear duty. Your course of life is incompatible with your position in the choir, and I sadly fear it reveals not only a social misdemeanour but a religious one—it is a mockery, a mockery of God."

The rector sat at a table with his head pressed on his hands. Pavey sat opposite him, and in his hands he dangled his bowler hat.

" You may be right enough in your way, sir, but I've never mocked God. For the betting, I grant you. It may be a dirty job, but I never ate the dirt myself, I never betted in my life. It's a way of life, a poor man has but little chance of earning more than a bare living, and there's many a dirty job there's no prosecution for, leastways not in this world."

" Let me say, Pavey, that the betting counts less heavily with me than the question of this unfortunate little boy. I offer no judgment upon the matter, your acknowledgment of him is only right and proper. But the fact of his existence at all cannot be disregarded; that at least is flagrant, and as far as concerns your position in my church, it is a mockery of God."

" You may be right, sir, as far as your judgment goes, or you may not be. I beg your pardon for that, but we can only measure other people by our own scales, and as we can never understand one another

266

entirely, so we can't ever judge them rightly, for they all differ from us and from each other in some special ways. But as for being a mocker of God, why it looks to me as if you was trying to teach the Almighty how to judge me."

"Pavey," said the rector with solemnity, "I pity you from the bottom of my heart. We won't continue this painful discussion, we should both regret it. There was a man in the parish where I came from who was an atheist and mocked God. He subsequently became deaf. Was he convinced? No, he was not—because the punishment came a long time after his offence. He mocked God again, and became blind. Not at once: God has eternity to work in. Still he was not convinced. That," said the rector ponderously, " is what the Church has to contend with; a failure to read the most obvious signs, and an indisposition even to remedy that failure. Klopstock was that poor man's name. His sister— you know her well, Jane Klopstock—is now my cook."

The rector then stood up and held out his hand. " God bless you, Pavey."

"I thank you, sir," said Dan. " I quite understand."

He went home moodily reflecting. Nobody else in the village minded his misdeeds, they did not care a button, and none condemned him. On the contrary, indeed. But the blow had fallen, there was nothing that he could now do, the shock of it had been anticipated, but it was severe. And the pang would last, for he was deprived of his chief opportunity for singing, that art in which he excelled, in

that perfect quiet setting he so loved. Rancour grew
upon him, and on Saturday he had a roaring audacious
evening at " The White Hart " where, to the tune of
" The British Grenadiers," he sung a doggerel:

> Our parson loves his motor car
>   His garden and his mansion,
> And he loves his beef for I've remarked
>   His belly's brave expansion ;
> He loves all mortal mundane things
>   As he loved his beer at college,
> And so he loves his housemaid (not
>   With Mrs. parson's knowledge.)
>
> Our parson lies both hot and strong,
>   It does not suit his station,
> But still his reverend soul delights
>   In much dissimulation ;
> Both in and out and roundabout
>   He practises distortion,
> And he lies with a public sinner when
>   Grass widowhood 's his portion.

All of which was a savage libel on a very worthy man,
composed in anger and regretted as soon as sung.

From that time forward Dan gave up his boozing
and devoted himself to the boy, little Martin, who, a
Thasper joker suggested, might have some kinship
with the notorious Betty of that name. But Dan's
voice was now seldom heard singing upon the roads
he travelled. They were icy wintry roads, but that
was not the cause of his muteness. It was severance
from the choir; not from its connoted spirit of
religion—there was little enough of that in Dan
Pavey—but from the solemn beauty of the chorale,
which it was his unique gift to adorn, and in which

he had shared with eagerness and pride since his boyhood. To be cast out from that was to be cast from something he held most dear, the opportunity of expression in an art which he had made triumphantly his own.

With the coming of spring he repaired one evening to a town some miles away and interviewed a choirmaster. Thereafter Dan Pavey journeyed to and fro twice every Sunday to sing in a church that lay seven or eight miles off, and he kept it all a profound secret from Thasper until his appearance at the county musical festival, where he won the treasured prize for tenor soloists. Then Dan was himself again. To his crude apprehension he had been vindicated, and he was heard once more carolling in the lanes of the Vale as he had been heard any time for these twenty years.

The child began its schooling, but though he was free to go about the village little Martin did not wander far. The tidy cluster of hair about his poll was of deep chestnut colour. His skin—Meg said—was like "ollobarster": it was soft and unfreckled, always pale. His eyes were two wet damsons—so Meg declared: they were dark and ever questioning. As for his nose, his lips, his cheeks, his chin, Meg could do no other than call it the face of a blessed saint; and indeed, he had some of the bearing of a saint, so quiet, so gentle, so shy. The golden ring he no longer wore; it hung from a tintack on the bedroom wall.

Old John, who lived next door, became a friend of his. He was very aged—in the Vale you got to

269

be a hundred before you knew where you were—
and he was very bent; he resembled a sickle standing
upon its handle. Very bald, too, and so very sharp.

Martin was staring up at the roof of John's cottage.

" What you looking at, my boy ? "

" Chimbley," whispered the child.

" O ah! that's crooked, a'nt it ? "

" Yes, crooked."

" I know 'tis, but I can't help it; my chimney's
crooked, and I can't putt it straight, neither, I can't
putt it right. My chimney's crooked, a'nt it, ah,
and I'm crooked, too."

" Yes," said Martin.

" I know, but I can't help it. It *is* crooked, a'nt
it ? " said the old man, also staring up at a red pot
tilted at an angle suggestive of conviviality.

" Yes."

" That chimney's crooked. But you come along
and look at my beautiful bird."

A cock thrush inhabited a cage in the old gaffer's
kitchen. Martin stood before it.

" There's a beautiful bird. Hoicks! " cried old
John, tapping the bars of the cage with his terrible
finger-nail. " But he won't sing."

" Won't he sing ? "

" He donn make hisself at home. He donn make
hisself at home at all, do 'ee, my beautiful bird ?
No, he donn't. So I'm a-going to chop his head off,"
said the laughing old man, " and then I shall bile
him."

Afterwards Martin went every day to see if the
thrush was still there. And it was.

Martin grew. Almost before Dan was aware of it the child had grown into a boy. At school he excelled nobody in anything except, perhaps, behaviour, but he had a strange little gift for unobtrusively not doing the things he did not care for, and these were rather many unless his father was concerned in them. Even so, the affection between them was seldom tangibly expressed, their alliance was something far deeper than its expression. Dan talked with him as if he were a grown man, and perhaps he often regarded him as one; he was the only being to whom he ever opened his mind. As they sat together in the evening while Dan put in a spell at turning chair—at which he was astoundingly adept—the father would talk to his son, or rather he would heap upon him all the unuttered thoughts that had accumulated in his mind during his adult years. The dog would loll with its head on Martin's knees; the boy would sit nodding gravely, though seldom speaking: he was an untiring listener. " Like sire, like son," thought Dan, " he will always coop his thoughts up within himself." It was the one characteristic of the boy that caused him anxiety.

" Never take pattern by me," he would adjure him, " not by me. I'm a fool, a failure, just grass, and I'm trying to instruct you, but you've no call to follow in my fashion; I'm a weak man. There's been thoughts in my mind that I daren't let out. I wanted to do things that other men don't seem to do and don't want to do. They were not evil things—and what they were I've nigh forgotten now. I never had much ambition, I wasn't clever, I wanted to live a

simple life, in a simple way, the way I had a mind to—
I can't remember that either. But I did not do any
of those things because I had a fear of what other
people might think of me. I walked in the ruck with
the rest of my mates and did the things I didn't ever
want to do—and now I can only wonder why I did
them. I sung them the silly songs they liked, and
not the ones I cherished. I agreed with most everybody, and all agreed with me. I'm a friendly man,
too friendly, and I went back on my life, I made
nought of my life, you see, I just sat over the job like
a snob codgering an old boot."

The boy would sit regarding him as if he already
understood. Perhaps that curious little mind did
glean some flavour of his father's tragedy.

" You've no call to follow me, you'll be a scholar.
Of course I know some of those long words at school
take a bit of licking together—like elephant and
saucepan. You get about half-way through 'em and
then you're done, you're mastered. I was just the
same (like sire, like son), and I'm no better now.
If you and me was to go to yon school together, and
set on the same stool together, I warrant you would
win the prize and I should wear the dunce's cap—all
except sums, and there I should beat ye. You'd have
all the candy and I'd have all the cane, you'd be king
and I'd be the dirty rascal, so you've no call to follow
me. What you want is courage, and to do the things
you've a mind to. I never had any and I didn't."

Dan seldom kissed his son, neither of them sought
that tender expression, though Meg was for ever
ruffling the boy for these pledges of affection, and he

was always gracious to the old woman. There was a small mole in the centre of her chin, and in the centre of the mole grew one short stiff hair. It was a surprise to Martin when he first kissed her.

Twice a week father and son bathed in the shed devoted to chair. The tub was the half of a wooden barrel. Dan would roll up two or three buckets of water from the well, they would both strip to the skin, the boy would kneel in the tub and dash the water about his body for a few moments. While Martin towelled himself Dan stepped into the tub, and after laving his face and hands and legs he would sit down in it. " Ready ? " Martin would ask, and scooping up the water in an iron basin he would pour it over his father's head.

" Name o' God, that's sharpish this morning," Dan would say, " it would strip the bark off a crocodile. Broo-o-o-oh! But there: winter and summer I go up and down the land and there's not—Broo-o-o-oh!—a mighty difference between 'em, it's mostly fancy. Come day, go day, frost or fair doings, all alike I go about the land, and there's little in winter I havn't the heart to rejoice in. (On with your breeches or I'll be at the porridge pot afore you're clad.) All their talk about winter and their dread of it shows poor spirit. Nothing's prettier than a fall of snow, nothing more grand than the storms upending the woods. There's no more rain in winter than in summer, you can be shod for it, and there's a heart back of your ribs that's proof against any blast. (Is this my shirt or yours ? Dashed if they buttons a'nt the plague of my life.) Country is grand year's end to year's end, whether or no. I once lived in London—only a few weeks—and for noise, and for terror, and for filth—name o' God, there was bugs in the butter there, once there was!"

But the boy's chosen season was that time of year when the plums ripened. Pavey's garden was then a tiny paradise.

"You put a spell on these trees," Dan would declare to his son every year when they gathered the fruit. I planted them nearly twenty years ago, two 'gages and one magny bonum, but they never growed enough to make a pudden. They always bloomed well and looked well. I propped 'em and I dunged 'em, but they wouldn't beer at all, and I'm a-going to cut 'em down—when, along comes you!"

Well, hadn't those trees borne remarkable ever since he'd come there?

"Of course, good luck's deceiving, and it's never bothered our family overmuch. Still, bad luck is one thing and bad life's another. And yet—I dunno—they come to much the same in the end, there's very little difference. There's so much misunderstanding, half the folks don't know their own good intentions, nor all the love that's sunk deep in their own minds."

But nothing in the world gave (or could give) Dan such flattering joy as his son's sweet treble voice. Martin could sing! In the dark months no evening passed without some instruction by the proud father. The living room at the back of the shop was the tiniest of rooms, and its smallness was not lessened, nor its tidiness increased, by the stacks of merchandise

274

that had ſtrayed from Meg's emporium into every corner, and overflowed every shelf in packages, piles, and bundles. The metalliferous categories—iron nails, lead pencils, tintacks, zinc ointment, and brass hinges—were there. Platoons of bottles were there, bottles of blue-black writing fluid, bottles of scarlet—and presumably plebeian—ink, bottles of lollipops and of oil (both hair and caſtor). Balls of ſtring, of blue, of peppermint, and balls to bounce were adjacent to an assortment of prim-looking books—account memorandum, exercise, and note. But the room was cosy, and if its inhabitants fitted it almoſt as closely as birds fit their neſts they were as happy as birds, few of whom (save the swallows) sing in their neſts. With pitchpipe to hand and a bundle of music before them Dan and Martin would begin. The dog would snooze on the rug before the fire; Meg would snooze amply in her armchair until roused by the sudden terrific tinkling of her shop-bell. She would waddle off to her dim little shop—every ſtep she took rattling the paraffin lamp on the table, the coal in the scuttle, and sometimes the very panes in the window—and the dog would clamber into her chair. Having supplied an aged gaffer with an ounce of carraway seed, or some gay lad with a packet of cigarettes, Meg would waddle back and sink down upon the dog, whereupon its awful indignation would sound to the very heavens, drowning the voices even of Dan and his son.

" What shall we wind up with ? " Dan would ask at the close of the lesson, and as often as not Martin would say: " You muſt sing ' Timmie.' "

This was " Timmie," and it had a tune something like the chorus to " Father O'Flynn."

O Timmie my brother,
Best son of our mother,
Our labour it prospers, the mowing is done ;
A holiday take you,
The loss it won't break you,
A day' s never lost if a holiday 's won.

We'll go with clean faces
To see the horse races,
And if the luck chances we'll gather some gear ;
But never a jockey
Will win it, my cocky,
Who catches one glance from a girl I know there.

There 's lords and there 's ladies
Wi' pretty sunshadies,
And farmers and jossers and fat men and small ;
But the pride of these trips is
The scallywag gipsies
Wi' not a whole rag to the backs of 'em all.

There 's cokernut shying,
And devil defying,
And a racket and babel to hear and to see,
Wi' boxing and shooting,
And fine high faluting
From chaps wi' a table and thimble and pea.

My Nancy will be there,
The best thing to see there,
She'll win all the praises wi' ne'er a rebuke ;
And she has a sister—
I wonder you've missed her—
As sweet as the daisies and fit for a duke.

Come along, brother Timmie,
Don't linger, but gimme
My hat and my purse and your company there ;
For sporting and courting,
The cream of resorting,
And nothing much worse, Timmie—Come to the fair.

On the third anniversary of Martin's homecoming
Dan rose up very early in the dark morn, and leaving
his son sleeping he crept out of the house followed
by his dog. They went away from Thasper, though
the darkness was profound and the grass filled with
dew, out upon the hills towards Chapel Cheary. The
night was starless, but Dan knew every trick and turn
of the paths, and after an hour's walk he met a man
waiting by a signpost. They conversed for a few
minutes and then went off together, the dog at their
heels, until they came to a field gate. Upon this
they fastened a net and then sent the dog into the
darkness upon his errand, while they waited for the
hare which the dog would drive into the net. They
waited so long that it was clear the dog had not
drawn its quarry. Dan whistled softly, but the dog
did not return. Dan opened the gate and went down
the fields himself, scouring the hedges for a long time,
but he could not find the dog. The murk of the
night had begun to lift, but the valley was filled with
mist. He went back to the gate: the net had been
taken down, his friend had departed—perhaps he
had been disturbed ? The dog had now been missing
for an hour. Dan still hung about, but neither friend
nor dog came back. It grew grey and more grey,
though little could be distinguished, the raw mist

obscuring everything that the dawn uncovered. He shivered with gloom and dampness, his boots were now as pliable as gloves, his eyebrows had grey drops upon them, so had his mouſtache and the backs of his hands. His dark coat looked as if it was made of grey wool; it was tightly buttoned around his throat and he ſtood with his chin crumpled, unconsciously holding his breath until it burſt forth in a gasp. But he could not abandon his dog, and he roamed once more down into the miſty valley towards woods that he knew well, whiſtling softly and with great caution a repetition of two notes.

And he found his dog. It was lying on a heap of dead sodden leaves. It juſt whimpered. It could not rise, it could not move, it seemed paralysed. Dawn was now really upon them. Dan wanted to get the dog away, quickly, it was a dangerous quarter, but when he lifted it to his feet the dog collapsed like a scarecrow. In a flash Dan knew he was poisoned, he had probably picked up some piece of dainty flesh that a farmer had baited for the foxes. He seized a knob of chalk that lay thereby, grated some of it into his hands, and forced it down the dog's throat. Then he tied the lead to its neck. He was going to drag the dog to its feet and force it to walk. But the dog was paſt all energy, it was limp and mute. Dan dragged him by the neck for some yards as a man draws behind him a heavy sack. It muſt have weighed three ſtone, but Dan lifted him on to his own shoulders and ſtaggered back up the hill. He carried it thus for half a mile, but then he was ſtill four miles from home, and it was daylight, at any moment he might meet somebody he would not care to meet. He entered a ride opening into some coverts, and, bending down, slipped the dog over his head to rest upon the ground. He was exhausted and felt giddy, his brains were swirling round—trying to slop out of his skull—and—yes—the dog was dead, his old dog dead. When he looked up, he saw a keeper with a gun standing a few yards off.

" Good morning," said Dan. All his weariness was suddenly gone from him.

" I'll have your name and address," replied the keeper, a giant of a man, with a sort of contemptuous affability.

" What for ? "

" You'll hear about what for," the giant grinned. " I'll be sure to let ye know, in doo coorse." He laid his gun upon the ground and began searching in his pockets, while Dan stood up with rage in his heart and confusion in his mind. So the Old Imp was at him again!

" Humph! " said the keeper. " I've alost my notebook somewheres. Have you got a bit of paper on ye ? "

The culprit searched his pockets and produced a folded fragment.

" Thanks." The giant did not cease to grin. " What is it ? "

" What ? " queried Dan.

" Your name and address."

" Ah, but what do you want it for. What do you think I'm doing ? " protested Dan.

" I've a net in my pocket which I took from a gate

279

about an hour ago. I saw summat was afoot, and me and a friend o' mine have been looking for 'ee. Now let's have your name and no nonsense."

" My name," said Dan, " my name ? Well, it is . . . Piper."

" Piper is it, ah! Was you baptized ever ? "

" Peter," said Dan savagely.

" Peter Piper! Well, you've picked a tidy pepper-carn this time."

Again he was searching his pockets. There was a frown on his face. " You'd better lend me a bit o' pencil too."

Dan produced a stump of lead pencil and the gamekeeper, smoothing the paper on his lifted knee, wrote down the name of Peter Piper.

" And where might you come from ? " He peered up at the miserable man, who replied: " From Leasington "—naming a village several miles to the west of his real home.

" Leasington! " commented the other. " You must know John Eustace, then ? " John Eustace was a sporting farmer famed for his stock and his riches.

" Know him! " exclaimed Dan. " He's my uncle! "

" O ah! " The other carefully folded the paper and put it into his breast pocket. " Well, you can trot along home now, my lad."

Dan knelt down and unbuckled the collar from his dead dog's neck. He was fond of his dog, it looked piteous now. And kneeling there it suddenly came upon Dan that he had been a coward again, he had told nothing but lies, foolish lies, and he had let a great hulking flunkey walk roughshod over him. In one astonishing moment the reproving face of his little son seemed to loom up beside the dog, the blood flamed in his brain.

" I'll take charge of that," said the keeper, snatching the collar from his hand.

" Blast you! " Dan sprang to his feet, and suddenly screaming like a madman: " I'm Dan Pavey of Thasper," he leapt at the keeper with a fury that shook even that calm stalwart.

" You would, would ye ? " he yapped, darting for his gun. Dan also seized it, and in their struggle the gun was fired off harmlessly between them. Dan let go.

" My God! " roared the keeper, " you'd murder me, would ye ? Wi' my own gun, would ye ? " He struck Dan a swinging blow with the butt of it, yelling: " Would ye ? Would ye ? Would ye ? " And he did not cease striking until Dan tumbled senseless and bloody across the body of the dog.

Soon another keeper came hurrying through the trees.

" Tried to murder me—wi' me own gun, he did," declared the big man, " wi' me own gun! "

They revived the stricken Pavey after a while and then conveyed him to a policeman, who conveyed him to a gaol.

The magistrates took a grave view of the case and sent it for trial at the assizes. They were soon held, he had not long to wait, and before the end of November he was condemned. The assize court was a place of intolerable gloom, intolerable formality, intolerable pain, but the public seemed to enjoy it. The keeper swore Dan had tried to shoot him, and the prisoner contested this. He did not deny that he was the aggressor. The jury found him guilty. What had he to say? He had nothing to say, but he was deeply moved by the spectacle of the Rev. Scroope standing up and testifying to his sobriety, his honesty, his general good repute, and pleading for a lenient sentence because he was a man of considerable force of character, misguided no doubt, a little unfortunate, and prone to recklessness.

Said the judge, examining the papers of the indictment: " I see there is a previous conviction—for betting offences."

" That was three years ago, my lord. There has been nothing of the kind since, my lord, of that I am sure, quite sure."

Scroope showed none of his old time confident aspect, he was perspiring and trembling. The clerk of the assize leaned up and held a whispered colloquy with the judge, who then addressed the rector.

" Apparently he is still a betting agent. He gave a false name and address, which was taken down by the keeper on a piece of paper furnished by the prisoner. Here it is, on one side the name of Peter Pope (Piper, sir!) Piper: and on the other side this is written:

3 o/c race. *Pretty Dear*, 5/- *to win.* *J. Klopstock.*

Are there any Klopstocks in your parish?"

" Klopstock!" murmured the parson, " it is the name of my cook."

What had the prisoner to say about that? The

prisoner had nothing to say, and he was sentenced to twelve months' imprisonment with hard labour.

So Dan was taken away. He was a tough man, an amenable man, and the mere rigours of the prison did not unduly afflict him. His behaviour was good, and he looked forward to gaining the maximum remission of his sentence. Meg, his mother, went to see him once, alone, but she did not repeat the visit. The prison chaplain paid him special attention. He, too, was a Scroope, a huge fellow, not long from Oxford, and Pavey learned that he was related to the Thasper rector. The new year came, February came, March came, and Dan was afforded some privileges. His singing in chapel was much admired, and occasionally he was allowed to sing to the prisoners. April came, May came, and then his son Martin was drowned in a boating accident, on a lake, in a park. The Thasper children had been taken there for a holiday. On hearing it, Pavey sank limply to the floor of his cell. The warders sat him up, but they could make nothing of him, he was dazed, and he could not speak. He was taken to the hospital wing. " This man has had a stroke, he is gone dumb," said the doctor. On the following day he appeared to be well enough, but still he could not speak. He went about the ward doing hospital duty, dumb as a ladder; he could not even mourn, but a jig kept flickering through his voiceless mind:

> In a park there was a lake,
> On the lake there was a boat,
> In the boat there was a boy.

Hour after hour the stupid jingle flowed through

his consciousness. Perhaps it kept him from going
mad, but it did not bring him back his speech, he was
dumb, dumb. And he remembered a man who had
been stricken deaf, and then blind—Scroope knew
him too, it was some man who had mocked God.

> In a park there was a lake,
> On the lake there was a boat,
> In the boat there was a boy.

On the day of the funeral Pavey imagined that he
had been let out of prison; he dreamed that someone had been kind and set him free for an hour or two
to bury his dead boy. He seemed to arrive at Thasper when the ceremony was already begun, the
coffin was already in the church. Pavey knelt down
beside his mother. The rector intoned the office, the
child was taken to its grave. Dumb dreaming
Pavey turned his eyes from it. The day was too
bright for death, it was a stainless day. The wind
seemed to flow in soft streams, rolling the lilac
blooms. A small white feather, blown from a pigeon
on the church gable, whirled about like a butterfly.
" We give thee hearty thanks," the priest was saying,
" for that it hath pleased thee to deliver this our
brother out of the miseries of this sinful world." At
the end of it all Pavey kissed his mother, and saw
himself turn back to his prison. He went by the field
paths away to the railway junction. The country had
begun to look a little parched, for rain was wanted—
vividly he could see all this—but things were growing, corn was thriving greenly, the beanfields smelled
sweet. A frill of yellow kilk and wild white carrot
spray lined every hedge. Cattle dreamed in the

grass, the colt stretched itself unregarded in front of its mother. Larks, wrens, yellow-hammers. There were the great beech trees and the great hills, calm and confident, overlooking Cobbs and Peter, Thasper and Trinkel, Buzzlebury and Nuncton. He sees the summer is coming on, he is going back to prison. " Courage is vain," he thinks, " we are like the grass underfoot, a blade that excels is quickly shorn. In this sort of a world the poor have no call to be proud, they had only need be penitent."

> In the park there was a lake,
> On the lake . . . . boat,
> In the boat . . . . . .

Luxury

EIGHT O'CLOCK OF A FINE SPRING morning in the hamlet of Kezzal Predy Peter, great horses with chains clinking down the road, and Alexander Finkle rising from his bed singing: " O lah soh doh, soh lah me doh," timing his notes to the ching of his neighbour's anvil. He boils a cupful of water on an oil stove, his shaving brush stands (where it always stands) upon the window-ledge (" Soh lah soh do-o-o-oh, soh doh soh la-a-a-ah! ") but as he addresses himself to his toilet the clamour of the anvil ceases and then Finkle too becomes silent, for the unresting cares of his life begin again to afflict him.

" This cottage is no good," he mumbles, " and I'm no good. Literature is no good when you live too much on porridge. Your writing's no good, sir, you can't get any glow out of oatmeal. Why did you ever come here ? It's a hopeless job and you know it ! " Stropping his razor petulantly as if the soul of that frustrating oatmeal lay there between the leather and the blade, he continues: " But it isn't the cottage, it isn't me, it isn't the writing—it's the privation. I must give it up and get a job as a railway porter."

And indeed he was very impoverished, the living he derived from his writings was meagre; the cottage had many imperfections, both its rooms were gloomy, and to obviate the inconvenience arising from its defective roof he always slept downstairs.

Two years ago he had been working for a wall-paper manufacturer in Bethnal Green. He was not

poor then, not so very poor, he had the clothes he
stood up in (they were good clothes) and fifty pounds
in the bank besides. But although he had served the
wall-paper man for fifteen years that fifty pounds had
not been derived from clerking, he had earned it by
means of his hobby, a little knack of writing things
for provincial newspapers. On his thirty-first birth-
day Finkle argued—for he had a habit of conducting
long and not unsatisfactory discussions between
himself and a self that apparently wasn't him—that
what he could do reasonably well in his scanty leisure
could be multiplied exceedingly if he had time and
opportunity, lived in the country, somewhere where
he could go into a garden to smell the roses or whatever was blooming and draw deep draughts of happiness, think his profound thoughts and realize the
goodness of God, and then sit and read right through
some long and difficult book about Napoleon or
Mahomet. Bursting with literary ambition Finkle
had hesitated no longer: he could live on nothing
in the country—for a time. He had the fifty pounds,
he had saved it, it had taken him seven years, but he
had made it and saved it. He handed in his notice.
That was very astonishing to his master, who esteemed
him, but more astonishing to Finkle was the parting
gift of ten pounds which the master had given him.
The workmen, too, had collected more money for him,
and bought for him a clock, a monster, it weighed
twelve pounds and had a brass figure of Lohengrin
on the top, while the serene old messenger man who
cleaned the windows and bought surreptitious beer
for the clerks gave him a prescription for the

instantaneous relief of a painful stomach ailment. "It might come in handy," he had said. That was two years ago, and now just think! He had bought himself an inkpot of crystalline glass—a large one, it held nearly half a pint—and two pens, one for red ink and one for black, besides a quill for signing his name with. Here he was at "Pretty Peter" and the devil himself was in it! Nothing had ever been right, the hamlet itself was poor. Like all places near the chalk hills its roads were of flint, the church was of flint, the farms and cots of flint with brick corners. There was an old milestone outside his cot, he was pleased with that, it gave the miles to London and the miles to Winchester, it was nice to have a milestone there like that—your very own.

He finished shaving and threw open the cottage door; the scent of wallflowers and lilac came to him as sweet almost as a wedge of newly cut cake. The may bloom on his hedge drooped over the branches like crudded cream, and the dew in the gritty road smelled of harsh dust in a way that was pleasant. Well, if the cottage wasn't much good, the bit of a garden was all right.

There was a rosebush too, a little vagrant in its growth. He leaned over his garden gate; there was no one in sight. He took out the fire shovel and scooped up a clot of manure that lay in the road adjacent to his cottage and trotted back to place it in a little heap at the root of those scatter-brained roses, pink and bulging, that never seemed to do very well and yet were so satisfactory.

"Nicish day," remarked Finkle, lolling against his

doorpost, "but it's always nice if you are doing a good day's work. The garden is all right, and literature is all right, and life's all right—only I live too much on porridge. It isn't the privation itself, it's the things privation makes a man do. It makes a man do things he ought not want to do, it makes him mean, it makes him feel mean, I tell you, and if he feels mean and thinks mean he writes meanly, that's how it is."

He had written topical notes and articles, stories of gay life (of which he knew nothing), of sport (of which he knew less), a poem about "hope," and some cheerful pieces for a girls' weekly paper. And yet his outgoings still exceeded his income, painfully and perversely after two years. It was terrifying. He wanted success, he had come to conquer—not to find what he *had* found. But he would be content with encouragement now even if he did not win success; it was absolutely necessary, he had not sold a thing for six months, his public would forget him, his connection would be gone.

"There's no use though," mused Finkle, as he scrutinized his worn boots, "in looking at things in detail, that's mean; a large view is the thing. Whatever is isolated is bound to look alarming."

But he continued to lean against the doorpost in the full blaze of the stark, almost gritty sunlight, thinking mournfully until he heard the porridge in the saucepan begin to bubble. Turning into the room he felt giddy, and scarlet spots and other phantasmagoria waved in the air before him.

Without an appetite he swallowed the porridge and

T

ate some bread and cheese and watercress. Watercress, at least, was plentiful there, for the little runnels that came down from the big hills expanded in the Predy Peter fields and in their shallow bottoms the cress flourished.

He finished his breakfast, cleared the things away, and sat down to see if he could write, but it was in vain—he could not write. He could think, but his mind would embrace no subject, it just teetered about with the objects within sight, the empty, disconsolate grate, the pattern of the rug, and the black butterfly that had hung dead upon the wall for so many months. Then he thought of the books he intended to read but could never procure, the books he had procured but did not like, the books he had liked but was already, so soon, forgetting. Smoking would have helped and he wanted to smoke, but he could not afford it now. If ever he had a real good windfall he intended to buy a tub, a little tub it would have to be of course, and he would fill it to the bung with cigarettes, full to the bung, if it cost him pounds. And he would help himself to one whenever he had a mind to do so.

" Bah, you fool! " he murmured, " you think you have the whole world against you, that you are fighting it, keeping up your end with heroism! Idiot! What does it all amount to ? You've withdrawn yourself from the world, run away from it, and here you sit making futile dabs at it, like a child sticking pins into a pudding and wondering why nothing happens. What *could* happen ? What ? The world doesn't know about you, or care, you are useless.

It isn't aware of you any more than a chain of mountains is aware of a gnat. And whose fault is that—is it the mountains' fault? Idiot! But I can't starve and I must go and get a job as a railway porter, it's all I'm fit for."

Two farmers paused outside Finkle's garden and began a solid conversation upon a topic that made him feel hungry indeed. He listened, fascinated, though he was scarcely aware of it.

" Six-stone lambs," said one, " are fetching three pounds apiece."

" Ah !"

" I shall fat some."

" Myself I don't care for lamb, never did care."

" It's good eating."

" Ah, but I don't care for it. Now we had a bit of spare rib last night off an old pig. 'Twas cold, you know, but beautiful. I said to my dame: ' What can mortal man want better than spare rib off an old pig? Tender and white, ate like lard.' "

" Yes, it's good eating."

" Nor veal, I don't like—nothing that's young."

" Veal's good eating."

" Don't care for it, never did, it eats short to my mind."

Then the school bell began to ring so loudly that Finkle could hear no more, but his mind continued to hover over the choice of lamb or veal or old pork until he was angry. Why had he done this foolish thing, thrown away his comfortable job, reasonable food, ease of mind, friendship, pocket money, tobacco? Even his girl had forgotten him. Why had he done this impudent thing, it was insanity surely? But he knew that man has instinctive reasons that transcend logic, what a parson would call the superior reason of the heart.

"I wanted a change, and I got it. Now I want another change, but what shall I get? Chance and change, they are the sweet features of existence. Chance and change, and not too much prosperity. If I were an idealist I could live from my hair upwards."

The two farmers separated. Finkle staring haplessly from his window saw them go. Some schoolboys were playing a game of marbles in the road there. Another boy sat on the green bank quietly singing, while one in spectacles knelt slyly behind him trying to burn a hole in the singer's breeches with a magnifying glass. Finkle's thoughts still hovered over the flavours and satisfactions of veal and lamb and pig until, like mother Hubbard, he turned and opened his larder.

There, to his surprise, he saw four bananas lying on a saucer. Bought from a travelling hawker a couple of days ago they had cost him threepence halfpenny. And he had forgotten them! He could not afford another luxury like that for a week at least, and he stood looking at them, full of doubt. He debated whether he should take one now, he would still have one left for Wednesday, one for Thursday, and one for Friday. But he thought he would not, he had had his breakfast and he had not remembered them. He grew suddenly and absurdly angry again. That was the worst of poverty, not what it made you endure, but what it made you *want* to endure. Why shouldn't he eat a banana—why shouldn't he eat all of them ? And yet bananas always seemed to him such luxuriant, expensive things, so much peel, and then two, or not more than three, delicious bites. But if he fancied a banana—there it was. No, he did not want to destroy the blasted thing! No reason at all why he should not, but that was what continuous hardship did for you, nothing could stop this miserable feeling for economy now. If he had a thousand pounds at this moment he knew he would be careful about bananas and about butter and about sugar and things like that; but he would never have a thousand pounds, nobody had ever had it, it was impossible to believe that anyone had ever had wholly and entirely to themselves a thousand pounds. It could not be believed. He was like a man dreaming that he had the hangman's noose around his neck; yet the drop did not take place, it did not take place, and it would not take place. But the noose was still there. He picked up the bananas one by one, the four bananas, the whole four. No other man in the world, surely, had ever had four such fine bananas as that and not wanted to eat them ? O, why had such stupid, mean scruples seized him again ? It was disgusting and ungenerous to himself, it made him feel mean, it *was* mean! Rushing to his cottage door he cried: " Here y'are! " to the playing schoolboys and flung two of the bananas into the midst of them. Then he flung another. He hesitated at the fourth, and tearing the peel from it he crammed the fruit into his own mouth. wolfing it down and gasping: " So perish all such traitors."

293

When he had completely absorbed its savour, he stared like a fool at the empty saucer. It was empty, the bananas were gone, all four irrecoverably gone.

"Damned pig!" cried Finkle.

But then he sat down and wrote all this, just as it appears.

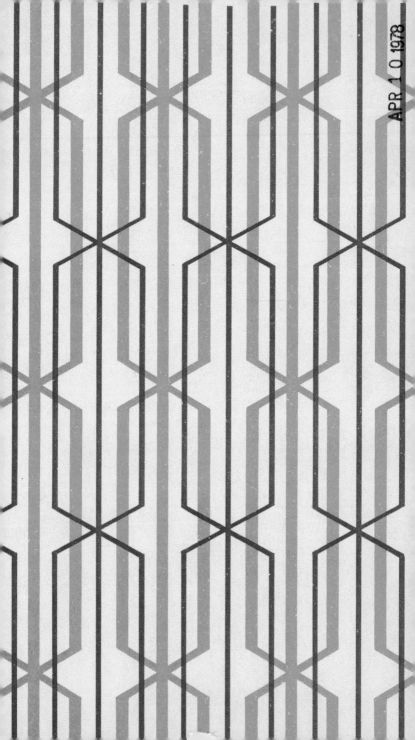